Steven Lang is the author of two novels, *An Accidental Terrorist* (UQP, 2005), which won both Queensland and New South Wales Premiers' Literary Awards, and *88 Lines About 44 Women* (Viking, 2009), which was shortlisted for both the Queensland and New South Wales Premiers' Literary awards for fiction. He and Chris Francis co-direct Outspoken in Maleny, presenting conversations with well-known authors. Steven's new novel will be published by UQP in July 2017.

an
accidental
terrorist

Steven Lang

UQP

First published 2005 by University of Queensland Press
PO Box 6042, St Lucia, Queensland 4067 Australia
Reprinted 2006, 2016

www.uqp.com.au

Typeset in 11.5/14.5pt Bembo by Post Pre-press Group, Brisbane, Queensland
Printed in Australia by McPherson's Printing Group

This project has been assisted by the Commonwealth
Government through the Australia Council, its arts
funding and advisory body.

Sponsored by the Queensland Office of Arts and
Cultural Development.

Cataloguing in Publication Data
National Library of Australia

Lang, Steven, 1951–.
  An accidental terrorist.

  ISBN 978 0 7022 5955 5 (pbk)
  ISBN 978 0 7022 3988 5 (pdf)
  ISBN 978 0 7022 3991 5 (epub)
  ISBN 978 0 7022 3989 2 (kindle)

  I. Title.

  A.823.4

For Chris

one

He watched the Fairlane make a wide turn and head back the way it had come, the tail-lights glinting on the wet tar. Too late, then, to change his plans. He bent to put an arm through the strap of his backpack and shouldered its weight, went up the steps of the hotel. The lobby was narrow and cold, less grand than the establishment's name might have suggested. A blue coin-operated phone in the corner was being used by a man with a ponytail, his voice echoing in the empty space. Kelvin pressed the small electric buzzer beside the office window which had attracted the sign, *Ring Bell*, but if doing so had any effect it was not immediately apparent, although the man using the phone stopped talking. The sound of men's voices emanated from behind a set of doors. When Kelvin looked across at the man he was holding the receiver against his chest.

The publican appeared in the office window, asking what he wanted.

'A room.'

'Come through then,' he said, pointing to the doors.

Kelvin made to push through to the Lounge, pleased to be

released from the gaze of the other man; except the swing doors caught his bag and held him there, half in, half out. He was obliged to stop and unhook the thing – all his worldly possessions – wrestling it through while the twenty or so men present, interrupted by the little drama, observed this young man with the face that gave an appearance of turning in on itself; the confluence of eyebrows and eyes and nose being almost too intense, and this, when complimented by the mouth, with its full sharp-edged lips, making the whole appear overly sensitive, too feminine, too – a risky word here for a man – too beautiful. He gave a small self-deprecating laugh and made a little bow. The men, not given to acknowledging the humour of strangers, returned to their drinks.

The place had had a makeover. It was no longer the beer and tile trough it was in the sixties and early seventies. It had been carpeted, colonised by groups of round wooden tables and chunky chairs, the dark patterned walls decorated with a mixture of fishing and logging motifs – glass balls snared in old nets alongside rusty cross-cut saws, sepia photographs of stocky men next to trees of unlikely girth; of slim three-masted schooners out in the bay. All the history of the coastal town displayed, but as decoration: the picture of a killer whale breasting a wave no more significant than the plastic lobsters.

Kelvin doubted Nev would approve the chairs. His father had liked to stand to drink, the sloping lip of the glass held daintily between his thumb and forefinger, a cigarette cupped in the other hand with the lit end turned inwards, the way he

2

learned on the boats, stabbing the air with the remaining three fingers to make a point.

'You got a problem, mate?' one of the men along the bar said.

'Sorry mate,' he said, 'just dreaming.'

'You're not from around here, are you?'

The question indicating more than it might seem, for Eden was now primarily a logging town, not enamoured of the newcomers, those who had once been called hippies but were now referred to as greenies. Not that Kelvin, short-haired, clean shaven, looked the part.

The men at the bar themselves bore scant resemblance to those depicted in the photographs on the wall; over the generations their upper bodies had become heavier at the expense of the lower. The mechanical nature of their work had done it, machine operating, truck driving, the relentless use of only the muscles of the arms and shoulders. It gave them the aspect of flightless birds, their swollen bellies perched on skinny legs.

The man who had spoken was wearing a blue singlet and shorts, thongs.

'Just passing through,' Kelvin said, adding, as a kind of bona fide, 'looking for work.'

'Right,' the man said, but with justifiable disbelief, for Kelvin was there only for the night, and that by mistake.

Hitching out of Melbourne that morning, heading for Sydney, he'd taken the wrong road. The disaster with Shelley had so confused him he hadn't noticed. The only thing he'd been sure of was that he was leaving. It wasn't until he'd got a lift from an RAAF man going to Sale that he'd realised he was on the Coast Road, not the Hume, and even then he hadn't considered he would have to go through Eden. It was only later, when he had passed Orbost, and then Cann River, when they came to the turn-off to Mallacoota, the Bellbird Hotel slipping by amongst the tall trees, that it came home to him.

He had refused the joints the man and woman in the Fairlane offered, it was too soon after Shelley for that, but the stuff must have seeped in anyway, disarming him. The driver was one of those men who think everyone should be excited about whatever it is that's got them going; raving on about some science fiction book he'd read, about modern music versus old, about the country back of Eden.

'People think they have to go overseas to find paradise,' he said. 'White people have been doing that ever since they came here. They just don't get it. They don't see *this* is the place. Paradise is right here, this is where it is.'

After a while he stopped talking and pushed a cassette into the deck. Johann Sebastian Bach. You had to give him that. And what with the old music winding up and up, and the tall trees and the talk of paradise, Kelvin had been taken by the desire to say that he knew what the bloke had meant. That this was, indeed, God's Own Country. That he'd grown up here. He couldn't ever remember wanting to say that. Perhaps that's what being away does to you: the body remembers the place and the mind forgets the pain. Eden had never been a place he wanted to lay claim to.

He said nothing. He looked out the window at the trees, more trees than you could ever imagine.

The men at the bar weren't finished with him.

'See that bloke over there,' another in the group said, pointing. 'The bloke in the denim shirt?'

'Yes.'

'If you're after work, he'll help you.'

'Right,' he said, turning back to the bar and the bottles behind it as a way of saying that the conversation was over, but, because of his lie (you would have thought he would have known better by now), was obliged sooner or later to approach the table where the man in the denim shirt, a rugged type, mid-thirties, was sitting with a noisy group of younger men.

He looked up at Kelvin, waiting for him to speak.

'I was told you had work,' he said, waving his hand in the direction of the men by the bar.

Denim Shirt looked past him. 'That's right. You plant trees?'

'What sort of trees?'

'Penis fucking radiata,' a sandy-haired fellow said, and laughed, pleased with his joke, looking around to see how it was received.

'Pine trees, seedlings,' Denim Shirt said.

Kelvin stood on the edge of their circle, their little pine-planting clique. 'I don't know, how hard can it be?'

'You haven't fucking tried it,' the same man said, and this time raised a laugh.

'We leave from out the front at six. It's five days on, two days off, flat rate, six-fifty an hour all up. You interested?'

Kelvin thus caught, having to decide. But then it was always like this, this was how it happened, he'd be going along and a door would open and he'd go in, or he wouldn't, as the case might be. But mostly he would, if only because the door was there, for no other reason. This time, however, it was different. This time he was standing in the bar of the Australasia in Eden, the pub he'd sat outside as a child for more afternoons than he cared to remember, bribed by his father or mother into waiting with a lemon squash and a bag of chips.

'I'll give it a shot,' he said.

'We won't wait,' Denim Shirt replied. 'If you're there, you're there.'

two

At 6 am the air was cold enough to make the breath steam. He stomped his feet on the pavement, recalculating the dollars-for-hours ratio for a week's work, stuffing his hands in his pockets, looking up and down the main street for the pick-up. There was something strangely temporary about the town which could not be solely attributed to the great length of vacant spaces marked out for central parking. With the exception of the hotel every building was cheaper and tackier than the next, as if the occupants had originally intended to stay only for as long as the whales, or the fish, or the trees lasted, and hadn't had much hope even for that.

The transport was a beaten Toyota troop carrier. The Denim Shirt, Al, was at the wheel. Kelvin pushed his bag under the feet of the men and climbed in the back.

They went south on the highway out of town, turning inland on an interminable dirt road, ascending and descending, winding and bumping past the shapes of dark-barked trees, the gears grinding, the men shaken against each other and the metal walls. Dust percolated throughout the cabin and collected on the outside of the back window so there was nothing to see except the chipped paint and the other men, their closed-eyed, unshaven faces thick with sleep.

Kelvin knew these men. Or if not them then others like them. He'd worked with them on fishing trawlers out of Darwin. Men called Stevo and Anthill, or Davo and Bill, strong men with few brains who yet – and this was the hard part – had lives just as rich as his own. This being the bit he always had difficulty with: the difference between the mass of humanity, even in the shape of a small town, and the individuals within it, each with their own story. He could smell the alcohol on them. After shore leave the men would return to the boats rancid and surly from the drinking, bragging and aggressive, taking days to sweat it out. Chances were, it had been on him too. He wasn't blind to the family connection in the work, but that was not why he'd chosen it; it had simply paid well, without demanding more than time and labour; because often enough he was as stupid as the rest of them.

The French girl, Yvette, was a case in point. She'd blown into Darwin as crew on a pleasure yacht and stayed. After they'd been going together a while they shared a flat for several weeks, and it had been Kelvin's first time like that with a woman. Domestic. Her idea had been to get work on boats up through the Pacific Islands, she'd almost talked him into leaving with her. She had wanted to take him around the world, to Paris, to her home in Lyons, and show him, her Australian boy, what it was really like to be alive, and he might have gone, the passport issue aside, except that he had woken up next to her one morning, she had been really very pretty, small, a sweet face, her lips whitened by the sun, nice breasts, nice parts, a body so tight it felt as if her skin could hardly contain it, as if there was no room for anything more inside, he woke beside her and he ran his hand across that skin and she had been smooth and brown and hard, and he had thought, It's over, just like that. He was bored, nothing more to it. He was twenty-one years old working fishing trawlers in the Arafura Sea and fucking a pretty French girl and smoking Thai sticks and he had a problem that sailing around the world would not have fixed.

He started hitching south. He'd been in Darwin long enough. He was not, generally, burdened by connection. He liked being able to move to new places, to make new friends, meet women, then move along. The only exception to this rule had been Shelley, and it had been too long since he had heard from her, he didn't even know where she was. Melbourne he guessed. He imagined her in a penthouse, cocktail glasses on the bar, a beautiful long, shimmering dress, a view out over the glinting city.

It took three days to reach Tennant Creek and he spent two more there, standing beside the road. Every car that passed condemning him for leaving Yvette. So much so he might almost have turned back. Instead he paid out valuable currency for a bus ticket to Alice Springs, and then, suddenly urgent to keep going, paid out more to take the train the rest of the way south.

Except that the train proved to be a line of flatbeds hauling trucks to Port Augusta with only one ancient passenger carriage tacked onto the end. Sometimes it hardly went faster than a walk. He smoked cigarettes on the little veranda at the front of the carriage. He'd never conceived there could be so little in a landscape, even less than in the open sea. The brightness hurt his eyes. Part of him would have liked to stay out there, without even the carriage window between him and the desert, but the loneliness was too much for him, the lack of anything except the splintery boards to push against too frightening. Out there, without another woman to take her place, he was unable to deny that he missed Yvette with a fierce pain. He had had to work hard to remember the claustrophobia her tight body had induced, to remember why it was he'd thought she was the stupid one.

When they came out of the forest the sun was up. Peering forward he caught glimpses of a wide green valley with fields that climbed to timber on the ridges, a broad sandy river, several isolated houses made from weather-washed timber, a post-office store, corn growing on the flats. The remnants of a town.

'Coalwater,' the driver said and turned across the river on a rattling sleeper bridge.

The men stirred. They coughed and stretched and lit cigarettes. They swore and opened the small sliding windows and spat into the moving air.

An even smaller road followed the river for a while, rising slowly onto the ridge and into the trees. After a time it came out in another valley, into a broad stretch of cleared land.

A creek was marked by a curving line of scrub. An old home-stead had a driveway of ancient gums leading down.

'Here we are then,' Al said. 'Anthill, put the billy on will you mate.'

The work was dreadful. Heavy machinery had been over the ground, trailing a deep-ripping plough, and the trees were planted in the narrow bands of disturbed earth it had left behind.

The process was simple, take three paces, insert the spade, push with the boot, extract a seedling from the shoulder bag and free it from its little pot, place it in the ground and firm with the boot, take three paces . . . but the ground was broken and steep and the plough lines took no heed of topography, marching up and down the slope. The shoulder bag was heavy, swinging forward every time he bent with the spade or the tree, and there were flies, a small swarm of them that seemed to have worked out their own routine, most of them resting on his back, drinking his sweat, taking it in turns to be the two or three that bothered his eyes and nose. Over the next rise, or perhaps the next, was the end of the row, at which point it was time to stand up and stretch, to walk past the straggling group of men to an empty row and start back down again.

It was the sort of work that is designed to induce a hatred of the land and everything in it. And if not hatred, at least indif-ference, which in terms of land is just as dangerous. Yet every time Kelvin reached the far end – an elevated region with views out over the valley – a feeling of elation took hold. He stopped and breathed and looked out, searching for the landmarks that might place him. The property must once have been magnificent, with rolling paddocks and dark gullies bounded on three sides by forest. It sloped gently down to the distant Coalwater, rising on the other side to a grand bush-covered mountain one whole end of which was bare rock. It was the combination that did it to him, the fields *and* the trees, the broad sky overhead. He adjusted the strap on his shoulder, brushed the flies from his face and began again.

They had been joined by some men from a neighbouring community which Stevo, the comedian, referred to as Hippie-dom. At lunch they all sat together on the grass in the shade of the giant gums near the homestead. The hippies were thin and tall and well tanned, dressed in denim jeans or old army pants, like the Eden men, except they were bearded and long-haired and their shirts had once been fancy Indian things with embroidery at the collars. They spoke, too, in the same way, using the same coarse, cutting humour, except from their mouths it sounded strangely false. If the other men hadn't been there Kelvin would hardly have noticed, but beside them it appeared to be a kind of studied ignorance. As if the hippies thought putting on this vernacular granted them membership of the workers' club.

When they'd finished eating, the hippies announced they were going for a walk. They went around the back of the homestead.

'A walk my arse,' said Anthill.

'Fucken drongos,' Stevo said. He mimed holding a joint to his mouth and sucked in loudly. He lay back on the grass, crossed his booted feet and yawned. He put his hands behind his head, amongst the tousled mass of blond hair, and closed his eyes. His face, vaguely familiar, was almost handsome in a larrikin way, except for, or perhaps because of, a certain cruelty.

Kelvin would have liked to go with the hippies, not because of any particular affinity with them, simply out of the desire for a joint. A smoke, never mind that he'd promised himself he'd give it away, would have helped this kind of work, easing the passage of the afternoon. He could have gone; he'd seen their invitation – the meeting of eyes and the slight tilt of the head – but he'd been too slow to move. It had felt like it would be premature to abandon the company of the Eden men.

Stevo stirred himself. He pointed towards the house. 'How come you put up with these cunts, Al?'

Al was engaged in the process of extracting a packet of Winfield Blue from his shirt pocket.

'Al?'

'They do the work,' he said, the cigarette between his lips.

'You know what they're doin' don't ya? It's not like you need to stretch your fucken legs.'

'It's not exactly a workplace health and safety issue,' Al said.

'They're all on the fucken dole, growing marijuana out there.' He turned to Kelvin. 'You watch out for them mate. They'll be onto you.'

'How come?'

'Just watch it. They're full of shit, mate.'

13

'Look who's talking,' Al said.

'I say what I think,' Stevo said.

'See the fucken wimmin,' Anthill said. He was a small man, Stevo's sidekick, narrow in the face, but also in his manner; it was unclear whether his nickname derived from his christian name or his appearance.

'What about the women, Anthill?' Davo said, smirking. He cupped his hands over his chest. 'Is it the tits you like, swinging free?'

Anthill grinned, showing his yellow teeth.

'You fucking wish,' Davo said.

When he saw they were laughing at him Anthill lowered his head.

'Fucken greenies,' Stevo said.

'They're just people,' Al said.

'Jackshit.'

'I'm not going to argue with you.'

'You'd waste your breath.'

Anthill kicked Stevo's leg. The others had come out from behind the homestead. When they reached them they sat on the logs, smiling, as if sharing some secret joke, like a row of jackanapes. One of them, apropos of nothing, said, 'Right.'

'Yeah,' another agreed.

'Shall we then?' Al said, standing.

The afternoon was harder than the morning. The swinging bag wore a strip of flesh off his shoulder and there were blisters

14

on his hands. Every step involved placing his foot on broken ground, up or down, neither easier than the other.

Stevo came abreast of him, planting two trees for every one of his.

'Buggered, mate?'

'A bit,' Kelvin said.

'Thought you'd be. You don't look like the type.'

Kelvin stopped. 'What type is that?'

'No offence, mate,' Stevo said. 'You don't look like you done much of this shit.'

'More'n you'd know,' Kelvin said.

'I reckon I seen your face somewhere,' Stevo said.

That would have been eight, nine years ago in school, Kelvin thought, having placed him now, an older boy, a bully even then. 'You been to Sydney?' he said. 'That's where I come from,' working the lie, watching it work.

'Up the Smoke, eh? That's what I meant. It's not like this up there, is it? Not so hard.'

Stevo pulled out a packet of rollies and made a cigarette, offered the pack to Kelvin. 'I was up there once,' he said. 'Got some cousins who live in Strathfield. You know Strathfield?'

'Sydney's a big place.'

If he'd had more energy Kelvin would have mustered up some real dislike for the man, but he was too tired. He rolled a cigarette and lit it, then picked up his spade.

'I'm going slow,' he said, 'I better get back to it. Thanks for the smoke.'

Stevo watched, leaning on his tool.

'See that bag,' he said, 'you need to tie it back. Bastard the way it swings around. Use a bit of baling twine. Some in the truck.'

three

It is the usual crowd, but for once she does not care. The main house is warm and light, full of people and noise and the smell of cooking. Some days she hates the isolation of her life so much she is grateful for any distraction.

She hangs the kerosene lamp behind the door, telling Suzy to shoo – such a shy dog, tangling herself between her legs, eager to leave, too scared to go, a thin whippet of a thing – and goes directly to the kitchen, weaving her way through the chairs around the long table, smiling, nodding to everyone. Andy, the new man, is sitting by himself, reading, his skinny legs in stove-pipe jeans sticking out from the armchair. He glances up at her as she passes and she raises her hand to him as a concession to politeness. In truth she cannot bear the man, neither the look of him nor his manner. Nor does she imagine he holds a higher opinion of her.

Eva leans forward for a kiss, floured hands held out to the side to avoid spoiling her clothes. Yes, she'd love some help, would she cut the apples? She's making a crumble. Always this staple food, beans and rice, fruit and vegetables, the room thick with the blue smoke from the frying pan even as Eva pats out more lentil burgers between her plump fingers.

Jessica washes her hands and sets up at the bench, looking out on the room, safe behind her job with the apples. The main house is the only building with electricity. The bare bulbs hanging on their cords expose the paucity of the furnishings. It is a group house, shared by all, owned by none.

Before long Eva comes back and says not to bother peeling them, just to core and slice. 'It's only a crumble,' she says.

'It's no trouble,' Jessica replies, but then sees that saying this has upset Eva. As if Jessica's insistence on peeling some apples is a deliberate attempt to put her down. As if it were a class issue or something. The problem is, she thinks, that in the last year and a bit she's managed to lose the social skills for even the simplest operation. She's hardly been in the room five minutes and already she's put everyone offside.

When she first visited the Farm, researching material on alternative communities for *Making Waves*, the Greenpeace magazine – the one, she always said, putting herself down, that goes out to everyone who supports them whether they want it or not – these people had seemed fascinating, a wonderful assortment of eccentrics who had not only thought about things but had acted on their conclusions. She had jumped at the opportunity to buy in.

How quickly they have become simply human.

Martin is in his usual position at the head of the table. He and Sally are talking to Jim and some man she doesn't know, sitting with his back to her. Their children are playing a game which involves running through the room yelling, cardboard tubes like swords in their hands. There are several other couples, they're almost all couples, except for Jim, and Jim, being congenitally opposed to monogamy, doesn't count.

Sally brings the stranger over.

'This is Kelvin,' she says. 'We picked him up hitchhiking on the way back from Melbourne. I just knew he would end up here.' She gives a silly feminine laugh, delighted by her own prescience. 'Jess and I go way back,' she says to the man, pleased to be the author of their connection, to, in some way, claim them both.

Jessica puts down the peeler and offers to shake his hand, looks up and meets his eyes, notices that he is more than simply pretty. But young. Looking her over. She blushes. The pale skin of her face, with its famously rosy cheeks, goes embarrassingly pink. He says he's working on the pine plantation (a fact not designed to endear him to her, but then he isn't to know). He's just passing through.

And before anything else can happen Jim comes over and he puts an arm around the young man's shoulder too, as if he, like Sally, wants to state some sort of ownership. She picks up the knife again.

'You're not still planting pine trees, are you Jim?' she says.

'That's where I met this bloke. Thought I'd rescue him from the Eden boys.'

Jessica cuts into an apple, quartering it. With a smaller knife she takes out the core, cutting from the flower, like her mother taught her, popping out the small ellipse of seeds.

'We're almost finished Rosehill,' he says, bumbling on.

Jim's a big man, with great wafts of jet-black hair on his head and face, and a kind of hauteur, generated as much as anything by his size and his plummy voice. At first she'd thought he was cold and distant, a snob, but it's not so; when he feels safe he is, in fact, like a Labrador pup, all over everyone without any apparent awareness of how they might feel about it. He contains oceans of indiscriminate friendship, some of which is clearly lapping around the stranger.

'It's great country over there,' he says to her. 'You should see it, I had no idea. The Coalwater does a long loop in this direction. That hill on the other side of the property runs right down to it.'

She likes him well enough. She even slept with him a couple of times – almost impossible not to, he is like a force of nature, but equally transient. He loves walking, and this is their common ground. They share the process of exploration, telling each other what new creek they have followed up, what clearings they've found. Tonight she is scratchy, she has no time for it.

'So you're planting right down to the river? They've cleared right to the edge?'

'They didn't have to,' Jim says. 'There wasn't much growing there, a few scraggly gums, a bit of wattle and ti-tree.'

She cuts into another apple. 'Which they removed so as to get in a few more of their fucking pine trees.' The fuck word somehow louder and dirtier, more like a swear word, when it comes from her mouth. But Jim is oblivious to even this message, he's arguing the point.

'Reforesting some of that land isn't going to hurt the river,' he says.

'Reforesting with an exotic, Jim. One that will adversely affect river flows. You know that as well as I do. It's called the Coalwater. Why do you think that is? Because before white people came here it ran deep and black.'

There are three people standing on the other side of the bench, Jim, Sally and Kelvin, there is a whole room full of people, but she no longer cares, she's had enough, although of what is not quite clear. The tiny scene with Eva perhaps, or Sally's silliness, her disappointment in them all when seen through the eyes of this new man. Everything really; the blue smoke from the lentil burgers and the ugliness of the room combined with the knowledge that she's going away to Sydney in a couple of weeks to do something important. Even if it's only for a little while.

'Come on Jessica,' Jim says. 'You know I don't like what they're doing any better than you.' He gives a little laugh to defuse the situation, turning to the others for support.

'The difference is you work for them.'

'They're the only gig in town.'

'Big deal.'

'It is a big deal,' he says, the words coming out loud, momentarily silencing the room. 'Some of us have to work for a living.'

'What's that supposed to mean? That I don't? Are you saying that your need for extra cash justifies you doing anything, as long as it's the only gig in town?'

21

Jim glances at the others again, but Sally has turned away. She's checking out Martin who is talking to the children. Perhaps he's trying to get them to shut the fuck up. Some hope. Kelvin is blank-faced, neutral.

'Of course not,' Jim says. 'But this isn't so bad. They're planting the things anyway, why shouldn't I work? It's not like it's the chipmill −'

'It *is* the fucking chipmill.'

'Bullshit. It's nothing to do with the mill. It's the softwood industry. It's based in Bombala −'

'It's the same thing exactly, different owners but working hand in hand. We should be out there stopping them, not working for the bastards.'

Jim's shoulders drop. It's another aspect of his puppy nature: instead of fighting, he rolls over and shows his belly.

'Shit. I'm sorry,' she says, her anger melting at the gesture. 'I just get pissed off seeing all these plantations. In another twenty years this place will look like Bavaria.' She looks at her pale hands on the board and the slices of fruit, browning. 'I didn't mean to go off at you. But this is serious stuff. We have to make a stand.'

'That's right, we have to make a stand,' Andy says, calling out from where he is slumped in his chair.

He gets up, scattering the dogs. He's tall and good-looking, but in a mechanistic way, in the same way a mannequin is good-looking, his hair tied back in a ponytail, his strong chin disguised by a scrappy beard. He moves in the room with force. She doesn't like the way the others, even the dogs, yield to him.

'How do you propose we do that, Jess-i-ca?'

He likes to say her name so that it comes out as three syllables, as a child might, as if he's constantly undermining her.

'I have my own ideas about that An-*du-rew*,' she says. Perhaps that's what's missing from his handsomeness: the eyes. His eyes are clear, even startling, but they lack even the beginnings of compassion.

Eva has left the stove and is standing to the side. 'Are those apples done yet?' she says.

'Oh, yes. I mean, nearly, I've four left to do.'

'Well give me the pot and I'll get them started.'

She bustles in, all self-righteous perspiration and flour, swinging the big pot over to the stove.

'Guess it depends what you want to take a stand against,' Andy says.

'The rape of our forests,' Jessica says, distracted by Eva, the words out before she can stop herself, 'by anyone or any organisation. The chipmill in particular.'

'The rape,' Andy says, savouring the sound. 'You feminists love that word, don't you?'

Jessica picks up another apple and begins peeling it. The little pieces of green skin fall on the board.

'You don't have to be a feminist to want to stop the exploitation of our forests.' There is an alarming teariness in her voice.

'So what do you want to do about it?' Andy asks.

To her surprise he's not going in for the kill.

'Lobby. Demonstrate; occupy the forests, not work for the bastards.'

'Very good, but not very, what d'you call it? Effective. They cut it down and you write letters. Fat lot of good your letters to Telecom have done. I don't see any telephones, do you?'

'We don't just write letters, we organise meetings, we get people involved.'

'More fucking words,' Andy says. 'They fuck with our forests, you talk about it.'

'Sounds like you guys could do with a smoke,' Martin says, pushing in, handing a joint to Andy who takes a long pull, looking at Jessica all the time, then offers it to her, the smoke still in his lungs.

She pushes it away. 'Contrary to popular opinion I don't think marijuana is the solution to every ill,' she says.

For a moment Andy demonstrates what appears to be honest amazement, then bursts into laughter, smoke emerging from his nose and mouth, caught in his hair so that he seems to be alight, bending over and coughing and laughing, slapping his thigh. The others join in.

'No, but it helps,' he says.

Nothing has been achieved. She should have stayed at home. Better to be lonely than to fuck up like this every time. She can no longer hold back the tears. She is acutely conscious of the young man. She turns away, lifting her apron to her cheeks.

Andy comes around the bench. She tries to turn even

further away but this would expose her to the others. He puts a hand on her shoulder, speaking quietly into her ear.

'If you're serious, come up and talk about it.'

Then he is gone, still laughing.

four

It is the drumming which eventually drives Jessica from the room. No other community activity is so completely guaranteed to alienate her. She doesn't mind the singing or the music they make with guitars and flutes and mandolins. There is a joyous anarchy in the loud cacophony which emerges when everyone plays together. The drumming is something else; it is a tight rhythmic rant, a disowning of the individual to the beat of the tribal which, in this case, means playing along with or behind Martin, the master musician, the one who holds it all together. It is the most significant way in which he maintains his position of authority. Jessica's inability to keep time, her lack of desire to even attempt to do so, more neatly confirms her status as outsider than the altercation with Jim.

As she gathers her things, readying herself to slip out the kitchen door, Suzy is instantly beside her, standing her paws on Jessica's hips. She strokes the dog's head and whispers reassurance, looking around to see if she needs to say goodbye to anyone, but there is no one. They are, anyway, lost in their syncopation. Tonight there seems to be some kind of competition taking place between Martin and Andy. They are sitting next to the fire, across from each other, drums lodged between their legs. Their palms beat the skins but their eyes are locked, not so much playing with each other as vying for dominance.

She steps out onto the veranda with her dog, lonely and disappointed.

The young man, Kelvin, is sitting in the dark on an old bed, the coal of a cigarette gleaming.

'I'm sorry,' she says, doubly embarrassed now, fumbling for the doorhandle. The attraction had been so obvious and she had behaved so badly in front of him. 'I didn't mean to disturb you.'

'You're not,' he says. 'Cigarette?'

'I don't.'

Suzy investigates him, sniffing at his trousers, and he puts his face down next to hers. Jessica holds onto one of the posts. The silence, which is not silent because of the drums, freezes her tongue.

'Nice dog,' he says.

He rubs her hindquarters and the dog develops that pained expression she adopts when feeling blissful, a complete abandonment to the moment, accompanied by an overwhelming wish to withdraw, or at least not to be observed.

'She loves attention,' Jessica says, but thinking, really, what a slut she is. 'You're not a drummer then?'

He shakes his head, 'I never mastered the technique.' Suzy

sits down next to him, but slowly, leaning against his leg, one eye on her mistress.

'I was about to go home,' she says. 'I'm not so good at being social, out of practice, you know.' She is devoid of clever phrases, wishes she could have come up with something other than she was about to leave, because now she will have to.

'I liked what you said before, inside,' he says.

'About pine planting? I didn't think I was very supportive of the idea.'

'Hey, it's a job. I've only been doing it for a week.' He bends down again and says some nonsense words in Suzy's ear. 'Besides, I thought that planting trees had been officially declared good.'

'There's trees and trees.'

'So I've heard.'

'So you've been told.'

'Yes.'

There's a bit of play in that, a bit of the ball going backwards and forwards over the net; she has even managed to laugh at herself.

'I meant I liked what you said about dope. That it's not the cure for everything.'

He is, she realises, actually trying. She spends so much time inside her own mind that sometimes she forgets to look out. The young man is there, in front of her, his masculinity arrayed before her in all its studied carelessness; and as soon as she sees it, the fall of the cloth of his shirt across his chest and belly, his naked forearm, she feels the pull of desire, perhaps that's too strong, curiosity, she feels the pull of strong curiosity, holding her on the veranda.

'I'm not anti-drugs,' she says, seeming to feel it is important he should know that, although as soon as she's said it she wonders why. She *hasn't* been anti-drugs, she's smoked and dropped as much as the best of them. But that's in the past. Perhaps this is where her frustration at the group stems from. Their indolence. All that talk about doing stuff in the forest is just words, stoned raves. Dreams. She's heard it all before. She prefers the hard yards of organisation, it's something she has a gift for, but it's not one that's appreciated on the Farm. Inside the drumming reaches some sort of crescendo. A woman, probably Sally, lets out a high quavering wail, an ululation, like an African. Jessica would be at a loss to say how bad it makes her feel.

'You want to come for a walk?' she says

'Sure.'

The moonlight is still weak so they keep to the road, Kelvin in one tyre track, she in the other, her lantern abandoned beside the door of the main house because she hadn't the courage to cross the room to get it. Their feet crunch on the gravel and he asks her questions and she finds herself answering, if only to fill in the space between them, but it's complex, because if she has to explain what she's doing on the Farm then she has to go back a long way – there's the time she spent in London, and then what happened when she came back to Melbourne, her sad history of married men – and she's not sure she should be telling a stranger these things.

She had wanted to be a solicitor. She had even completed her degree, but then had found she couldn't stand being an articled clerk for even a single day, let alone a year. She had been accepted by an old and venerable firm but had lasted just one afternoon. She'd been assigned to the stacks, and all those folders tied up with ribbon, the rows and rows of cases, each one no doubt a brick in the edifice of the law of precedence, seemed to lean in on her, suffocating her. She suddenly couldn't bear to think of them as her life. She ran off to London; to escape her family, the law, whatever, to be a writer, which, in the event, meant working in pubs and becoming someone's lover . . . there was no end to the need for everyone, apparently, to fill their lives with events, not only the big ones but also the little, ordinary ones, every minute filled with the imperative of doing. On the Farm these expectations are largely absent. On the Farm there is silence. Of course there are social pressures, perhaps even more intense because of the smallness of the group, but she still manages an unusual level of isolation. And if she resents the other people on the Farm, or has regrets, disappointments, about living here, they do not stretch to the landscape. She loves it. She loves the hills and the forest and the simple rhythm of her life. A clarity has settled in her, not just in her brain but also in her hearing; she can sense sounds beyond the reach of everyone else. In the safety of this separated world she gives herself over to them as she might to a lover.

She realises, with the young man Kelvin by her side, that this quiet is what she had craved back at the main house, and in her social ineptness she has managed to drag him along with her so that now she still can't hear it. Except, of course, it's her who's doing the talking, she's the one filling in the spaces. He's the one who's listening, who's got her talking.

At the creek they turn up the steep hill towards her ridge.

'Do you mind if we stop talking for a while?' she says. 'Sometimes I just like to hear the night.'

So then there is only the grate of their boots on the gravel road. The moon is in its first quarter and the light is softer than it will be in another week, when the shadow's edges will be cut by a knife. Tonight they are indistinct and the sense of the valley opening out all around them as they climb is given as much by a vacancy of air as by vision. Released from the need to explain anything she is all at once glad to be there in the night with him, alone. She puts out a hand and interlaces her fingers with his, pulls him off the road onto a path. She ducks beneath branches, leads him out onto one of the granite slabs, away from the trees. To where the whole world is laid out below them.

There is no wind. Night noises reverberate around them; this is the silence she loves. Far below there is a sort of echoing plash, she knows the sound but has never managed to identify it. It's an unknown noise, one that can only be heard by a kind of wilful listening, something akin to the exercise of imagination, which grants it an unusual power; the sound – this thing that is smaller and more abstract than anything she knows – enters her, rather than the other way around, and, once inside, expands, refusing to admit to the boundaries of

31

flesh. It stretches her, including within her the whole valley, the hills, the sky, even the people, those distant drums, the man beside her, the dog, everything.

'Can you hear it?' she says.

'Yes,' he replies, and it doesn't matter what he is referring to, not then, not while their hands touch and the white air holds them on the face of the world.

'Where do you live?' he asks.

'Not far from here. I'll show you.'

five

He woke in her bed, a woman's bed, surrounded by women's things: bottles, jars, jewellery, clothes, scarves; a woman's smell, that subtle litany of scents both natural and refined.

A several-paned triangular window lodged near the ridge pole spilled a line of sunlight, exposing, in its angular course, the room's unusual geometry. She was asleep beside him, head turned away, hair arrayed on the pillow. He had not realised there was so much of it. As if drawn by his gaze she rolled towards him, put a hand on his chest, palm open, feeling him, confirming his reality, then swept back the hair, revealing her face, cheek pressed against the pillow. A woman's face. Very close, puffed with sleep. Her arm displacing the covers so that he saw, also, a swelling of breast, white against the white sheet.

She opened one eye and smiled. He watched the whole thing: her being asleep, opening her eye and, concurrent with that, her smile. Her expression did not pass through any stages on the way, did not stop at doubt, confusion, concern or fear, went directly to smile. Such unaffectedness could only provoke in him an instinctual terror. Kelvin needed time to respond to things. And despite his attempt to conceal it, and using only one eye, she saw his reaction. The smile faded.

All at once she was up and out of the bed, her back to him, naked, bending over to find a sarong, covering up before he could see more of her, just the briefest glance allowed, pale freckled skin, swelling of buttock, smooth strength of thigh; then she was on the ladder, descending.

She had not been so coy in the night. 'Slow down,' she'd said, her hands on his chest, 'there's no rush,' lying beneath him, her breasts golden in the candlelight, her face softened by pleasure, his cock in her, 'Slow down, we've all night,' reaching up to touch his cheek, open-palmed, her fingers all over his face, rubbing it, and he had wanted it there, he'd nuzzled her hand with his face. 'Am I pretty?' she'd asked and he'd looked down at her again. 'Yes,' he'd said, and meant it, because she was; not just pretty but beautiful.

The room was long and rectangular. The bed in a loft at one end. The walls were unlined, the weatherboards simply nailed to the outside of the framing timber, the ceiling the same, except for a layer of silver insulation paper next to the iron, now sagging between the rafters, tarnished bronze by smoke. The kitchen was a series of timber slabs with shelves underneath that lacked cupboard doors. There was a pair of camping gas rings and an old slow combustion stove.

She came back inside with Suzy at her feet and he swivelled around in the bed, lay on his belly, watching; this new view of her. She was putting water to heat and mixing something in

34

a bowl. In one seamless movement she raised her arms and wound her hair into a rope, forming a precarious turban, tumbling at the edges. She glanced up at him and the smile was there again, her mouth open, white teeth flashing, blue eyes bright in the sunlight. This time he was ready, waiting for it.

'Do you like pancakes?' she said.

He liked waking in women's rooms, in women's houses. He liked the way they inhabited them. It was not just the bedroom. Jessica was evident in every portion of the structure. There were bits and pieces arranged in displays on tops of cupboards, on narrow shelves nailed in between the exposed studs; odd things: wooden boxes, shells, bits of tree and root, old biscuit tins, pictures from children's books pasted onto card, whole wings from dead birds. And then there were the books, whole shelves of them. After years in Darwin that in itself was an attraction.

Kelvin had lived in share houses, bunkhouses, aboard boats, in other people's homes, but he'd never accumulated things. To have gathered things would have hindered his capacity to move, but would also in some way have defined him. He could not afford to do what she had done. In this house she was on display, reflected in its objects. Her life visible at a single glance. Beneath the loft was the area where she wrote, a single table with a chair and a manual typewriter, the walls lined with bookshelves. 'Not published yet,' she had said, showing him around, a candle in her hand, standing close to the table in case he looked at anything. 'Well, a few articles,' averting her eyes when she spoke, then bringing them back with unnerving directness, challenging him to doubt her.

For the previous week he'd been sleeping in the bunk rooms of the old homestead at Rosehill, in a tall thin room entirely lined with unpainted pine boards, the building full of the raucous bastardry of men who lacked the company of women. At lunch on the third day he'd got up and gone with the hippies for a smoke.

On the fifth day, when it had become apparent he was going off with Jim for the weekend, Stevo had been unable to resist a comment, 'Sucked in mate,' he'd said, 'sucked in.'

He sat at the small table in the kitchen. She stood at the stove, still in her sarong, still naked beneath it. Her crepes were good, served with lemon and sugar, everything about this woman was good.

'My mother used to make these,' she said, 'every Sunday without fail.' She flipped a pancake. 'Nowadays it's just Suzy and I. *She* thinks she's in for a pancake. See?' The dog was sitting at her feet, alert to every movement. 'What sort of person would make a pancake for a dog? I'm not that sort of person, am I, Suzy?' She was not really talking to him, it was more a kind of play-acting, the dog glancing around quickly, ears swivelling. 'Did your mother cook?' she said suddenly, catching him out, so that he gave his standard answer.

'I never really knew her. She died when I was young.' The

one designed to shock and, by doing so, dissuade further enquiry. If that one didn't work the next one usually did. 'Cancer,' he added with head slightly bowed, eyes to the floor.

'That's awful,' she said. 'So who, I mean, where did you grow up?'

'In Sydney. I was raised by my father.'

'Just you and him?'

'Yes.'

'What did he do?'

'He's a bookseller. I don't have much to do with him these days.'

He ate his pancake.

Jessica poured more mix in the pan. 'I'm sorry. It's none of my business.'

That much was true.

'Don't worry about it,' he said.

'I don't have much to do with my parents,' Jessica said. 'They don't approve of this. They think I should be in Melbourne, practising law.'

He toyed with something he'd found on the table. It was a little Russian doll, the smallest piece of a series that must once have been stacked inside each other. His silence propelled her on.

'I was a good Jewish girl – always did what my parents wanted. Well, up until a point. They still have hopes. When I left London and came back to Melbourne they thought I'd come to my senses, but I took a part-time job at Greenpeace instead. Then I came up here.'

He still didn't speak. He was listening, or looked as if he was but you wouldn't have wanted to test him on comprehension.

'So that's my life.'

She sat opposite him with her pancake, her tea in its cup and saucer, no two in the place alike. She ate. People seemed to need to tell each other these things. They weren't satisfied just to be with each other, they had to fill everyone in on their history. As if anyone wanted to know, as if anyone had a right to ask. He had never been to London, had never left Australia, had no idea what the world was like. If he'd gone with Yvette he might have found these things out.

When she was back at the sink Kelvin went and put his arms around her, kissing her neck, taking the weight of her breasts in his hands. She tilted her head back and leaned against him. He wasn't good at talking but he could do this. The tap was running. He fumbled at the knot of her sarong.

'Not now,' she said, wriggling free.

He stepped back, confused.

She turned off the tap, propped herself against the bench.

'You're a strange one, aren't you?' she said.

'Am I?'

'Yes.' No humour there. 'What are your plans? I mean today.'

'I don't have any. I was supposed to hang out with Jim.'

There it was: the opportunity to leave and have it be her choice.

'Would you like me to go?'

'Do you want to?'

'I asked you first.'

She wiped her hands, adjusted the sarong. Raised her eyes; that directness again. 'No, I don't want you to go. Not yet anyway.'

He had nothing to do with his hands. 'I could stay,' he said.

'What about Jim?'

'He'll keep.'

'Good,' she said, 'that's settled then. I'll have a shower, then we can go for a trip, a picnic. An adventure.'

six

The old Holden was a car designed by men for men. Within its sparse simplicity Jessica appeared excessively fragile, her fingers thin against the shiny plastic of the steering wheel, her back straight, her chin jutting forward so that she could see over the bonnet. The manipulation of the column shift in conjunction with the clutch was a major event. In the house she had seemed larger, at least as big as him.

On the narrow farm road they came face to face with a panel van.

'Andy,' she said, nudging the car over to the side, the passenger wheels precarious on the broken edge of a wash.

The van squeezed alongside and stopped, Andy with his arm resting on the window frame, leering in at them.

'Great day, isn't it?' he said. He looked past Jessica to Kelvin. 'I'm heading down the coast.'

'Right,' she said.

'Where you two off to?'

The question could easily have been seen as one of common courtesy, but Jessica did not seem to take it that way.

'We're going to pick some plums.'

Andy looked behind him down the road. There was only forest that way.

'At Cooral Dooral,' she said.

'Never been out there,' Andy said. 'I must make the trip some day.'

Jessica gave no indication as to how this suggestion affected her. 'We have to get going,' she said.

'Okey-dokey. Did you think any more about what I said last night?'

'I'm not interested, Andrew. I have my own way of going about this thing.'

She had not turned off the motor. She engaged the clutch and pulled the lever down into first. She waited for Andy to draw forward so she could go but he made no move. She raised herself up in the seat to see the road more clearly and began to roll forward, squeezing the big car into the gap, both hands placed nervously on the top of the wheel. Kelvin could see she was not going to make it. Andy had not moved. The front wheel began to slip. The heavy car lurched sideways. Andy, only then seeing the possibility of damage to his own car, pulled forward, but it was too late for Jessica. There was a dark scraping sound from beneath their feet. Jessica pressed the accelerator to the floor, lurching back up onto the road with a roar of gravel.

'Bastard,' she said, braking hard, throwing Kelvin onto the dashboard. 'Sorry,' she added, continuing on, glancing in the mirror.

41

The car seemed to have suffered no damage.

'What the fuck was all that about?' Kelvin said.

'He's just a prick, that's all.'

They came down to the ford. She stopped and changed back into first.

'As if Carl would let him out there. He's a weasel that guy, a fucking weasel.'

Kelvin was going to say that he looked familiar but decided against it. Sometimes it seemed everyone here reminded him of someone else. As if there were only a limited number of versions of people in the world.

As Jessica pushed the car into the water the grating of metal on rock was repeated, followed by a sudden staccato burst of unmuffled motor.

'Bastard,' she said again, 'fucking bastard.'

seven

Carl heard it before the dogs. He was standing at the kitchen bench, the coffee pot on the stove, taking the black liquid in one of the small cups the way he had learned in Italy. It was difficult for him to sit to take a meal, not from fear – he was not that driven – but from laziness. The rigmarole of transferring from pot to plate, plate to table outweighed any benefit which might accrue from sitting by himself. It was simpler to stand at the bench, a book propped open against the backboard at a distance which suited his eyes.

He lifted his head. The dogs, alert at least to *his* every nuance, perked up their ears. When the sound of an engine became clear they put on a great show, jumping up and racing out of the house. At another time he might have laughed. Instead he called them to quiet with an urgency they heard and obeyed. The noise was wrong, too loud for the distance. He thought at first it might be a helicopter, its rotor blades chopping up the sound, throwing its distorted echo off the hills.

He checked the house. An instinctual reaction. From outside

he watched the opposite hill through a pair of binoculars. After several minutes he glimpsed a grey Holden, lurching over the ruts.

He went to the other end of the veranda. By leaning out he could keep the car in view as it followed the track down to the old workman's cottage and stopped. She must have come over for the plums and lost her muffler on the way. That was all. Two people got out; he couldn't identify anything else. Jessica wouldn't bring just anyone, but the other person meant almost certainly she wasn't coming to visit.

He was prey to layers of conflicting feelings: relief, annoyance at the disruption, yearning, disappointment that she wouldn't come, irritation at that, and underneath it all a surge of loneliness which threatened to grow and infect everything.

He'd spent the morning in the north-west paddock. From where he stood he could see where he'd been working, knocking out the regrowth, pushing it into piles, burning it in windrows. The grass was starting to come through, almost electric green beside the black piles of ash; superphosphate green, she called it. There was pleasure to be had in just the sight of it, the clean line along the edge of the forest, the darkness of the big gums, the thought of the fence he would build with split posts, the tractor resting near where he would put the gate. It should have been enough to stop him going to see her, but it wasn't.

Bugger the fence, he thought, thinking in Australian.

This time the dogs were ahead of him. They ran backwards and forwards between the Toyota and the house.

'Right,' he said, waving a hand. They gave a single excited bark and jumped onto the tray, shuffling for position.

She was standing next to the car with her hair tied back, wearing home-made pants and a blouse, one hand resting on the open window, the other fending off the dogs who were running between her and her silky bitch.

'Hi,' she said.

'Jessica,' he replied, but his eyes were on the man over by the old trees.

'Kel,' she called, 'come and meet Carl.'

Well-built, handsome, he guessed, though not much more than a boy. Clean eyes hardly glimpsed because he hid them when they shook hands, tilting his head down and mumbling. Nothing in the hand either, a limp thing, a wet fish; someone should teach him that before he got much older.

Carl couldn't say he felt too pleased to be introduced to the new, the younger, replacement.

'Thought we'd better get the plums before the birds,' she said.

'I heard you. Thought you were a column of tanks. Come over to the house when you're done and you can put her on the ramp, we'll take a look.'

He turned to the boy. 'Where you from?'

'Sydney,' Kelvin said.

Evidently he thought this would suffice. Carl waited.

'That was a while ago, I've been around, I was up at Cairns, and in Darwin. You're from the States aren't you?'

45

'I was.'

Carl assumed Jessica had filled him in. If she hadn't then the clothes should do it. He wore old fatigues around the farm and still kept his hair cut like a soldier's, crew on the top, almost shaved above his ears and around his head. He had even, he did not think it was taking things too far, managed to find an old pair of dog tags to wear inside his shirt.

He backed the Toyota under the trees so they could stand on the tray to pick the plums. The fruit was small and stony but sweet. Jessica said she was going to make jam, but it would be a dangerous brew for the teeth, full of pips.

Carl got Kelvin to drive the car onto the ramp, then made coffee while they waited for the metal to cool. The afternoon sun was on the valley; the mixed breeds of cattle, Hereford, Murray Grey and Brahmin, dotting the paddocks.

Jessica was organising some sort of protest. She wanted him to come along. But even if things had been different she'd have had no hope. He would have thought she knew that by now. She had, after all, got as close to him as anyone; although what she had almost found out was not the truth about his past, but the truth about his feelings. In the end he had resisted even that. For her sake. To protect her. Out of love. That he hadn't told her was proof enough. That he had suppressed the temptation to invite her to live with him in his highland fastness, to come live with him and be his wife, raise Brahmin-cross cattle and dogs, hell, even children.

'A funny thing,' she said, drinking the coffee, the boy off to the side as if it was the most normal thing in the world. 'You know the muffler? I ran into Andy on the road, poking his nose into everything. I had an argument last night with Jim, at the main house, a stupid thing. Andy bought into it, said if I wanted to take action against the mill I should come see him.'

'What did that mean?'

'They were talking about putting spikes in logs, the usual shit.'

'What did you say?'

'I told him to get fucked. He was on about it again today – that's how come I went off the road. He wanted to come out here too. He didn't say as much but you could tell.'

Only a month before Carl had gone to Bega for the cattle sales. Afterwards, against all practice, he'd allowed himself a beer. He'd been leaning on the bar when someone had come up behind him and said, 'G'day, Frank.'

It took months to grow into a name, adopting it so that when he heard it he would turn, naturally, seamlessly, as if he'd worn it all his life. And if that was hard to do, it was even harder getting rid of it. The requirement not to turn, to pretend he didn't hear, to avoid even the flinch, the tightening of the shoulders which is the giveaway, which is what they're looking for, is almost impossible to achieve.

The man touched his arm. Only then could he allow himself to respond, finding himself faced with Gazza in all his glory, the sleeveless T-shirt displaying the tattoos on his upper arm, the semi-shaven face, the calf-high boots and tight black jeans, the mullet. 'Sorry,' Carl said. 'Do I know you?' holding out his hand. 'It's Carl . . .'

At least he caught on quickly.

'Carl,' he said, 'that's right, sorry mate, remember me? Gazza? Cairns?' Taking his hand in his meaty paw.

'Gaz. That's right. Must be what, three, four years? How is it? What brings you to these parts?'

Gazza so pleased at the coincidence that it was necessary to have a drink. There'd been a time when he might have had the strength to refuse, but he'd softened. The crop they had grown together had paid for Carl's farm, several beasts, a four-wheel drive and enough to get by on, at least for a while. Gazza hadn't fared so well. He'd gone back to his old mates, always trying for the next big deal, importing smack, except this time it turned out the cops were onto them. He hadn't got caught but he'd lost it all. 'Everything 'cept the car. I do a bit of travelling these days. Thought I'd come up the Coast Road. Less traffic, if you get my drift.'

Theirs had been what Carl called a business friendship, a partnership that lasted for the period of the agreement and was finished, done, completed, when it ended. Gazza was not so clear about things. He thought the whole world was his friend.

Over a beer Carl hoped to impress on him his need for privacy. Gazza was enough of a crim to understand, but the meeting worried him. If Gazza had found him, then others might. For almost three years he had been undisturbed. He had begun to think he could live a normal life, could go into a pub after the sales and talk cattle with the locals, could clear scrub from paddocks, build a dam, love his dogs, watch the dawn and the midday and the coming of night and not be attentive to the prerogatives of his past. The incident had reminded him that he hadn't been forgotten. That somewhere, in some office, on some computer, in some shoe box somewhere, the essential piece of information remained.

'That muffler oughta be cooled by now,' Carl said in the boy's direction.

Kelvin followed him out to the shed, a large open-sided structure cluttered with farm machinery, full of the smell of hay and cows and diesel, the dogs at his heels.

The ramp was a crude affair, a couple of slabs running up onto stumps. It was just possible for the two men to squeeze under the front end of the car.

'Do you know anything about these things?' Carl asked.

'No,' Kelvin said.

The exhaust pipe had come apart at a join. The separated ends were bent and rusted.

'They're filthy, dirty and recalcitrant, if you know what that means. Ornery if you don't. We'll need to make a sleeve.'

He went back into the shed and rummaged around, found a piece of old flat iron and curved the steel around the pipe, folded up the loose ends like lunch wrap, using a pair of multi-grips. Then he wound some wire around it and made a sling which he attached to the underside of the car.

'That should hold it.'

His fingers were black with the oil and the dust from the rusting pipe.

He was surprised about the boy, about her bringing him out here like that. She must have wanted Carl to look him over. He did not know what that meant. Perhaps she was asking him to become, or maybe it was an acknowledgment that he already was, a kind of guardian, someone who would look out for her, someone to run to in times of trouble. After they'd stopped with the sex she had got on with her life. She'd had no idea of the effect she'd had on him. She regarded him as a friend, useful for fixing or cutting or building, for listening to her endless stream of problems and plans. What did he get? Access? Perhaps. She was beautiful and young, lithe and natural, deeply intense. Just to have her around the house was enough. The smell of her. There was still the need for sex, but that could be managed elsewhere, even in a town as small as Bega. Now, he thought, she was asking him to go a step further, to include in this arrangement the new man, the one she was sleeping with.

'You don't talk much,' he said.

'There doesn't seem to be much to say right now,' Kelvin said.

'I like that, I can't abide chatter.'

He brought his gaze to bear on him, pinning him against the stump. He *was* good-looking. He could see what it was she liked about him, the freshness, the strong features as yet unmarked by lines. But there was something deeper, too,

50

unexplained. Kelvin's was a face waiting for something, for life to light it up. Presuming someone was home in the first place.

'If you've had enough of the pines I could use a hand out here for a few days. Fencing,' he said.

Kelvin thought about it for a moment. 'I'd like that.'

'Monday then,' Carl said, crawling out from under the ramp.

eight

Carl handed him a crowbar off the back of the tractor.
'Three foot deep,' he said, 'bout this round,' holding his hands the width of his shoulders apart.

Kelvin had never placed a strainer post. He thought he was fit from the pines but sinking a hole in debased granite proved a different manner of work, every millimetre of subsoil hard won with the bar, the shaft of octagonal steel grasped in two hands and launched at the base, released at the last moment to avoid the jar as it hit, picked up, its weight increasing in direct proportion to the number of times, and launched again. Blisters began to swell along the top of his palm and in the valley between thumb and forefinger before he was even halfway down.

Carl came over and looked in. 'Wider at the base,' he said.

The hole was deep. Kelvin rammed the bar into the sides near the bottom, sweat gathering in beads on his forehead.

Carl split posts. He'd cut the trunk of a tree into lengths and now he ran the blade of the McCulloch down the sides of each one, sectioning it, the saw bucking and screaming and grinding. When he was done he put it aside and took up a wedge, tapping it into the end-grain, then rammed it home with a nine pound hammer, swung hard. In the silence after each blow the log continued to creak, every fibre resisting the wedge. When the timber gave, the post sprang away from the heartwood, falling on the ground with a blunt musical sound. Carl pushed it away, picked up the wedge and began the process again. He worked steadily, relentlessly, managing to make the use of such a hammer look light. In the end all that was left of each log was a small central pole, ragged, like something naked.

Kelvin lay belly-down on the ground, reaching into the earth with his bare hand to scoop out the last of the loose dirt. He wondered if this could possibly be the way it was done. At least this time Carl was satisfied. He looked in, grunted, then dropped the bar into the hole, leaning it against one side. He brought the tractor over and backed up to one of the strainer posts, using the hydraulics to lift the end off the ground. Between them they managed from there to prise up the log, the base of it sliding down the bar, a great mother of a thing, a tree trunk, smooth and round, square-cut on the top.

When it was in they both put a hand on it, feeling its strength in the ground. They looked across the top at each other and smiled. They sat back and rolled a smoke, drank coffee from a thermos, stared out over the paddocks. It was an overcast day, the air warm and close, the flies heavy on their backs.

Kelvin looked down the path Carl had cleared for the fence.

'By week's end we'll have a line of wire strung,' Carl said. 'Where I come from the ground's so hard most o' the year you couldn't fix a post. Had to build fences that stood by themselves. Buck'n'rail. So cold in the winter the thermometers froze.' At times Carl's accent seemed almost a parody of itself.

Around lunch it began to rain. They had the two strainers stood, and a third, an in-line post, placed in a gully where it would hold down the wire when the tension came up. They abandoned the work, Kelvin riding the back of the tractor to the house, liquid with exhaustion.

Jessica had driven him to the crossing in the morning. Their second night in her home had been almost domestic, the lack of sleep playing on them, promoting a kind of softness, their bodies too tired for sex but too enamoured to resist. Working with Carl he had found himself subject to a strange and disconnected play of images, just within the range of consciousness. They were strangely banal, being no more than pictures: the flower garden outside her door; the view through the windscreen as they rounded a corner on the narrow forest road; the kitchen in her house. Nothing was happening in them, but they still had the power to tilt him off balance; they had a hidden emotional content which served to keep him half in her world, even while the tractor rumbled across the main paddock, the dogs running behind.

Carl took him in the house. Lunch was bread and cheese, more coffee, a simple affair made awkward by their presence together in the rudimentary kitchen. Out along the fence line they had been surrounded by unlimited space, the green fields sloping down to the dam, the eucalypt forest climbing into the hills, the very sky. Carl's presence had been something of a defence against such vastness. Within the walls of the house he was larger, formidable. Kelvin escaped to the veranda with a book, curling up on an old sofa that smelled of dog. Across the grey weatherworn floorboards, beyond the rail, the rain had begun to fall heavily, in sheets and gusts, obscuring the longer view.

In the evening they played chess. With the coming of the rain Carl had lit the fire as well as the stove to keep out the damp, but it made it so hot inside that they needed to prop the veranda doors open. Moths congregated around the lamps. They drank a beer and played and then drank a couple more. Carl replied to his attempts at conversation in monosyllables. Kelvin, losing, took affront, seeing in his opponent's silence a comment on his performance. He was an impulsive player, going in strong in an attempt to gain dominance of the board, pushing at Carl's pieces to prevent him from bringing his strategies to the fore. He failed to see Carl's defensiveness as a strategy in itself, drawing him into vulnerable places where he was open to attack.

Carl got up to rummage for food. He found meat in the fridge and put potatoes on the stove, poured oil in a pan and threw in rough-cut onions, stirring them with the point of his knife. Kelvin fiddled with the chessmen. It was a child's set, plain wood, the pieces shiny from handling. He was not sure what to do while Carl prepared the food. He was excess baggage, both a burden on this man and burdened by him. He stuffed the chess pieces in their little box but the heads of the bishops stuck out, he had to rattle them to make it close.

'You known Jessica long?' he asked.

'Some.'

'What about the others?'

'Oh, I know a few of them. Not much. I keep to myself. They're good neighbours, that's what matters, I don't get involved.'

Carl had a habit of leaving such long spaces between his thoughts that Kelvin was ready to ask another question by the time he got around to continuing. 'I have opinions but I keep them to myself,' Carl said. 'I like some of these people but I don't get involved in the day-to-day stuff. They have to have a referendum to figure out whether to grub out or spray the blackberries. I haven't got the time for that, I get on the tractor. I'm not good at meetings, committees. I like to get things done.'

He pushed the onions to the side and laid the meat in the pan, bent to find some plates, put knives and forks on the table.

'I spent a deal of time on farms like that back home in the late sixties, early seventies. People going back to nature. People looking for something. They grow up in the suburbs and they think something's missing and then they hear of this back-to-the-land stuff and they think, that's for me. So they come down here and straightaway they've got problems. They have to have a roof, they need wood to keep themselves warm. So they learn some things real quick, they build a house and a garden. It's good for them. They get their hands dirty. How do you take your meat?'

'How you do it.'

'Then here it is.'

He lifted a great slab out of the pan and brought it over to the table.

It came from a beast raised on the property, cut thick, cooked so it was still red in the centre.

'The trouble is once they've got the house, what are they going to do? Small-acre farming? You've got to be kidding. That went out in the Middle Ages. That's survival stuff, and these people are educated, middle-class. Physical work is good, but only as a kind of spiritual practice, not to make a living. So now they're out in the country and there's *still* something missing. So what do they do? They find a cause. Either that or they turn on each other. I try not to get involved.' He started to eat.

'Jessica's into organisation,' Kelvin said, assuming this diatribe was in some way directed at her. How could it not have been? Everything in his mind referred back to Jessica.

Carl raised his eyes from his food. 'Yeah?'

'All this stuff about wood-chipping. She seems to spend all her life in meetings.'

'You don't think much of that, huh?'

'I don't know. I'm like you, I don't like meetings.'

'Jessica's different.' There was an edge to Carl's voice.

'Hey, I like her,' Kelvin said. 'I'm just not into all this political shit.'

He was shocked to catch a look of disapproval, even malice, on Carl's face. The older man chewed on a piece of meat until apparently he decided there was nothing more to be gained from it. He took the morsel out of his mouth and laid it on the side of the plate.

'Pericles said . . . You know Pericles, don't you?'

'No.'

'The *Athenian*?'

'No.'

'Pericles said, "We do not say that a man who has no interest in politics is a man who minds his own business. We say that such a man has no business here."'

'Right,' Kelvin said, too quickly. He took a drink from his bottle. 'What's with you two?'

'We're friends.'

'Just friends?'

'These days.'

Kelvin smiled his broadest smile, white teeth flashing, a bit slow on the uptake but warned now, the ground laid out for him. At least he knew the bloke wasn't going to want him to fuck.

nine

The first time he'd seen Shelley he was thirteen years old and scavenging through bins behind a cafe in the Cross. Two boys roughly his age had come upon him and started to make a play of their find, taunting him, swearing at him, throwing empty cans at him, calling him a dog, a shit, a piece of fucking dogshit; like a song. Behind them, apparently indifferent, but watching, was a girl, licking an ice-cream cone. When she was finished eating she turned away. The boys abandoned their game and followed her.

At that point he could not remember when he had last spoken to anyone. He had left Eden several days before on the early bus, alone, *running away*, all his energies directed towards this part of the plan, all the lies and scheming and petty theft culminating in his presence next to the heavy glass of the bus window, nothing left for what might happen when he arrived. But by the time the Nowra train arrived at Central it was dark and raining, and the vague ideas he'd nurtured of working nights in a bakery or at the markets so that he could sleep in a park during the day were shown up for the adolescent daydreams they were. He walked out along Broadway, into City Road, the pavements slick and cold, a wind blowing against the shop windows. He cowered in a doorway when a police car slipped past. He waited for them to turn and come back, for the inevitable hand on his shoulder, but it never came. Instead he continued on beneath the streetlights, shivering, panic-stricken, exposed, until he found an abandoned warehouse. He crawled under the wire and into the building where at least it was dry, if horribly dark, stinking of urine and age. No one had been looking for him. The police were not draining the marshes, there were no men in yellow overalls walking in long lines through the scrub calling his name. He had made it to Sydney, alone, and no one had noticed or cared.

He watched the three of them go, sticking to the middle of the lane, shouting and laughing, the boys swinging around the older girl, engaged in a kind of dance with the tarmac, the blue-stone kerbs, the parked cars and the rubbish. He followed, and if they noticed they gave no indication. At Taylor Square they turned past the courthouse, out onto the brightness of Oxford Street, where they became suddenly smaller, as if in larger areas they knew how to become invisible. They took a side street next to the gay pub; when he reached its awnings he just had time to glimpse them slipping into a laneway down the back.

The street was ill-lit, part of some one-way system and subject to rapid bursts of determined traffic. The houses on either side were boarded up, their tiny front yards filled with rubbish. The laneway was even darker. He went right to its end and back again but there was no sign of them. He could not have said why he was there. The boys had tormented him with a violence made more intimidating by its casualness, and the girl had simply watched. But his small stash of money was gone and any illusions about the city long forgotten. He was hungry and cold and would have happily been found, happily been taken back to Eden and suffered the beating from Rick. At least he would have been owned. He sat in the laneway, furiously pushing a stick backwards and forwards in the dirt to stop himself from crying. He was stupid, stupid, stupid. The ground was hard-packed, the stick made hardly any impression on it. When he looked up a boy was watching him through a hole in the fence. Their eyes met and the boy said to someone behind him, 'It's the kid from the Cross.' Another voice said, 'Let's see,' and then there were a bunch of them, peering through the gap.

'You need a place to stay?' the girl said.

There were five of them living in the squat off Barwon Terrace. It was a cavernous place whose internal walls and floors and anything else of value had been stripped. What timber was left was being slowly cannibalised to keep the building warm and to cook the small amount of food they bothered to prepare themselves. Mostly they lived on takeaway, stuff they bought, augmented with anything they could pilfer. The girl was Shelley. She wasn't the leader, that honour went to Spic, an older boy, thin and keen, already skilled in the way of the street, to whom they paid allegiance and any money or goods they came by. In turn he divided up the spoils, keeping a larger portion for himself and in return offering protection from drunks and drug addicts, the casual flow of the marginal folk. Spic was number one but it was Shelley who held them together. She was close to sixteen, her hair cut short and ragged. She wore loose clothes whose bagginess concealed her fragility, the sleeves of her skivvy hanging down over her hands.

Kelvin stayed. He hung on, especially to Shelley, accompanying her wherever she went, and she accepted his adoration as she might that of a pet; because of her they all tolerated him, allowed him to drift with them through the streets, sitting on kerbs looking at people and discussing how it would be for them later, what kind of car they would have, what clothes they would wear. How they would spend the millions they were going to win in the lottery.

When she was preparing for work even Shelley didn't want his company.

'I'll come with you,' he said.

'Don't be stupid.'

'Why not?'

'Why do you think? I do it for guys.'

'You do what for guys?'

He really didn't know, or didn't want to think it possible.

'It's easy,' she said. 'They cruise past in cars. You get in, you jerk them off. There's nothing to it.'

She was applying a mask. She invoked strong feelings. He watched her and his heart rate increased, his limbs became loose and awkward. He tried to think of things to do or say to please her. He wanted to be next to her all the time. He loved her smell, was like a child beside her. But when he watched her doing her face it seemed that the features came apart from each other. Her eyes, her nose, her mouth became too big for the space they occupied. They were each individually perfect, but out of balance. He had to concentrate on just one bit at a time.

'I could do it too,' he said. 'I could do it for women. We need the money. I could earn some money too.'

'Women don't do it.'

'Why not?'

'Because.'

'How much do you get?'

'Ten or fifteen bucks for a hand job, twenty-five or thirty if they want to touch you, forty bucks for head.'

'What's that?'

'You don't know what head is?'

'Yeah, well, I do.'

'What is it then?'

He had no idea. With each addition to her face she was getting further away from him.

'I don't know,' he said.

'Well why d'you say you did, stupid? It's when you suck them off.'

'Yeah. Right.'

He did not believe her.

She stood up. 'Well that's me. How do I look?'

She had become someone else.

'Listen,' she said. 'You can come with me to the street, just

63

this once, okay? You can come and see what it's like. But you do what I say.'

William Street was broad and brash, running up to Kings Cross from the city full of the tail-lights of cars, the great neon signs at the top proclaiming the nature of the place; the Ferrari, Rolls Royce and Jaguar shops with their broad expanses of glass lining the boulevard. The bass beats blaring from car windows and the high-maintenance women in heels laughing loud beside men in shiny suits.

In a laneway running parallel things were not so bright. The boys who dressed as girls leaned against a concrete wall and pushed out their narrow hips in tight little skirts and frilly blouses. Men in cars crawled passed, hidden behind tinted windows, while a stream of invective fell against the glass and metal, was tossed backwards and forwards across the way from the red-rimmed mouths – a repetitive, harsh sound, like charnel birds interminably claiming territory.

When Shelley came by they turned it on her. They called her a slut, a little whore. They spat on the ground where she had walked. They told her to go elsewhere and swung their handbags on their little gold straps, suggesting to Kelvin, in falsetto voices, that perhaps *he* might like to stay.

Down the far end she stopped. She told Kelvin to piss off and went to the edge of the kerb. She opened her little bag and took out a compact, checking her lipstick in its tiny mirror, put it away and lit a cigarette, then, holding the pole of a parking sign, slightly raised one leg, stretching the cloth of her short dress, exposing her upper thigh. She stayed that way, talking to Kelvin hidden in a doorway, but not looking at him, talking as if she was addressing the cruising cars, telling him what she thought of them in saccharine tones, pouting her lips and bending forward to show her little cleavage, inviting them to come to her, to try a real girl, a teenage girl, to explore their teenage fantasies, the language of the street coming from her strange but rich in all its textures, the street dark and narrow, the glittering boys further up tossing smokes to each other while under their skirts their genitals smarted from the tape.

When a car stopped she told Kelvin to wait, she'd be back.

After an age she returned, pulling down the back of her skirt as she left the car, searching in her bag for make-up, a cigarette already in her mouth.

He wanted to know what she had done but she wouldn't tell him. She returned to her post, to her posturing, waiting for another door to open.

Kelvin watched the street as he might a film. With Shelley there it didn't touch him. These cars going by, their windows down or up, this concrete laneway, the backs of the buildings with their graffiti-stained roll-a-doors, the glittering transvestites themselves, were all harmless players in something designed for his entertainment. He had escaped from Eden and come to a place where things were real, where the adult world was shown to be the way he had always sensed it was, completely fucked up.

When she finished they went up the Cross together, just the two of them. She had money. They wove through the crowds, past the touts and louts, the glossy shops, moving together in the bright vigour of the street. They bought ice cream and walked back to the squat singing some stupid pop song it didn't matter how loud because there was no one who could hurt them.

He didn't see how it affected her. He saw her go out in the back yard in the night and wash herself with the hose and he thought it strange and asked her wasn't she cold, but it wasn't until he got in a car himself that he saw what she was washing off, that this world, too, had a way of getting under the skin, as if there were layers and layers of the stuff.

ten

A week later he comes back. Jessica was not certain he
would, or if she even wanted him to. He does not strike
her as the reliable type, not simply because of his age; he has a
fluidity to him, as if he is permanently passing through, own-
ing nothing, a clean slate, an empty vessel. The perfect zipless
fuck. It is part of his attraction. He hovers, naked, in the morning, at the top of the ladder, exquisite, smooth-skinned,
tight-bodied, white buttocks almost crude against the sun-
burned back. He knows she is watching. She can see that in
the way he holds his shoulders back, offering his best side. It
seems he is accustomed to being admired. She notes it, she
admires, but she could do without it, that vanity. It doesn't suit.
As if he is the peacock, she the Plain Jane. It's not the way it is.
He's just a boy.

She takes him into the forest to show him who's who.

She leads him across Gubra Creek and along the fire trail
which tracks its course. They get occasional glimpses of the
developments on the other side, Martin's sprawling structures,
his vegetable garden, much smaller from this vantage than it

appears close up; Andy's permanent tent in its sunless valley, the chimney smoking blue in the morning air.

She turns uphill, following a path of her own design, pushing through the debris of peppermint and dogwood, crashing on dried leaves and tassels of bark, the smell of eucalyptus cut with that of mustard or curry from the small leaves they brush against.

'This won't last long,' she says, anxious to reassure him, her guest.

The undergrowth gives way abruptly to open forest. This is where it begins.

The mountain rises in ridges, the slopes taken by stringybarks, *Eucalyptus muelleriana*, a name which her vague grasp of Latin attaches to the idea of women, although there is nothing especially feminine about them; they are, if anything, spectacularly asexual, populating the mountain's flanks with an ecclesiastical air, curiously still, vast cathedrals of grey trunks, fire-blackened at the base, clear underfoot, obscuring all view except of themselves.

They climb. He walks beside her, matching her pace, separating and coming back together as the terrain permits. She normally comes here alone, without even the dog, today tied up at home. She lives close to this. They all do, but most never enter it. The Farm is already wild enough. The mountain's geography can only be revealed by exploration, its contours only learned by touch. There are no landmarks, no paths, no signs. The given directions are up or down or across, and the latter is mostly impossible. The slopes are steep, and any attempt at a traverse leads the inexperienced walker into gullies of loose rock and bracken fern, tangled with vines. The best passage is along the line of the ridges.

She stops at the summit of a small rise in a series of indistinguishable rises. There is a ring of rocks and an old and blasted tree which once must have been taller than everything around. Kelvin sits to catch his breath. Jessica perches on a rock looking out, though there is nothing to see, only branches latticed against the sky. There is also, now that the crashing of their feet has ceased, no sound. This is not some crowded aviary, no mammalian haven. The ground is little more than bare rock. Ants with gold regalia on their backs chart their immediate territory with wilful incomprehensibility.

He is about to speak but she holds up a hand.

'Listen,' she says.

A wind is moving in the valley below. Down through the trees this current of air is tossing branches and leaves, engaged in a struggle to depart or stay, it is unclear which. The contrast between the stillness where they are and the turbulence below is startling; moreover, this patch of wind seems to be approaching, albeit not directly. It climbs, then veers off, then climbs again, like a searching animal, racing across the flanks of the mountain, swinging in one direction and then another. A cloud passes across the sun. Jessica is fixed where she was when she turned to him, her hand up, like a traffic cop, holding him with her eyes. Suddenly it is on them. Hot air sweeps over them; every twig, each leaf and branch, every molecule rattled by its passing. The sun breaks through, tossing myriad shafts of

light in their eyes. Then the wind is gone again. In its wake
kookaburras, unseen before, begin their clamour, barking out
their laugh in crazy elongated speeches, thrilling, strange.

He breaks from her eyes.

'Did you do that?' he says.

'No, it was only the wind,' she laughs, delighted. 'The air
spirits checking us out.'

'Did we pass?'

'I think so.'

He draws her to him. He wants to kiss her but she turns her
face away. It's not the right time for that.

The stringybarks yield to other species, silver-top ash, tall
trees whose black bark gives way to smooth-skinned, shining
limbs, sparse-leafed, their trunks leaning awkwardly into the
slope.

The first time she came here was by mistake, trying to find
the summit, following the ridges up and trusting in her faith
that any valley she dropped into would bring her back to
Gubra Creek and, eventually, the Farm. This particular rock-
strewn ridge, the trees so vast and far apart that their fallen
leaves could not manage to cover the ground, troubled her. It
seemed to hold some darker purpose. Its lonely asymmetry
was like a curtain drawn across the doorway of a deeper place.
She had shied away, dropping off the side of the ridge.

Now she takes the same route, but out of choice.

'I thought we were going to the top,' Kelvin says.

'There's nothing there,' she says. 'You can't see out or anything.'

'What's on the other side?'

'Cooral Dooral. Well, not exactly, that's way off to the north. But once you cross the ridge you're on that side. You take one tiny step either way when you're at the top and you come out in completely different country.'

'So let's go.'

'I want to show you something else.'

She takes his hand, guiding him down, but then has to release it to maintain her balance, the slope is so steep. Underfoot is loose, broken-edged rock. There are shrubs and young trees to grasp but some have vicious thorns. Below them is a tight mass of greenery, uninviting, impenetrable, difficult to reach. When they get close they are on ground so perpendicular that it appears to be literally underneath them, that they must step down into it, like entering water. Indeed, when they do so, the change is almost as radical and immediate. They push through and, after another hundred feet of scrambling, find themselves on a valley floor, a wide level place completely enclosed by the canopy.

In the half-light leopard-spotted trees rise up like pillars. The ground is an interwoven complex mosaic of roots and round pebbles.

'Wow,' he says, 'rainforest!'

'Is that what it is?'

'I guess so. I've seen it up north, near Cairns. But this is different.'

'It's my lost world. I always expect to see dinosaurs.'

Beside him a liana as thick as an elephant's leg curves down and then up again like a hammock.

'Do you like it?' she asks.

She had thought she was bringing this young man here to show him what was important, a kind of object lesson in the face of his own self-centredness. Now she feels like the one on display. Her vulnerability everywhere obvious. She goes to him, comes inside his arms, feels his breath in her hair. She raises her lips to be kissed and the touch of his are instantly hot and moist, as if he has been waiting. She places his hand on her breast, finds the bare skin beneath his shirt. He smells of all the branches and leaves and shrubs he has brushed against. Against his chest all her anxieties evaporate. She unbuttons his shirt, fumbling, unable to take time to look, her hands on his belly and chest. She undoes the belt on his trousers, the button, the zip, finds, tangled within, his cock, holds it with both hands, quivering. He undresses her and she sits on the curve of the hanging liana; she reaches up and grasps the strands of the vine for balance and he comes into her. She wraps her legs around him and pulls him to her. She is filled with the fecundity of the place, she is in the mountain being fucked by the forest in its darkest realms, her white skin glowing in the half-light. The vine sways, she curls her legs around his back, he sucks on her skin, licks at her neck, kisses and kisses her open mouth. And although she is lost in his touch, is like a cipher of his every movement, pushed hither and thither by his desire, she is also in him. She is the mountain, the forest, the crumbling broken-rocked slopes and the vines that hold them together, the wind in the open trees, the tracking ants, none of it is too large or too small to be encompassed in the act they share in this deep recess of the land.

When they are done he moves away. She stays, strung out on her vine. He lies on the soft damp leaves, she can see the broken pieces of them on his skin, but although they are rotting, crumbling, they bear no resemblance to dirt, they lie on him or about him but he is not altered by them. He is separate.

He opens his eyes. 'Shall we move on then? There's mozzies about.'

He is already gone. It is the way with men, but it always shocks her, their abruptness, their readiness for the next thing. She wants to stay here forever, or for at least a minute more. He has already left. A moment of doubt troubles her mind. Did she do the right thing? She so easily reveals herself to another, as if the bare essentials of herself are the greatest gift she can offer. It is, of course, what she was looking for from him. How often has she done this, taken someone into her private places in the hope that by doing so they might reveal theirs, and instead been left stripped bare? As if it will take her lifetimes to learn the nature of the word private, what it means, that it suggests things for her alone, for no one else.

Then he comes over, loose-limbed, and kisses her, still precarious on her vine. He runs his broad hand down her body and back up again, cupping her breast. There is an additional scent attached to him. He smells of her, her in the forest, and she is glad.

eleven

By the time he made it up to Carl's house it was seven-fifteen, Jessica's car was way back over the hill and he was already out of breath. Carl was on the veranda, waiting. After taking one look at Kelvin he said, 'Coffee?'

Kelvin nodded gratefully, collapsing in a chair.

'Too much screwing, eh?'

Kelvin glanced up, surprised at the coarseness, the failed attempt, if that's what it was, at Australian humour. Carl seemed equally embarrassed. Quite apart from any common history they might have had with the woman in question, they didn't know each other well enough.

'We went walking,' Kelvin said.

'Where?'

'Dunno, across the creek, up the hill.'

Carl got his maps out. He had a great stack of the things.

'Show me,' he said, moving the cups and unfolding them on the bench. It was his way of covering for his earlier comment. 'Maps,' he said, 'are the *most* beautiful things, they're the key to everything.'

To Kelvin they were meaningless diagrams, instruction manuals in a foreign language. He was simply glad of the diversion that kept them from the paddocks and the fence. He watched politely while Carl pointed out where his house was, where Cooral Creek wound down off the plateau, cutting its way through the hills, where Gubra Creek joined it below the ford. He showed Kelvin where the Farm was, and where he'd been the day before and how really everything was much closer to everything else than it looked, it was just the mountains got in the way so you had to go the long way around by road. Even aside from any difficulty with the maps, though, Kelvin was having trouble concentrating. He'd only been away from Jessica for an hour and already he missed her. He was unaccustomed to the intensity of his feelings. He didn't need a map to remind him of what had happened between them, he could think of nothing else.

Then, at the end of the day, while they were loading the tools onto the hold-all, the dogs around their heels, stretching and yawning and yapping, Carl decided to worm the horses.

Which, Kelvin thought, was the problem with the man. He was not just relentless, he was meticulous, obsessive. He'd said of the fence, 'When you look down the line you only want to see the nearest post,' and Kelvin had heard him but hadn't paid too much attention until Carl discovered he'd rammed one in squint, a hundred mil out of line, and two days later they'd had to go back and take the bastard out again, wrapping a chain around its base and hauling it up with the tractor's hydraulics, then redigging the hole to make it right. Kelvin had been working with him for more than a week, out in the paddock, living with him at night back in his old house, and he admired him, no doubt about that; there wasn't anyone he'd ever met who had his range of skills *and* the temperament to use them. He was not so much self-sufficient as self-contained. He appeared, and this was perhaps the most mysterious part for Kelvin, to have the roots of all of his needs within himself, to have a capacity to be satisfied simply with what was around. The trouble was he didn't seem to know when to stop. He had no idea when someone else's limit might quite genuinely have been reached. He always had to go the extra mile. They were in the top paddock and the horses were nearby so he figured to round them up, dismissive of Kelvin's objections.

'Won't take but a moment. I oughta've done it days ago.'

By the time they had them yarded the last of the sun was on the hills, a line of gold creeping towards the distant ridges. Carl went to the shed for the drench. Kelvin sat on a rail. In the mellow light the colours were deep and distinct, the dark water in the dam reflecting the silver sky, currawongs calling their songs back and forth across the valley, the air clear and sweet from the remaindered heat of the day. The four horses were confined in one pen, ears up and back, wide-eyed, watching for clues as to what would happen next. Carl came back with a device like a grease gun.

They took them into the next pen one at a time. Kelvin's

job was to hold the rope while Carl inserted the tube in the back of the horse's mouth and squirted. He stood next to the animal, so much larger than he had ever imagined now that it was here, right next to him, its sharp hooves stamping. The older pair were apparently resigned to the process, at least accustomed to the indignity, and tolerated his touch. The operation took only moments: he held them, Carl squirted the foul grey liquid, and then they were back out in the paddock, coming back to watch the action from the safety of freedom, their tails up in disgust.

The filly was only a yearling and flighty, terrified of the men, ears flat, eyes rolled back, lips curled; but when Carl approached, talking gently, she accepted the rope and allowed herself to be held while the drug was administered. When Kelvin let go she coughed and spat and stuck out her great tongue, shook her head and trotted out.

'Now you,' Carl said to the speckled gelding.

In the twilight the dun was turning this way and that against the rails, high-stepping, raising and lowering his head and snorting. A pair of those slow black march flies that favour the cool of evening were bothering his heels. He stamped a foot and swept his tail, the coarse hair brushing against a post.

Kelvin knew enough to stand stock-still in the centre of the yard, his arms by his sides, palms out, while Carl moved forward, murmuring. The horse backed himself into a corner, trying desperately to see this man with both eyes at once.

'Gently now,' Carl said, saying it again, softly, repeating it over and over, 'gently now,' getting up next to the gelding and passing the end of the rope under the beast's neck and then over while the horse stood his ground, quivering.

'Come now,' he said to Kelvin. 'Round to my left, that's right, slowly now, here, take the rope,' speaking in that same gentle monotone and yet, even with that, his voice possessing a shocking authority.

Kelvin took the rope. After three horses he was confident that he knew how to calm the beast. He placed his open palm on the gelding's neck, feeling, abruptly, beneath the short hair and skin, the hardness of the flesh, the terrible strength of the animal. He whispered quietly to him. He had allowed himself to nurture the belief that it was his empathy that had calmed the other animals. Carl reached the drench over from the rail and brought it up, saying, 'Hold his ear now. Hold him.'

His *ear*? Then the horse was up. He lifted himself into the air as if Kelvin was not there. His sharp hooves pawed the air around Kelvin's head. He shrieked and thrashed above him. Kelvin ran. He turned and ran. He clambered up on the rails as the horse came down and took off around the yard, circling as fast as he could within the confined space, pounding the ground, tossing his head, kicking up his hind legs, shuddering his breath.

Carl had not moved. The drench was still in his hand, the dropped rope at his feet. He did not look at Kelvin. When the horse began to slow he approached again, moving with that same quietness in the settling dust, bending to pick up the rope, stepping inside the horse's space, putting the rope around and calling Kelvin to come off the rail. He climbed down.

He crossed the dirt and came over beside them. He took the rope.

And once again the gelding was above him, so big, the white underbelly revealed amid the raking hooves, this ancient unnatural contract between man and beast shown for what it was – the animal was trying to kill him. Again he ran. Once again Carl did not falter. He waited until the horse calmed. There was, though, a harder set to his shoulders when he approached. But not in his voice. Gently, he spoke. As soon as he was inside the gelding's range the horse was up. Not waiting for the rope. His forelegs right about Carl's head, his face thrown back to the side, his mouth open, the pink gums bright against his flashing teeth. He didn't neigh, he screamed. Carl stood. As the horse came down, as his head came down, Carl punched him. He brought his fist around and punched the animal on the nose, directly, then immediately again, punching hard, with a sharp right swing. It was as if the world had come to an end. All the evening light and warm air and colours ceased. The horse was stunned. All his terror given form. Involuntarily he shat. A stream of turds. He tried to move away, backing into a corner, his buttocks against a rail, snorting, lowering his head, pawing at the ground. He was about to rise up again, and again Carl hit him. Then he stepped right inside his space and slipped the rope around, talking to him in that same gentle monotone, as if there had been no anger, as if nothing had happened at all, but calling him all manner of obscenity, gently, evenly, only stopping when he was ready for Kelvin.

'This time,' he said, 'hold the bastard. Take his fucking ear at the base and hold on. Don't let go.'

His fist hurt. He hadn't meant to hit the horse and he felt bad about it and about doing it in front of the boy. The horse would get over it but he wasn't sure the boy would, a thing like that can turn someone, just when you think you're getting their trust out it slips and all the work you've done, all the fine stuff, gets lost. The difficulty was that watching the boy was pretty much like watching himself at the same age. Although a less generous part suggested he had been like that at a *younger* time.

He drove deliberately. Kelvin's impatience was not his, he had nowhere to be and it was his truck, his suspension, his tyres. He'd been reluctant enough to drive him over the hill as it was, knowing full well that the boy was running from him and his hardness. Who wouldn't? But he'd like to have been able to explain. What? That it *is* a battle, that you can't let things, animals, people, the world in general, push you around. You have to stand up for yourself. Did Kelvin think this farm had fallen into his lap? Carl was negotiating the rough bit of road down towards the creek and the Murray Greys were there, they must have come down for their drink and they only moved when he was right on top of them, such pretty cattle, a lot of the Angus in them, stocky beasts that he'd reared from poddy calves, bottle-feeding them at night, though you wouldn't know it to look at them. He'd only been on the place three or four years but it was more his home than any-where in the world and that was because it was hard won, because it was beautiful when he came and was more so because he'd been there.

It was also possible, he thought, that Kelvin's need to see Jess had nothing to do with the horses. That, too, was something he recognised from his younger self, the need to be single-minded in the pursuit of a woman. That a man's desire for a woman could not be simple desire, it had to be grand passion. If he was not consumed by feeling then the event would somehow lack tenor, it would be nothing, not even a statement.

Carl couldn't have more than fifteen years on the boy and yet he felt immeasurably older, possessed of an almost parental desire to educate him, to communicate a small amount of his small wisdom. It was ridiculous to be thinking in that way after such a short time. But perhaps Kelvin was partly to blame. He generated this sort of feeling, he was like a vacuum, presenting an invitation to all and sundry to fill him up, to be the one who would affect him. It was probably what attracted Jessica.

The boy said nothing all the way over the hill and down through the forest on the other side; a rough bit of road, very sharp rocks, strange the way the geology of the place changed so radically so quickly. Then, at the Farm, he suddenly announced he'd get off at the end of Jim's road. He said he'd walk up to see Jessica later. Perhaps Kelvin had just needed to get away from him after all.

twelve

It was a relief to be out of the truck and in the night, walking with the full moon bleaching the road, making strange crisp black shadows out of familiar things. To be away from Carl and his obsessions. The cold air quickening his steps. As he approached Jim's he could see yellow light leaking out through the cracks in the wall. The house was barely more than a shack, a mishmash, a large one-roomed place built out of round poles and scavenged materials, sitting in its own little dell, different sections of wall made out of different materials, wattle and daub, weatherboards, sleeper offcuts. Various bits of cast-off machinery, old cars, a rusting tractor, littered its surrounds, glinting dimly in the moonlight.

Martin and Jim were playing a game of pool on the three-quarter-size billiard table Jim had picked up at a clearance sale, around which the house had been virtually built. Andy was in one of the armchairs, in front of a small fire, rolling a joint. Several instrument cases were scattered around the floor. Kelvin was directed to pour himself a beer, and as there were no glasses he found a tin mug which did little to alleviate a certain metallic taste peculiar to the brew. He stood by the table. Martin was bringing his habitual force to the game. When Andy was done with the rolling he lit the joint, but then held onto it for two or three puffs, as if he was alone, or wanted everyone else to know whose dope it was. When it was almost half gone, he passed it on with the admonition, 'Watch out, man, this is good shit,' squeaked out through a lungful of smoke.

They'd all been watching and waiting, too polite to comment, but the air was tense. Kelvin took a drag and passed it on, holding in the smoke for as long as possible, worrying about how he might get a joint to take away with him. He didn't want to turn up at Jessica's stoned if he had none to share. It seemed that Andy was the man with the stash and Andy, demonstrably, was not the generous kind.

He was right about the strength, though, the stuff wasn't just good, it was psychedelic. After just one puff Kelvin had the sense that the room, despite its strange and eclectic clutter, had become more spacious. Time, too, was becoming less rigid in its flow. He wondered if the others felt the same, or if it was just that way because he hadn't smoked for a couple of weeks. He put himself down to play the winner of the game, which turned out to be Jim, as you'd expect. But before he could set up the balls Andy came over. He was carrying a black canvas shoulder bag bought from a disposals store, the kind that had been designed for holding gas masks during World War II.

'Gentlemen,' he said. 'A scientific experiment.'

He took out a heavy glass jar with a screw-top lid and

placed it in the centre of the table. It was about two-thirds full of a slightly viscous liquid with hints of yellow and blue, enhanced by the light of the lamps.

'Mind the table!' Jim said.

'Right. The fucking table,' Andy said. He picked up the jar again. 'Well get us some paper then.'

Jim produced a wad of newspaper onto which Andy once again put his jar. He waited for a moment, glancing at them each in turn.

'Diesel,' he said.

Things seemed to be happening rather slowly and Kelvin thought he might have missed something. He looked at Martin and then Jim but could determine nothing from their faces.

'Now, look at this.' Andy rummaged in the satchel, bringing out a zip-lock bag of white crystals.

'Shit!' Jim said. 'Heroin.'

Andy looked at him and rolled his eyes. He unscrewed the lid of the jar and poured in the contents of the bag, closed it back up again. Then he picked up the jar and shook it vigorously.

The dope was so good it seemed to Kelvin that Andy's moving arms left an afterimage behind them.

Jim laughed, so perhaps he saw it too. There didn't seem to be anything else funny going on.

When Andy put the jar back down it appeared very similar to when he had first picked it up, except now there was a small residue of crystals in the bottom.

'Isn't that beautiful?' he said.

No one spoke.

'That was sugar,' he said, glancing at Jim. 'Out in the forest round here there's all sorts of machinery. There's dozers and sniggers and fuck knows what else. No security. I've checked. Now, you put this stuff in the fuel tank of one of those machines, you fuck it. I mean fucking completely fucked, all the fuel lines, the heads, you name it. When it gets hot the sugar caramelises and burns, it bakes on.'

'Right,' Martin said. Martin knew about these sorts of things. 'And?'

'It's fucking beautiful, isn't it? You'd need a chemical lab to tell the sugar's there. And once it's there there's no way of tracing where it came from. What I reckon is we go out one night with a drum of this shit and pour it in ten or twenty of the fucking machines. If we work as a team we could bring the mill to a standstill.'

Everyone looked at the jar. Kelvin glanced at Andy. He was enjoying himself.

'You're serious, aren't you?' Jim said.

'Fucking oath. How about you Jim-boy?'

When Jim had built the roof he'd used poles that were too small for the span so that when he put on the iron the whole thing had started to sag. He'd had to put a post in the middle of the room to hold it up. Throughout the demonstration he'd been leaning against it. You could see the criss-crossed axe marks where he'd cut the bark before peeling it off. Now he slid down the pole until he was sitting on the floor, his cue held up between his legs.

'I don't know,' he said.

'What's not to know?' Andy said. 'We've had this rave a hundred times. Isn't that right, Martin? Heh? This is the most simple beautiful thing I've ever heard of. Nobody loses except the mill. The machines are built by multi-fucking-nationals, they're insured by multi-fucking-nationals and owned by banks. They don't blow up, they just stop fucking going. No one gets hurt, nobody. It's foolproof. I thought we were against the mill. Or is it too fucking scary?'

'Damn right it is,' Martin said. 'It's not a game.'

'No, it's not, this is where we get serious. You write all the fucking letters you like, you're not going to stop them. The only thing that'll stop these bastards from cutting down every fucking tree between here and the border is to make it too expensive for them to keep going.'

'It's not that simple,' Martin said.

Andy turned away from the table, then swung back and took his jar off again.

'Must be time to play some more pool,' he said, 'some more *games*. I'll roll us another number.'

'Jesus,' Jim said.

Andy took out his little battered tin and started sticking papers together. 'It's a dark and lonely job,' he said. 'But someone has to do it.'

Kelvin found the balls in the pockets of the table and placed them in the triangle, alternating the big ones and the little ones, putting the black in its position behind the first ball then rolling the whole thing backwards and forwards over the felt until he was sure he had them in the right place.

'Since when did you become an environmentalist?' Martin asked.

Andy kept to his work in the armchair.

'Are you playing?' Kelvin asked Jim, who still hadn't moved.

'I've always been one,' Andy said, 'always *cared* about the planet. I told you I'd been up the Daintree. Now *there's* some blokes who're not afraid to say what they don't like.' He licked the paper on his joint and rolled it up, put it in his mouth to wet the thing and then regarded it with an expression of surprise. 'I've been driving around poking my nose into these logging dumps. You guys want to get out and about. Have a look. Get yourselves down to this thing Jessica's got organised in Nadgee. You want to know what a crime is, that's the place. A fucking disaster.'

'The difference is, Andy, they don't put you in jail for fucking up the forests, they do for fucking up machinery,' Martin said.

'And?'

'And I don't want to spend my life in jail. I don't want a bunch of loggers out here breaking my legs.'

'Wouldn't happen.'

Once again Andy held onto the joint. His stamina, or his resistance to the stuff, must have been phenomenal. He passed it to Martin who took a good toke himself then gave it to Jim.

'That's me,' Martin said.

'Come on,' Andy said, 'stick around, we haven't started yet, aren't we gonna play some music?'

'I don't feel like it.'

Evidently he'd been hanging on for just one more hit on the joint, because now he gathered up his things.

'Night all,' he said.

When he closed the door behind him it felt as though he had taken more than just himself from the room. For want of anything better to do Kelvin started the game. He hit the white into the centre of the pile and they split with a satisfying whack, but nothing went in.

Jim stood up and took a shot but his mind wasn't on the game.

'Jesus, it was only a suggestion,' Andy said. He came over and leaned against the post Jim had recently vacated. 'I thought we could do something, make a difference, you know, strike a blow for the trees.'

'You wouldn't want to get caught,' Jim said. 'They'd fuck with you something horrible.'

'No way you'd get caught. That's the beauty. Don't listen to Martin. He's just pissed off because he didn't think of it.'

'You got much of that dope?' Kelvin said.

Andy raised heavy-lidded eyes and met Kelvin's, then dropped them to the table again.

'For you, Kelvin, my man, *anything*.' He had that smile on again, a kind of leer, his lips curling away from his teeth.

'Just a little bit,' he said.

'I wasn't giving you any fucking more than that.'

thirteen

She is always surprised by the power of small things. Her garden, for example, exerts an influence far beyond its size or contribution to the table. She sits on the front step of the house in the morning with her tea, intending to stay only a moment, sees a weed and is lost; hours pass crouched on the path following back the brittle threads of chickweed to its roots beneath the straw.

Each age has its own approach to gardening. Until recently the idea has been to relentlessly work the soil, digging and turning and breaking, aerating and mixing the top layer, creating a friable bed in which to plant. Jessica is more modern. She repudiates the spade, mourns too deeply the lives of turned worms. They are the gardener's friends, she says, and adds mulch on the top, doesn't dig, lets the soil find its own balance. When the council slashes the roadside she goes out with Suzy and stuffs the back of her car with cut hay, trip after trip, harvesting the bounty of the long paddock. She lays it around the stems of tomatoes and sweet basil, corn, capsicums and aubergine. It is a kind of propitiation, an offering to the mysterious plant gods, perhaps more scientific than that of former times, but no less ritualistic. Parsley and marigolds line her beds; in the centre a circular herb garden boasts oregano, rosemary, lavender and geraniums, thyme and yarrow, pennyroyal and comfrey. Around the house it is all flowers, petunias and lobelia giving way to foxgloves and Queen Anne's lace, stock, coriopsis growing wild. She longs for warmer climes where she might grow gardenias, frangipani, ginger, the tropical flowers with their heavy scents.

It would, she thinks, be easier to be a gardener than to write. All day she is unable to settle. It is the fault of the early morning trip over the hill with Kelvin. It has interrupted her routine. She can't write so she gardens, except she knows too well that gardening is an excuse for not writing and is therefore forbidden, so instead she drives to town for the mail, to do some organisation. All twelve miles of dirt. No one has got around to changing the signs to kilometres: stone markers still count the miles. Surveyors are out along the road plotting some trajectory across the landscape. Perhaps it is for the long-awaited telephone. Bronzed men in long white socks and short shorts that ride high on their thighs peer into theodolites or hold up wands, their four-wheel drives pulled over at odd angles. Sexually she has been asleep. She has noted this, that without a man to focus on she does not get aroused. Her sexuality is not a thing in itself, it is a factor of the other's presence. If a lover leaves (and don't they all, isn't that the incredible lie at the base of every beginning?) she misses not just the man, the intimacy, the support; she misses, also, the sex.

But after a time, two or three months say, it gets easier, the feeling abates. She likes to think of it, her sex, as going to sleep, not dying but hibernating, waiting for the new spring. Her sister, during a slump in *her* sex life, always coarser, earthier, said, laughing deeply, 'I think I've healed over.' This is how it has been, and she has got used to it, has been pleased to be no longer subject to its ravening, its embarrassing hungers. When not overcome with loneliness and a sense of failure for having no man, she has managed to relish the focus it has brought to other activities, the breadth of connections she has developed. A relationship always has a tendency to dominate her life; she lets the other aspects go. How else could she have become such a force in the Forest Alliance?

She sits on the steps of the store waiting for the mail bus from Bega with the other Coalwater residents: Alice from over the river with her flock of screaming children and her lank hair and battered face; the storekeeper herself, Joy, a formidable woman with a husband to match; Old Jack in his shoes with the fronts cut out of them to make room for his toes. Coalwater is not a big town. Once upon a time it was bigger, but even then it was not what could be called large. Now it is spread out, ramshackle, lacking visible means of support. There is no industry and it is too far from anywhere to commute to work. The milk truck stopped coming when the quotas were introduced. The land, which back from the river was always marginal, has been given over to desultory steers and the rabbit. The only thing to happen in recent memory was the arrival of the hippies. The residents did their best to ignore them, convinced that their painted Kombi vans were a temporary aberration.

Old Jack was one of the few to give them the time of day. His farming days over, he sits on the veranda outside the store and talks to whoever will listen. Barrel-chested, skull-jawed, his grey hair cut to a Germanic stubble, his thin lips hardly move when he speaks. Great tufts of hair sprout from his ears. All his clothes are old, dark felt trousers, a striped shirt which at one time had a separate collar, beneath that a woollen vest, always the same regardless of season. The skin on his neck is thick, segmented, lizard-like. His eyes follow the hippie girls in their Indian print skirts with nothing on underneath, with their bare feet and their rings on their toes.

He has found out Jessica's surname, 'Coalwater Cohen, eh,' he says, 'come and sit here till the bus comes. It won't be here for a bit yet – the way the roads are Alby doesn't want to rush things.' He pats the wooden bench beside him and she accepts. 'It's a long time since we've had a Cohen living here. There was one when I was a young man, lived back of Mt Imlay.' He points to a hill in the south-east. 'A strong man he was. Used to come in here once a month for his bag of flour. He'd sling it on his shoulder, a hundred-weight bag, and set off back home again, walking, barefoot.'

She has heard the story before. She stretches out her legs and looks at her feet, her long toes dusty against the weather-worn boards.

'Out your way, now, that was good dairy country. One hundred twenty cows milked every day. Five ton of butter to

Eden once a month by bullock and dray. Before the war, milked by hand.'

He means the Great War, in which he was too young to serve. He coughs a deep throated damp cough. It pulls him over and as he leans forward he exposes a small area of pale skin at the base of his shirt, and this tiny piece of his body that has never seen the sun is enough to make Jessica suddenly aware of him as a man, not just a repository of arcane history. She has been asleep but Kelvin has woken her. The beast is stirring in its lair. Already it is starting to consume her thoughts.

After the mail she uses the public phone. She prefers the box near the school. There are only two in town, the one next to the store and the one perched on a hill with no shade, no protection from the elements at all, just a glass box with a door that behaves badly. But its isolation provides privacy as well as a fine view of the river, that wide expanse of sand with a stream of water threading its way amongst it, gathering in a pool under the bridge pylons.

As it turns out everything is set for the weekend in Nadgee, as well as for going to Sydney to speak to the All-Party Sub-Committee on the Native Forests of the South Coast of New South Wales. There was no need to come to town and she is angry about that, about allowing herself to be distracted from her work by this trip in the same way she permitted several hours to pass in the garden. It is all very well to laugh at writers for loathing their work, and for doing anything to avoid it, it does not mean she is *excused*.

When darkness falls she is at home. She makes a meal, feeds the dog, and Kelvin isn't there. Still she can't settle and she is angry at herself for wanting him, angry at him for coming into her life and disturbing her thus, for being who he is, for waking her. She tries to write and fails, tries to read and abandons it, ends up, in desperation, cleaning a kitchen cupboard. By the time he rolls up, against all expectation, stoned, smelling of tobacco and dope and beer, she is out of sorts, distant, critical.

'I missed you,' he says, settling himself on the couch, the makings of a joint on a low table in front of him, leaning forward with his knees spread wide to accommodate his arms.

'Did you?' she says, unbelieving, pissed off because she *has* missed him and, really, has no mind to smoke. Then he passes her the number he's rolled, offers her a match so she can light it, and she says she will, after all, share it with him, 'If only to be in the same place as you,' and pulls on it, holding the smoke in her lungs, testing the sensation the drug produces in her brain; finding it, surprisingly, good. She forgets what it's like, why they are all so committed to it, the sudden clarity it brings, the immediate and absolute awareness of what is important and the falling away of everything that's not. She raises her eyes from the coffee table and discovers that Kelvin is, in fact, right there; the object of her affections has arrived, and she laughs, a short bray directed entirely at herself but inducing in him a broad smile, his mouth twisting up to the left, transforming his face; he is, how could she have forgotten, beautiful.

Kelvin was talking about Carl when he handed her the joint, but she can no longer remember what he said. It doesn't matter. She goes around the little table to be beside him. That is the important thing.

Except, of course, it isn't quite that simple. She can make it next to him, into his warmth and smell – which from being disagreeable has somehow transformed itself into being *him* and therefore pleasant, satisfying, arousing – she can undress him, there, on the couch, she can let her hand, wide-fingered, drift across his chest and onto his belly, down towards the startling junction of his hips, his animalness undeniable, as is its effect on her. But it does not end there. The language they speak in this place is just as complex, more so perhaps, than that of words. She kisses him, he kisses her, his hands are on her body and, she thinks that it is a kind of meditation, this love-making, requiring concentration, not just a giving in to feeling, but a wilful seeking out. But perhaps it is just the dope, for her mind keeps wandering down vast historical/ philosophical paths, then back to Kelvin and his physicality, the hardness of his flesh beneath his skin, the hair on his legs, strong mountain-goat legs, the nest of his cock and balls, so admirable, his lips on her body like an insistent feeding thing, something that won't be denied. *He* doesn't seem to be prey to these ancient perspectives, unless, of course, as an aspect of his love-making itself, at which he seems so adept, so present, so *original*, such a strange description this last for an act which is, after all, the most banal, the most common. Old Jack's little bit of exposed skin had told her that; that was the revelation she had on the steps of the store, not such a startling one but at the same time momentous. Her long-dormant sexuality had shown her that there is no division between animalness and humanness. This was where she, and so many others, with their strictures and scriptures, their obsession with transcendence, had made their mistake: thinking people were animals dressing up, trying to hide their true nature, failing to understand the meaning of *love thy neighbour as thyself* when thyself was constructed in the image of God. Human beings, she thinks, making love to Kelvin, already are their true nature, the covering and the uncovering both, all at once; there is nothing hidden, there never has been, it's all out in the open.

The problem is that in the morning, driving him over the mountain, he is once again a chimera. She wonders, not for the first time, if he is a construct of her own imaginings. Was he ever there, did he really give rise to all those grand thoughts? She is not sure. That's the stupid thing about dope. She can't remember half of what the thoughts were, and what she can remember makes no sense. She places her hand on his thigh, feeling his leg through the thick denim, a solid thing.

fourteen

After that he went with Shelley whenever she worked. She no longer seemed to mind. He was her mascot, her protection from the jibes of the boys further up the street, from the things that might go wrong in cars.

The nights were hot and long. He sat in his doorway and watched the cars, watched her come and go. Eventually he grew bored. While Shelley was off doing tricks he stood at the kerb himself. A game, a dare. A car went past slowly, then came around again. On the third time the window slid down. He bent to look in. The driver was away across the other side.

'How much?' the man said.

'Twenty,' he replied, although for what he wasn't sure. He didn't care, it was more money than he'd ever had, it was what Shelley earned, and the man nodded and leaned over and opened the door, so he got in and when it was shut the driver made the window go up.

The man was wearing dark glasses and a kind of Elvis shirt, thick pale trousers with a perfect crease. The car seats were deep pile, there was deep pile everywhere, on the walls and the ceiling, along the dashboard, curved around the extra dials. The man was old. Lines on his face, grey hair. He was playing country and western on the radio; a funny-looking bloke, all narrow jaw and cheekbones, jutting teeth when he smiled. He drove a few blocks, stopping beside a park.

Kelvin wanted to do it right but didn't know how. He sat, rigid, thinking about the money and how to ask for it while the man undid his pants, tilted his chair back and pumped at his cock to make it big. A strange thing this, a man's cock, pale, thicker than he had imagined possible, with a sideways curve to it and a shiny purple head poking out from its rippled foreskin, veins on it.

'Well, come on then,' the man said.

Kelvin was about to reach out and touch it when the man said, his voice curiously high, 'You like that, don't you?'

Kelvin wasn't sure. It was curious, this little bubble, the inside of the car, all thick and resonant with the shag pile and the music and the man with his cock, with the night outside so effectively sealed away from them like it was only television. The man reached out and grabbed his shoulder, pulling him down towards his lap with surprising force, pulling him and then pushing Kelvin's face into his smell, the man's cock against his cheek, the smoothness and hardness of it hot against his skin, the coarse hair in his mouth and nose. It happened so suddenly that his arms were caught underneath him. The man was holding him amongst it, and his arms were tangled in the handbrake so he couldn't get away. He tried not to, but despite himself he started to gag.

He could feel the sick rising in his throat. He started to cough and retch.

'What the fuck?' the man said, lifting him back up and pushing him away with as much force as he had drawn him down; throwing Kelvin against the door, his temple hitting the glass. He fumbled for the handle but there was some sort of lock on it. He put his hand over his mouth to try to stop the sick, the bloke sitting up now and shoving at him, swearing at him, reaching over to open his door and tip him out onto the road. Then he was scrambling to get away from the wheels before the car took off.

The park was a small green square with a view out over Woolloomooloo, with a kids' playground next to a spreading fig. Kelvin pushed the carousel around, his feet thumping in the circled dust, running round and round and then jumping on, leaning out with his head back so that the lights of the bay below, the dark silhouettes of the buildings, the broad leaves of the fig tree, all flitted past, the speed of the spin lurching inside him, getting off and running again, then back on, sitting at its centre, perched on the apex of the cold rails, shiny with the hands of many children, letting it wind down.

It had happened so quickly. He had been chuffed at getting the ride. The inside of the car was great, cool, the soft seat, the dials, the music, the smell of it. He'd even liked the man. Kelvin hadn't even minded the business with his cock, that was what it was about, wasn't it? He could do that, it was only when the man pushed him that it went wrong, that he messed up. He'd have done it right if the guy had just given him time, he hadn't meant to fuck it up. Everything he did fucked up sooner or later.

The carousel had stopped. He was cold, perched there in a T-shirt. He put his arms around his knees, doubling himself, a process of making himself smaller, not larger, hunched against the cold. It was time to go but he found it difficult to move.

At the squat no one was home. He borrowed some blankets and huddled on his mattress.

When she got back Shelley was mad. She'd been looking for him everywhere. One of the trannies had told her he'd gone with a mark.

'What the fuck were you doing? I told you not to get in cars.'

He couldn't speak.

'What's the matter now?' she said.

'I'm cold.'

She felt him.

'No you ain't. You're not sick are you?'

'No.'

'What then? Did someone hurt you?'

She lifted his head so she could see his face, then she put her arms around him, Shelley, in her work clothes, smelling of cheap perfume and make-up and cigarettes, smelling of what she did with strange men, and despite himself he began to cry. He didn't know he was going to cry and once he started he didn't know how to stop, the shame of crying making him cry more, his head against the sequins of her dress, he could feel his tears wetting the cloth and he couldn't do anything about it, there were just these tears and Shelley with her arms around him, rocking him, not taking care, giving care, this girl who got in cars, who could do what he couldn't.

But nothing in Sydney stayed the same for long. Spic moved away, to the mythical North, promising that he would send for them when he'd made good. Without him the squat was soon uninhabitable, subject to the predations of other homeless and even, eventually, the council. The other boys drifted away. A pimp called Daz picked up Shelley in a car and took her off to a quiet place where he talked to her and while he talked he weighed a safety razor in his hands. What he said was that he thought it would be a shame to ruin looks like hers, and allowed she might continue working, if it was for him. 'And your little poofta friend and all. Not that I like that sort of thing. But if he's working then it has to go through me. I don't want to hear nothing else.'

He found them a place to live, a tiny house squashed between the back of two restaurants in Little Stanley Street. Generosity wasn't his motive. He sat with a group of men at a little metal table outside the corner shop. Shelley's business was vetted through him and she performed her services in the front room. Kelvin worked the Wall, albeit under some sort of protection.

The men in cars came in all shapes and sizes but they had certain things in common. Religion, something Kelvin was only vaguely familiar with, was never far from the surface. From the moment of their decision to let their cars steer them towards the Cross they were under the protective sway of desire. But, it seemed, the instant it was over they were once again subject to a harsher counsel. Often they turned on Kelvin, blaming him, calling him names, even, on occasion, asking him to get down on his knees with them and pray. Sometimes their vilification leaked over into the earlier part, their self-disgust so strong that even during the act they needed Kelvin to be the one begging for it. He went along. It was part of the deal. What drove the men was incomprehensible to him. He didn't bother his mind about it. Even after Daz's cut he was earning. The only thing he knew for sure was that until they came, the men were his. It was why you took the money first.

Glen Slattery was thick-waisted, short-legged, carefully and yet prissily dressed, wearing a toupee so glaringly obvious that it took on the force of a deformity; so single-minded in his spontaneous decision to follow his desire that he had not even cleared the passenger seat. Kelvin had to wait on the kerb while he moved the piles of books into the back. Several paperbacks fell onto the front floor.

It didn't happen in the car. Slattery drove them to Newtown, hardly speaking as they crossed the city. Kelvin picked up the fallen books, checking their titles in the passing streetlights, placed them carefully on the back seat. They entered a musty building from a laneway at the rear. There were more books in the corridor, books and periodicals were stacked on the floor, on sagging shelves in the filthy kitchen, on the stairs, in the upstairs room where there was a bed; dusty piles of them in no seeming order.

When it was over, Slattery seemed to lack any form of guilt.

'You like books do you?' he said.

He took him downstairs to the shop.

'You've come to the right place.'

Here was the epicentre of the smell that pervaded every room in the building. Slattery didn't turn on the lights and so, at first, Kelvin was not certain what he was seeing; a pale light slanted in from the street and illuminated an impossible conglomeration of objects. Books and more books, on shelves, yes, but rough affairs that had been added to and then added to again, getting higher each time, spawning buttresses that stood out into the room, themselves filled with books, creating, by their presence, alcoves; whole sections devoted, Kelvin would later discover, to different areas of study. Right then he was still coming to grips with what he was seeing. In the limited monochromatic light the room distorted – stretched in places and shrank in others. Slattery let him walk amongst it, running his fingers over the spines as though the business of the place was not words but rather some sort of bathhouse, a bookhouse for bathing.

Outside, beyond the glass, buses and trucks, taxis, passed in the night on King Street. In the darkness of the shop he was invisible. There had been no books in his mother's house. She had called her women's magazines books, but even as a small child he'd known real books were something more. The first time they'd gone to the mobile library together his mother had let him loose in the children's section. When she went to the counter with her pile he came with his own. 'Take those back,' she said, but the woman behind the counter, the same woman, incidentally, who drove the big bus, who had, therefore, a certain authority, said, 'It's all right, he can take those.' As if it was the most natural thing in the world.

'Take one,' Slattery said. 'Take a couple, no charge. No,' changing his mind, 'tell you what, if you like them and want more you can bring them back and I'll change them.'

'What's that?' Shelley asked.

'A book.'

'Really? Is that what it is, I'd never have . . .' Jumping onto him and digging her fingers into his side, grabbing the book from his hands when he was distracted and then holding onto it so tightly that to wrest it back would damage it, turning and turning away from him, opening it at random and reading aloud, slowly, painfully, like a child in class, '. . . what is this? What's a *granfalloon*?' Looking at the cover, '*Cat's Cradle*? Is this for babies?'

Now that there was just the two of them they hung out together in the afternoons. Shelley, it turned out, was fastidious. She liked to be clean. The tiny house had a tiny bathroom out the back, a cold place whose walls and floor were painted concrete, a hole in the floor for a drain that backed up when you spent too long in the shower. This last being attached to a gas-fired device they called the dragon. It was supposed to light itself automatically but the pilot light was faulty, it needed a match, a process that resulted in an eruption of flame. Shelley insisted on a shower before going to bed, dragging Kelvin in to light it for her.

Sometimes, at the end of the night, they would share a joint in the little loft room they used as a bedroom. Shelley always had stories to tell, about the marks, about the other girls, what Lola had said to Denise, what Denise had said back, who was in Daz's favour, what another pimp had done to one of his girls. It was different along the Wall. The boys didn't speak to each other, there was just Darlinghurst Road and the fig trees overhanging, the squashed fruit underfoot and the furtive looks, the constant eye out for the police and always the fear and the excitement of where the night would take him, the men it would bring with their need to look at him, to touch him, the softness of their lips on his skin.

'I had one from Brisbane,' she said. 'Wants me to go up there. Says I could be an exotic dancer. Gave me his card.'

'What sort was he?'

'The usual, a creep. Lots of hair. Hair all over him, dark, like. Said I wouldn't have to fuck. I reckon it'd be good, living in Brisbane, it's hot up there, not like here. What d'ya think?' She stood up and pirouetted around the room like a ballet dancer, on her tiptoes, in one of her moods. 'I did dance at school. *Pleeyays* and all that.' Standing with her heels together, toes pointing out, turning her head to the side like an Egyptian and bending at the knees for him. 'Hairy, he was, like a fucking ape.' Laughing. After the night's work and the dope the only thing to do was laugh.

Kelvin had become attuned to her. He had learned to

recognise the days when she was up, 'hyper' she called it, full of plans for this and that; and the other ones, the days when everything was woeful, when you may as well slit your wrists because nothing was ever going to be any better, there would never be a way out. He had learned to ride them both out. In the early hours they'd go to sleep, lying together on a mattress on the floor, side by side, touching only hands like brother and sister, like, Kelvin thought, Hansel and Gretel, waiting to be eaten.

He took her to Slattery's shop. From the street, in daylight, it was dowdy, unattractive, the window displaying sun-bleached paperbacks and old car manuals amidst dead flies. There were a couple of little baskets in the doorway, almost blocking the entrance, offering romance novels for ten or twenty cents each. Inside it was just books, old books and the smell of old books, and of Slattery himself, nearly hidden behind the counter, smoking, marking up, with nicotine-stained fingers, the sales in a tall thin journal. Several people were browsing the shelves and a tinny radio was playing something classical.

'Who's this?' he said.

'Shelley,' Kelvin replied. 'My friend.'

'Very nice,' pulling two syllables out of the one in the second word. 'So you liked the books?'

Kelvin felt the presence of the other people in the shop.

'And now you want some more.' He pointed along the shelves. 'Try over there.' Then just to Kelvin, under his breath,

'Come back after five, without your friend, and I'll give you something else for your trouble.'

'Queer as a hatful of arseholes,' Shelley said in the bus back to the city. 'And the hair. How disgusting was that, eh? Did you see the dirt? You wonder how people live like that, don't you?'

Kelvin read the books. He read the ones Slattery gave him and the ones he chose himself and he went back for more. Most often he went in business hours, sometimes on the bus, sometimes walking. He liked to walk in the city, passing through the different regions, as separate from each other as different nations. Often as not he had money in his pockets, and a little dope in his system. Everywhere there were people rushing from one place to another, locked into some grind. He, Kelvin, was free to move around. On one of his walks a dog attached itself to him. It didn't so much follow him as just choose to walk awhile beside him. Together they went the full length of Cleveland Street, crossing the lights at the railway bridge where Regent Street comes in, all the way up to Victoria Park. Apart from Shelley it was the closest he ever came to another being in all that time; this easy, unspoken sharing of an hour's walk. There was, of course, Slattery, but Slattery was a special case. Some afternoons Kelvin would curl up at the back of the shop and read there. It never occurred to him to offer money for the books. It was the characters in the novels that he knew, not the people in the city he moved amongst, not even Shelley, who couldn't go with him into the pages, he tried to take her but she didn't see the point. She disapproved of his friendship with Slattery. She spent her days in the city proper, perfecting what it meant to be a woman, studying it in magazines and emporia. And if he failed to notice Slattery's passion for him, the way he fawned on him, it was because that side of things was a different world. Kelvin had the knack of separating one from the other. If, on occasion, he gave way to Slattery's desire, he did it for a fee. It was a transaction, not the payment of a debt. And it was none of Daz's business either. Slattery was his.

fifteen

If the predominant feature of the far south coast was trees, forest without apparent end, then Nadgee State Forest, after the Timbillica fire, was its opposite.

They came out amongst its devastation without warning. The road continued on through the blackness, a long ochre ribbon, tracing the curves and undulations of the ridge lines, but the overarching forest they had travelled through was gone. The fire had taken everything. The slopes carried not charred forest but no forest at all, the geography of the place exposed with stark cruelty. The young regrowth with its broad volatile leaves had been too closely bunched together to survive the extreme heat. All that was left were thin bare stalks, and not many of those.

It was what Jessica had wanted them to see.

Their route led them on and out into this black desert, until it was all around them, as far as the eye could see. Above them, like a taunt, was the undisturbed translucent blue of the sky. Jessica's friends from the Forest Alliance were parked atop the ridge, leaning against a dilapidated yellow Datsun. Below them a vast bowl stretched, at the centre of which one stark leafless tree remained. The woman, Katya, was wearing dark loose clothing, perhaps with the intention of disguising her weight, although, Kelvin thought, quite possibly such considerations never entered her mind. She had a thick mass of curly hair and a harsh turn to her mouth. Perhaps it was just the light. It was still before eight but it was already inordinately bright. The man was a noted botanist but had the appearance of a hippie, bearded and long-haired, shabbily dressed. He laid out maps on the ticking bonnet of Jessica's Holden, running his fingers along the contours, locating them on their blasted hill.

Kelvin looked out over the valley. He was an appendage, idle and aimless, an hour early for the events of the day, his feeling of uselessness made more acute by a heightened sense of desire for Jessica. The day had produced a new version of her. She was all efficiency, their relationship sidelined. She was articulate, precise, impatient, better presented than her companions.

Besides, he was having other problems with the place. He pushed at the impossibly clean line between the blackened dirt and the gravel of the road with his foot. He could see the nubs of the root boles where the trees had been. New leaves were already poking through, their tips glistening purple against the ash, as if to demonstrate some parable of resilient Nature, Nature the undefeated, even here. Except, Jessica's friend had explained with a certain doom-laden pleasure, this development was another disaster in the making. The sprouting leaves would give rise not to new trees but to a mass of suckers, not a forest but a dense thicket, fuel for another fire in several years to come. 'The bastards were so sure of themselves they didn't even leave the seed trees behind. They had it all worked out,' he said.

'You see this sort of shit and you want to put them up against the wall,' Jessica said.

Two beige Forestry Commission Toyotas came around the hill, a grand plume of dust in their wake. Further back, strung out in dribs and drabs, was a long line of cars.

'Jesus, look at that would you,' Katya said. 'We should have organised a bus.'

There was a moment of confusion with the forestry officers, two of whom were young, while the third, in the slightly more battered vehicle, was an older man with the face of an amiable drinker. Jessica assumed he was in charge, but after a brief introduction he cleared the air.

'Don't mind me,' he said. 'I'm the shit-kicker. It's Mark you want to be talking to.'

The young officers, a man and a woman, shiny in their pressed khaki with their badges sewn on the shoulders, waited while this was sorted out, then came forward to shake hands with the sincerity of Mormons. Mark was even younger than Jessica, with short blond hair and blue eyes hidden behind sunglasses, a jaw whose length was exaggerated by the shortness of his upper lip. When he smiled his top gums were nervously revealed.

'Good of you to come,' Jessica said. 'I'm sure you had better things to do with your Saturday morning.'

He dismissed her attempt at politeness with a brief nod. 'No problem,' he said.

The cars disgorged a raggle-taggle of people, several men wearing loose T-shirts, drawstring pants and sandals, some with the customary heavy beards and long hair, but others, too, balding, thin and professorial. Most of the women had something in common with Katya, if not in size then in seriousness, although there was one who was striking, a long slim being with a child on her hip, making the day seem more interesting, the cause more worthwhile, in that seemingly effortless way of beautiful people, just by her presence.

Jessica stood on the raised edge of the road and gathered the crowd together, introducing Mark, offering him the opportunity to speak.

'It's great to see so many people interested,' he said in a hearty we're-all-in-this-together tone. 'As you can tell, it's been pretty serious through here. What we're hoping to do today is to see how the forest and its inhabitants are responding to it, but we also want to have a look at some sites the fire missed, islands, if you like, that were protected for various reasons.'

The sheer horror of the place and the uninterrupted brightness of the sun had subdued everyone before he'd even begun. They listened to him as they might a tour guide, and he, taking advantage of it, set out to give the impression that this event was organised by the Forestry Commission itself.

'What we have here is forty-seven thousand hectares of forest, that's about a hundred thousand acres in the old lingo, bounded on one side by the sea, on the other by the Pacific Highway. On November 10, 1981, after several days of strong winds a fire was started in the south-east corner at a place known as Timbillica –'

'In one of your bark dumps,' a man called out.

Mark stopped. He glanced at his companion and pushed his sunglasses further onto his nose. He smiled his peculiar little smile.

'Well, there's some evidence to suggest that's the case but we're still not certain, we're waiting for the results of an enquiry.'

'A whitewash. It was you lot did this.' He was a tall man with long naturally curly hair and a nervous way of speaking. Even though he had the audience behind him his heckling came out as a kind of petulance.

'I think,' Jessica said, stepping in, 'we should let Mark speak.'

'No, I think the gentleman has a point,' Mark said, in control of things; they must have trained him for such eventualities. 'I think there are big lessons here for forest managers. I'd go as far as to say that I think mistakes were made. When we started clearing here we were working on a two thousand acre front . . .'

Kelvin had hoped to get close to the woman with the child on her hip but found himself instead on the edge of the group beside Katya and the botanist, who, in what seemed an uncharacteristic gesture, spat onto the black dirt. 'He's a sap,' he said. 'The guy knows nothing. They move staff around every two or three years just so's no one's responsible.'

His gob of spit sat on the ash, unabsorbed, milky and thick.

'What the fuck is a two thousand acre front?' Katya said,

louder, turning some heads. 'What is that, eh? It doesn't mean anything, does it? It's fucking garbage.'

Kelvin turned his back on the crowd. In the wide curve of the valley the remains of an old road could just be discerned. It followed a contour of the bowl ending in a flat circular area perhaps halfway between the top of the hill and the base. Below it a small creek began its meander downwards, its banks delineated by a thicket of white stalks, the only variation from black in the whole vista.

His father had worked the boats out of Eden. Nev had been saving up for his own licence, but when the quota system came in, limiting the number of fishermen, he'd missed out. He put the money down on a rig instead and started hauling for the mill. It paid well and the work was steady. There were a lot of trees, even cutting at that rate. Within a few years there had been five log trucks with *McIntyre Haulage, Eden* on the doors in gold lettering. Not that Kelvin knew much about it. During one of his mum's bad spells Nev hooked up with Daphne from the pub. His mum and he had had to do by themselves after that. There wasn't any money but there weren't, also, the fights.

It was years before Nev, probably at Daphne's instigation, started picking Kelvin up and taking him over to his new home. Their kitchen had tiles on the walls, an electric stove and a fridge, running hot water. There was a bathroom and even, wonder of wonders, a television. Daphne, a thin, pretty, frail woman with no children of her own, made biscuits for him and tried her best to be whatever it was she thought a stepmother should be. None of it made any difference. He didn't want to be there.

Once Nev turned up in the big Kenworth. A driver was sick and he was on for the day so he thought he'd take his boy along as offsider. Kelvin climbed up in the cabin and perched there with the motor thrumming beneath him, unsure what to say, convinced that whatever he did would be wrong, sitting in the noise and the smells, that complex mix of oily rags, interior plastic seating, cigarettes and sweat. Nev held the edge of the wide wheel with his belly as he drove, winding up and down between the gears. He reached over and tweaked Kelvin's arm, nodding at the road ahead and laughing – there was no possibility of conversation anyway because of the noise – showing his white teeth at the pleasure he felt in the great truck roaring beneath them, the air breaks screaming out their wind like injured whales. Kelvin had never seen him so happy.

The team was working a coupe of old forest south of the town. There was a D9 pulling the logs up to the dump, and a Volvo snigger, one of those four-wheeled machines with an articulated waist and a great pair of horizontally opposed tongs on the front, a thing like an enormous demented yellow ant, which stripped them of their bark and loaded them onto the truck. There were five or six men on the site, two or three in the forest with their Stihls, felling and cutting, the different notes of the saws screaming their woe, the trees falling one after another with a strange ease that never lost its ferocity.

The dozer driver let him run out the chain which wasn't a chain at all but a wire rope which he dragged out behind the machine and looped around the trunk of the fallen tree, getting down on his knees amongst the crushed leaves and branches and the smell of new-sawn log, to push the heavy hook under, then standing aside to watch the machine winch it out of the gully regardless of all obstacles, dragging it up to the bark dump, leaving a curved muddy slick in its wake. The whole operation imbued with a wonderful casual brutality, a great show of might. He would have worked there all day for nothing, just to be part of it, but a forestry officer came down and told Nev to get the boy out of it.

'He's my boy,' Nev said.

'And?'

'He's right with me.' Pausing. 'I'm Nev McIntyre.'

The officer looked at Nev and then at the door of the truck and back again.

'Don't care who you are,' he said. 'Get the boy out of here.'

So he was made to sit in the cabin again, feeling it shudder and rock as each log was loaded, listening to the warning horn on the snigger bleat as it backed to and fro. After that, just as he knew he would be, Kelvin was always in the way, useless, a bloody nuisance. He'd been thirteen years old, he'd forgotten that, forgotten that the outing had been his father's concession to his birthday, delivered several days late and without notice, and had also been the last time he'd seen him.

Behind him Mark was talking up the Forestry's new environmentalism: small coupe sizes and a patchwork system of allocation, strict guidelines for contractors and heavy penalties for infringement; spelling out these changes as if the Forestry hadn't fought against them at every turn. First you oppose something with all your might and then, when you're defeated, you make out it was your choice. Perhaps it had always been that way, Kelvin didn't know, he didn't seem to know very much really, except that this was the place he had come to with his father, this bowl or somewhere very like it, and that he'd loved the experience, at least the first part, and yet here, eight or nine years on, was the result. He was adrift on a sea of contradictory positions. He'd only come there because of Jessica, his feelings for the place were no more than his feelings for her. Or had been.

The group started to move off but he was fixed where he was. He stared into the valley. Jessica waved at him to come but he ignored her. She left the crowd and went to him, wanting him to walk with her, a little impatient, angry at all of Mark's bullshit, her mind in five places at once, talking over the top of anything Kelvin might have thought to say.

'. . . as if they aren't doing the same sort of shit right now . . .' Tugging on his sleeve. 'Are you coming?'

'I've been here before,' Kelvin said.

'Haven't we all.'

Barely listening.

'No, I mean here, before it was like this.'

He had no idea why he should want to tell her this, his most closely guarded secret.

'I came here with my father.'

117

'On holiday?'

She was already moving away, the crowd were fifty metres off, that was where she was supposed to be, where she, in fact, wanted to be. She didn't need to know these things at all – it was still possible to retract, a tiny lie would do it, just the word yes would suffice.

'No, I came here with my dad, he was hauling for the mill and he took me along with him. It was my birthday.'

Jessica was never very good at covering up feelings, her face was like a constantly shifting weather map of her moods. A moment before, it had shown a certain serious officiousness, an expression which included several states of mind – efficiency, an understanding of the gravity of the situation, a certain self-importance, but also a measure of irritation that she should be dragged away from the main event – all of which was, in an instant, overlaid by confusion.

'You told me your father was a bookseller in Sydney.'

'Not that father, my real father. I grew up round here.'

'But you told me . . .' She stopped. She swung her head around to see where the others had gone, perhaps to see if anyone could hear them, then brought herself back around. 'I don't get it. Is all the other stuff bullshit?'

She'd missed the point. This wasn't about that. It was about being here, in this place, where everything had been stripped away. On the ridge, on the edge of the road, his shoe black with dust, with the sun rendering everything flat and hard and difficult.

'No,' he said.

She didn't let him say anything more. 'Don't bullshit me, Kelvin. Whatever you do, don't do that.' She started to walk away. 'I haven't got time for this now. We'll talk about it later.' Dismissing him as if she was his mother or his schoolteacher and he was stupid; getting further away from him. 'I have to look after these people.' So that he was doubly abandoned, his attempt to reach out slapped down. He was a stupid child, stupid for telling the truth, stupid for lying in the first place, stupid for thinking anyone cared.

sixteen

In the car on the way to the beach – part of a convoy – Jessica refused any attempt at conversation, the air between them as thick as the fog of dust from the cars ahead. She drove with intense concentration, only breaking her silence to swear at the slowness of the pace. Kelvin confined himself to staring out the side window. The passage of cars along the road had, over time, coated each and every individual leaf on every single tree on both sides with the fine white dust. He wondered how they survived.

At Saltwater the protesters, their work done for the day, were preparing to swim, to eat lunch, to have a smoke and sleep off the afternoon. Jessica slammed her door and walked off towards the beach.

Kelvin noted and followed, but slowly. Clearly it was a day for remembering. He'd been to this place too. Pre-Rick and the twins he'd guess, just him and his mum, camping at Christmas down here at the beach. Over to the left there was an inlet, it would come into view in a moment, an almost-freshwater lagoon where they'd fished and swum – his mum running into the water in a tiny bikini shrieking with exaggerated laughter, trying to get him to come in too.

Jessica came back to him.

'I'm going for a walk,' she said. 'Will you come?'

Several people were already setting up. Jim and Andy were tossing a frisbee and threw it to Kelvin as he passed. He caught it and spun it back, finding that even in that short space of time Jessica had got ahead of him. He sprinted to catch up with her.

'What's he doing here?' she said without even glancing back.

'Who?'

She didn't answer.

'Andy? He wanted to see Nadgee, I guess, see what you're on about.'

Again she let it hang.

'He doesn't like the chipmill any more than you do,' he said. 'It's true, I've talked about it with him.'

'In a pig's arse.'

The fire hadn't made it down this far. They were on a strip of sand bordered on one side by thick bush and on the other by the great, the wondrous ocean, prussian blue, iridescent green, clean white where the waves broke. Jessica was walking fast on the hard sand close to the edge, aiming for a small avalanche of water-washed boulders and a craggy headland of red dirt rock. Captain Cook, when he visited in the late eighteenth century, had named this place Disaster Bay, the larger thing, not just this little beach. The volcanic nature of its geology was everywhere evident, the sharp bubbles of rock softened by the ages, not eradicated. A wide horizontal shelf skirted the headland, creating a kind of groin where deep water lurched. Jessica stood on its edge, a sea-wind lifting her hair.

'So,' she said. 'What's all this about?'

'What?' he said.

'Don't shit me, Kelvin.'

He found a small level space and sat with his hands hanging loose between his legs. He did not want to be interrogated by her. He was still caught up with these new memories. If she'd been open to it he would have liked to have told her about them. When he had given way to impulse and spoken to her about his father he had been prepared for anything but anger.

'I want to know why you felt you had to lie to me.'

The rock was broken and serrated and she couldn't find a place for herself to sit that was close enough to speak to him yet far enough away to express her outrage, so she remained standing, twisting this way and that in the wind.

'Come on. I want to know who you are.'

Her anger made it just too hard.

'I don't want to talk about it,' he said.

She turned away, turned back. 'Well fuck you then. Fuck you.'

He looked up. For a moment he thought she was going to leave and for an instant of that he didn't care. He was overcome by a profound exhaustion. Who did she think she was?

'Listen Kelvin. You want to hang around with me, you have

to talk to me. Ask me anything you want, I'll tell you. What you see with me is what you get. I'm a real person. I might not be all I want to be but I'm not a fabrication, I'm not something I made up to get people to like me.'

'You didn't tell me about you and Carl.'

She had not expected that. He saw that. She had thought she had him cornered. She fumbled for words, he could see her thoughts racing, trying to figure out how he knew about this, and what that meant.

'I would have told you if you'd asked.'

'But I didn't know to, did I?' He surprised himself with the viciousness of his tone, as if it mattered a damn what she'd done with Carl. 'I didn't think the first day we met you'd take me to visit your ex-lover. And set me up with him.'

'I didn't set you up with him. He's a friend. I didn't think it was important.'

'Well I didn't think it was important that I was born in Eden. You never asked. What's so fucking significant about it anyway?'

'You were born in Eden?'

'I didn't tell you that?'

'No.'

'Well, there you go then.'

She doesn't know what to do with her body. There doesn't seem to be anywhere to put it while her mind tries to digest this information. Some part of her is aware that her fury stems from what happened in Nadgee: the fire, the Forestry, the sheer ignorance and ugliness of it all, and that these feelings have somehow got caught up in what's happening here. She feels, at the same time, horribly exposed out on this shelf, as if not only are her footings collapsing beneath her, but that everyone on the beach can see her falling apart. She hasn't even had time to think about *what* he's told her, just the lie, and, she supposes, inherent in that the failure of everything she's been dreaming about for the last few weeks. It's only her anger that stops the disintegration. But Kelvin's not talking, he's not even looking at her. If this goes on much longer she'll have to leave. Just go. Let him sort it out for himself.

This beach was where it had started. The other people camping had all been families: mothers, fathers, children, grandparents, uncles and aunts, you name it. He and his mum were the only ones without a dad. They'd had to borrow other dads to help. Kelvin would've liked to have been able to manage it himself but some things were just beyond him. Even as they were unpacking the car, the first afternoon, when she was dragging the heavy canvas tent out of the back a man offered to lend a hand. 'Here, I'll get that,' he said, stepping in between them and the car so Kelvin had to stand back, a man dressed only in shorts, Bob or Barry or Ray, his chest covered in coarse hair that extended down onto the arms; Barry pulling out the tent with ease, slinging it up onto his shoulder, saying, 'Now where do you want this?' Kelvin confused by the extraordinary rush of emotions this simple event inspired; admiration, envy, annoyance, but also awe, because he saw, suddenly, his mum, beside the man, how small she was, his mum, small, separate from him, her hands in the pockets of her shorts, short shorts, the tails of her shirt tied in a knot below her breasts, her belly showing, trying to be something. So often, it seemed, she tried too hard. She didn't really know what she was supposed to do, as a mother, or even as an adult. As if she was making it up as she went along, like she was a little girl the same age as him and it was all a game in which they took turns to play the grown-up. Except that he knew the truth, he was the one who had to keep up the pretence, to run into the water after her so that no one would notice she was acting. But this time was different. She was the reason why Barry was there. Bob, Barry and Ray, other people's dads, wanted to be there, gathering firewood, lighting fires, carrying water because of her. He was old enough to see that, and, at least on some level, had known why. That holiday had been both the summit and the end of the golden time. The time when his mum was well and it was just the two of them, that time after his father had left and before Rick came.

He'd always believed he'd run away after the fight with Rick. He'd completely forgotten about the day in the truck with his dad. Rick had been drunk. The twins were crying. This was a long time later. The twins had been born by then and the sickness had come back. Rick and his mum were arguing. Kelvin was standing in the doorway of the little brown kitchen. It was night. The twins were screaming in a room behind him, some noise had disturbed them, probably the same thing that had woken him. Rick had hold of his mum and he was shaking her. She wasn't responding. She looked frail, lifeless, her dark hair hanging over her face. The only reason he knew she was alive was that she had a tailor-made cigarette smoking between her fingers. Kelvin went in and grabbed Rick's arm. He didn't think, just did it. Rick hit him. Smacked him right in the face so that he thought he must be broken, hit him so hard he went down and his mum screamed so he got up again and came at him a second time and this time Rick told him he was a useless piece of shit, just like his father, and pushed him away across the room, into the television set, knocked it right over so it smashed. He'd got cut on the elbow by the glass, had to go to hospital for stitches. He remembered that day clear enough but somehow he'd managed to forget about the day in the truck. It wasn't that long after the fight. He'd had this fantasy about his dad being better than Rick. He'd had this fantasy about his dad since long before Rick even came on the scene. But it wasn't so, his dad was worse, that was what he'd been scared of in the truck, that was what had been wrong with Daphne's house. There'd been no place for Kelvin, no safe place.

He looked up at Jessica. She was still standing in front of him, her arms crossed. He wanted her to stay. But he wasn't sure he could make her. He had that same impossible sense of never being enough for anyone who ever mattered to him.

seventeen

'See those people down at the mill,' Carl said, over dinner, 'they're like the dogs here: the only thing they understand is a force of equal or greater measure. Your little demonstration don't count for shit with them. What you did was based around the idea that someone cares. The owners don't even know it happened, they probably don't even know where Nadgee is. It's *that* insignificant. They're not interested in negotiation, they *do*, others *talk*. Talk is weakness for these guys; if you want to talk they know they got you beat.'

Kelvin ate his meat and potatoes. They had finished the fence that day, even though it was the last thing he'd felt like doing; stringing the wire out through the holes that they'd drilled in the posts with a great steel auger attached to the chainsaw. Winding up the tension with fence-pullers. It didn't bear consideration.

'What you need,' Carl was unusually talkative, as if Kelvin's distance was drawing the words out of him, 'is an economic argument. The mistake the hippies make is thinking this has something to do with ideology. Hell, it hasn't even got to do with wood-chipping. You've got to learn to take the ideology out of it. Wood-chipping just happens to be where the money is today, and it's only there because it gives a good return on capital. Soon as that stops happening they'll take it somewhere else.'

If Kelvin was listening at all it was only from the point of view of how such an argument would work against Jessica, how it would sound when he said it to *her*, what her arguments would be in return. She was bound to have some. He'd say what Carl had said, believing it, and then she'd cite another dozen examples he'd never heard of about effective nonviolence in India or Norway, or in Tasmania for God's sake, and he wouldn't have a hope. After the weekend he wasn't sure he had a hope anyway, and under normal circumstances that wouldn't have mattered – if someone, if a woman, for example, didn't like what she saw, there was no reason to hang around. There were plenty of others, just look at the pretty one at the demo. Except this time it did.

'What y'all have to do, if you want to stop this shit, is make it unattractive in an economic sense. Now, you can do that by regulation, or by direct action, those are your two choices, but whichever you choose it's gonna be slow, a matter of attrition, you've got to be in it for the long –'

'Carl,' Kelvin said, 'do you think you should tell anyone everything about yourself?'

Carl made a kind of snorting sound, interrupted mid-sentence. It was his turn to sit. He constructed a well-proportioned serve on his fork, plastering the potato on top of a piece of meat before putting it in his mouth. He raised his eyes to Kelvin and dropped them again, went to cut some more meat, stopped, finished what was in his mouth.

'So this is what's up? You've been as much use as a racoon all day. Listen, it depends on a lot of things, doesn't it? Depends on what you got to tell, depends on who you're telling it to and why. What is it you don't want to tell her?'

'Just stuff.'

'And?'

Kelvin had been about to tell Carl. As if having once broached the subject it had suddenly become common property and everyone could know, which wasn't the case at all. He'd almost blurted it out. He'd wanted to.

Instead he said, 'I know about you and her.'

'What about us?' Carl replied, frowning, in a tone which suggested that perhaps in this case attack wasn't the best tactic for defence, that what had worked with Jessica wouldn't work here.

'That you had a thing.'

'And?'

Carl stood up from his side of the table and Kelvin thought he might have been about to come around and hit him, or pick him up and throw him out the door. Instead he went to the kitchen and reached up to a top shelf where there was a bottle of whisky.

'D'you drink this stuff?' he said.

'From time to time.'

He poured a half-inch into two tumblers, and handed one to Kelvin. He clinked the two glasses together and drank.

Kelvin took a sip and swirled it around his mouth, savouring it, then knocked the rest back in one gulp, feeling the heat radiate out from his chest.

'I already figured you knew. I near enough told you myself.'

'Is that why you hired me?'

'Why?'

'Because I was with her.'

'Does it matter? Listen, if you hadn't been with her you wouldn't have set foot on the place, it's as clear as that. Did she ask me to hire you? No. I could've used some help on a fence. You were there.' Carl poured another shot into their glasses. 'You know, just because she's into that, doesn't mean you have to be.'

Kelvin thought about that, 'Yeah, but I like her.' He took another drink of the Scotch, slower this time. 'I mean, I really like her.'

'Can it be that bad?' Carl said, and laughed, the kind of laugh which is meant to diffuse the situation, but when Kelvin looked up at him whatever was on his face killed the laugh. Carl tilted his head to the side, curious. Kelvin swirled the last bit of Scotch in his glass.

'Listen, there isn't anything you could have done that I haven't done worse,' Carl said. 'I mean it.'

He offered him the bottle.

'I was born and raised in Eden,' Kelvin said.

'This Eden, here?'

'Here.'

Once he'd started it wasn't so hard, the story simply

unravelled itself, not only the bit where he ran away and met Shelley; that much he'd told Jessica. But what happened after that. What happened when they went on the street, Slattery, the whole thing. The whisky helped but really it was just good to talk, to let it out. Carl was a good listener. He didn't interrupt but he was there and Kelvin could feel the attention drawing out the words.

He was in the flat above the shop when they heard the banging. There was often noise from the street, drunks falling asleep in the doorway, the odd demented customer who believed they needed after-hours service. But this was persistent. 'It's a fucking second-hand bookshop,' Slattery said, 'not an out-patients.' But he went downstairs and Kelvin heard the bolt being drawn, then a female voice. Shelley. Worried.

She was in her work clothes, a tight skirt and top, calf-high boots, rushing up the stairs, her lipstick mussed. 'You have to get out of here,' she said. 'Daz's coming.'

Slattery coming up behind her, small and plump in corduroy pants and baggy jacket, semi-blond wig like the pelt of a cat, saying, 'It's your little friend,' seeing the expression on Kelvin's face, 'Here, what's going on?'

'He's on his way now. Lola told him.'

She was speaking very fast, standing in the middle of what was probably the living room of Slattery's flat but was, in fact, just an extension of the greater collection of magazines and newspapers and books he gathered around him, only with sofas included. She was slurring her words. Several times he had to ask her to repeat herself. She'd told Lola about Kelvin seeing Slattery. Lola was in trouble with Daz because of a boy *she'd* been seeing so she'd told him about Kelvin to get herself off the hook and now Daz was on his way to sort Kelvin out.

Slattery was panicking, 'Who is this guy? What does he want? What've we done? What's he going to do to Kelvin?'

'He's found out Kelvin's been fucking you and not cutting him in on it and now he's going to cut Kelvin,' she said.

It all seemed horribly clear. The stories Shelley told about the violence used against whores by their pimps had never seemed to refer to him, they were just some sort of street lore. Now the compartments he'd had neatly separated were bleeding into one another and the outcome had the force of certainty. He found it hard to move. There was nowhere to go, he may as well stay where he was and take whatever was coming. Shelley was urgent, however, hustling Kelvin down the stairs.

'We'll go out the back way.' She turned to Slattery. 'We need money. How much have you got?'

'Money,' he said. 'I haven't got any money.'

'You must have some. We need it, to get away.'

He was scared, all in a dither. 'What will he do to me?' he asked.

'Depends if he finds you. You've got a car, haven't you? You can drive us to the station. Lock up. Go somewhere. Call the cops for all I care, tell them your shop's being burgled. Just don't tell them you've been fucking little boys. How much money can you give me?'

'There's the float.'

'How much is that?'

'About a hundred dollars.'

'That'll do.'

'A hundred dollars!'

'We need it, we have to go now. He's watching our place. I'm saving your *life*. What's a hundred dollars?'

Kelvin had never seen her this wild: deeply intense, almost manic, her eyes large, her face drawn. He wondered if she was on something. If so then she was holding it well. When she turned her focus on Slattery he was unable to resist. He took out his wallet and seemed to have no difficulty finding the money, but he drew the line at driving them to the station.

'I can't leave the shop,' he said. 'They could damage it. They could set fire to it.' He put a hand on Kelvin's shoulder. 'You will be careful, won't you. It's my books you see . . . I have to stay. You understand, don't you?' He closed the door behind them. Then opened it again, pulling Kelvin back towards him. 'You will call, won't you?' he said. Then he closed it and locked it, turned out the lights.

They were left in the narrow passage between the door and the tin fence with only a distant streetlight to guide them across the back yard, stepping over its rubbish, under a broken Hills Hoist. Shelley took his hand. Her skin was cold, he thought he could feel her fear through his fingers.

'Quickly now,' she said.

133

Out in the street, under the lights, with people around, it wasn't so bad. Shelley waved down a cab and told the driver to take them to Central. He asked to see their money first.

Kelvin wanted to know where they were going, but she wouldn't discuss it. 'What about our things?' he said.

'You can't go back there.'

'But the money,' whispering because the taxi driver could hear. They'd been saving a little, not much, because money seemed to just disappear.

'I've got that,' she said, patting her boot. 'That's all we need.'

It was only when they were on the train, going north, when they'd passed out of Sydney, when out in the dark they could see trees, the Hawkesbury River, that she started to laugh.

'Did you see his face?' she said. 'Did you see his face? Laugh? I could've fucking died. His toupee almost fell off.'

Loud peels of high-pitched laughter in the rail carriage, other people looking their way. She put her hand on Kelvin's shoulder in parody of Slattery. 'You will call, darling, won't you?' and burst into laughter again. She *had* told Lola about Kelvin, she said. And Lola *was* in trouble and she couldn't trust her and she thought sooner or later she'd blab to Daz about it so they had to get out. 'Besides,' she said, 'I had to get you away. I mean, he was weird, wasn't he? I mean, the whole fucking thing was weird. I didn't like it at all.' Laughing. Sitting opposite him in an all-night train heading somewhere he'd never been before and laughing, and Kelvin was furious with her for fooling him into thinking Daz was coming after him with a razor, for the real fear he had felt, for telling Lola about it in the first place. Yes, she said, yes, but Daz would have found out one day, sooner or later, Kelvin was so stupid, and look, now they were gone, they never had to see Daz ever again, she'd look up the ape-man in Brisbane, he'd give her a job as a dancer in a nightclub and neither of them would ever have to fuck for money again.

And it was true, the idea appealed, getting up and leaving, no attachments. It was the kind of thing he'd imagined himself doing while leaning against the Wall. He was fourteen and on a train going to a city where nobody knew him, with Shelley, and after a while he laughed too. It was good to have Slattery's hundred dollars and not to have his hands fumbling him that night, he'd never do that again, he'd never fuck again for money. He pulled out the book he'd taken from Slattery, already dog-eared, by a man called Heinlein, about a man from Mars who sees the world as it really is. He looked at his reflection in the window and back across at Shelley and smiled.

'I saved you,' she said.

This was another one of her moods. Combined with some pharmaceutical. She would be back down the next day, scratchy and sore and difficult, but her play that night had been extraordinary, standing in Slattery's flat giving her performance. She was leaning against the window so that he could see her face and this slightly blurred reflection beside it, both of them wanting his approval and there was no way he could withhold it. Sometimes he loved her so much. There was nothing back in their little house he would miss, nothing at all.

'So, what happened?'

'Shelley met with her man. He got her work as a dancer.

'And?'

'She ended up going with him.'

'Where?'

'Sleeping with him, living with him. Perhaps she got over the hair, I dunno.'

'And you?' Having to draw it out of him.

'I didn't fit any more. I was a bit older, you know, and Shelley was doing well. She didn't need me any more.'

'You were well out of that,' Carl said.

'I was?'

'He was a fucking pederast.'

It was late and the table was littered with the detritus of whisky and cigarettes. Kelvin cleaned a pathway through the spilled ash with his forefinger, then crossed it with another pathway whose sides blocked the first one. There seemed to be many different answers he could give but none that were appropriate.

'I went up to Cairns,' he said. 'Then there was Cyclone Tracy so I went to Darwin. There was work for builders' labourers, and people up that way don't ask so many questions. I stayed. That's how I ended up on the boats.'

'Did you keep in touch with Shelley?'

'Bits and pieces, some postcards.'

Kelvin was winding down, he didn't want to talk any more. He wanted to keep the bit about Melbourne and Shelley to himself. It wasn't anyone's business but his own.

Out on the veranda the night was clear and cold. A moon in its last quarter cast a yellow glow. Carl sat on the steps with the dogs. It had been a cheap trick with the whisky and no doubt he'd pay for it. He could feel the alcohol in him like a sickness. Maisie came over to see what the matter was and laid her head on his thigh and he was immensely grateful for the gesture. Down in the paddock a cow lowed. Jessica had, it seemed, a knack for choosing the difficult ones. It was not the whisky or the cigarettes or exhaustion that ailed him. The boy's story had woken something and now it was sitting on his chest, compressing it, making it difficult to breathe. He played with the dog's ear, ran his fingers along the flow of her pelt.

Kelvin had broken custom. He had revealed himself, and the man he'd chosen to give his confession to was the very person whose story could not be told, who could not afford the luxury. He couldn't even write it down, hide it in some vault. He had tried that. For several weeks he had filled exercise books with his scribbles, hiding them each night under the floor. But if they found him they would look there, they would look everywhere, it went without saying. There were other people involved. So he'd burned the books, scattered the ashes. He had to live with the choices he'd made. But the boy's story had pricked him, alerted him to his isolation. Carl was acquainted with loneliness, how in the early evening or in the small hours of the morning it would fall on him. He knew, also, that the feeling would pass, that fighting made it worse. He had come to understand how it was better to surrender; but even knowing that it was hard, and no amount of familiarity with its ways had taught him to deal with the words it whispered in his ear. Still, loneliness was his beast and no one else's. When he made peace with it there was, on occasion, at its darkest point, a moment of beauty; one tiny instant during which everything in the world seemed to be in the right place at the right time. Out on the steps, with his dog beside him, his arms wrapped around his knees, he wondered if it would come.

They were down by the dam the next afternoon, fiddling with the pump, when he heard a motor. It had been one of those days in which inanimate objects conspire to malfunction, when nothing fits, spanners are the wrong size, threads cross, the simplest thing, a pencil, goes missing and will not be found. He went to the glove box and dug out the binoculars and watched until he caught a glimpse of a white van on the little straight by the creek. There was some sort of decal on the side. Immediately, irrationally, he felt the fear in him, liquefying his stomach, heightening his senses. Where had it been hiding to come up as quickly as that? Was that what his melancholy had really been about? And the day's reluctance? The problem was what to do with the boy.

No. The thing to do was not to panic. It could still be

nothing. At the curve before the second ford he got another look. A blue logo on the passenger door.

It proved to be a Telecom van, driven by a uniformed technician complete with clipboard and name tag, the dogs, as well they might, staking him out, their hackles up, barking.

'I'll handle this,' he said to Kelvin, yelling at the dogs.

The man climbed out, nervous.

'Howdo,' Carl said.

'I'm looking for Cooral Dooral Station,' he said. He checked his clipboard. 'Carl Tadeuzs.'

'You've found him.'

The technician held out a hand, said the name that was on the tag. He took in the dam, the paddock, the house a few hundred metres above them.

'It's just a courtesy call,' he said. 'We're going to lay cable for your neighbours, see, and we're making a visit to the properties round about to offer you the chance to connect – while the equipment's in the district.'

'I'll be right thanks,' Carl said.

The Telecom man checked his clipboard again, 'There's only a nominal charge involved, sir, the same as you'd pay for a connection in the city. I think it's about a hundred and forty, fifty dollars.'

'I don't need a phone.'

They stood for a moment longer, the three of them in a little huddle next to the van. He had hoped his tone would finish the thing but the man made no move to go.

'We've got a pump to fix here,' he said. 'So you won't mind if we get back to it.'

'Not at all sir. Nice place you've got. I wonder if I might trouble you for a signature. Just to say that we did offer you the service.'

'Sure. Kelvin, my hands are filthy, will you sign for me?'

Kelvin stepped forward.

'It should be the property owner, sir.'

'He'll do it on my behalf,' Carl said.

The technician went back to his truck and sat in the cabin, making notes. He stayed there a full five minutes.

'You don't want the phone?' Kelvin said.

Carl gave him what he hoped was a withering look.

Watching the van go he thought that he had been right to feel the fear, that the fear was and always had been his friend, his fear was what had kept him alive thus far. He'd allowed it to go to sleep, he'd become attached, he'd settled down in one place and now something was happening and he would have to move again and he did not want to.

The pump was still disconnected, the big plastic bucket of fittings tipped out on the ground beside it, the thick recalcitrant black snake of polypipe curling out of the ground.

'Let's clear up this mess,' he said. 'We'll fix this when I get back from Bega with the right bit.'

Kelvin looked at him.

'I know,' he said, 'but the day's fucked, isn't it? I need those gates, I'll go to the co-op tomorrow and get a fitting while I'm there. Let's have a coffee.'

He had to get rid of the boy, tell him something, take him out of the loop. He sat in the cabin of the Toyota staring at the brown earth of the dam, the brown water, the useless pump, the stained aluminium feed-pipe nosing down the steep bank. Kelvin was beside him, the dogs in the back. Waiting.

A moment before he had been so deeply immersed in this place that he'd forgotten everything else. He clattered the diesel into life and nudged it up the hill to the house.

'I'll take you over the Farm later if you like, won't be much happening around here for a few days. You probably won't mind that, eh? You can come back Monday.'

On the mountain, in the evening, Kelvin asked him if he was in trouble.

He shrugged. 'Not as such, no more'n usual. But thanks for asking.'

He could feel Kelvin's eyes on him.

'By the way, about last night,' it was the first mention of it, 'appreciated you telling me what you did. Meant a lot to me. But about Jessica, I've no clue as to you telling her that stuff, that's something you'll have to figure out. One thing though,' Kelvin still not talking, staring straight forward through the windscreen while the truck wound along the old road, tree ferns spilling over the edge, Carl wondering about how it would be possible to put this without sounding false, 'she's a good woman. There's not so many like her.'

eighteen

'Here,' Kelvin said, pointing to a cul-de-sac with perhaps twelve houses, each with their unpainted boards curling up, children's toys clustered around the stumps; outside one an aluminium dinghy on a trailer; in the driveway of another a logging truck, its bogey wheels tucked up behind the cabin like dog's balls, the rig almost bigger than the house.

Jessica pulled onto the gravel edge across from the entrance and took his hand in a gesture that was probably meant to demonstrate compassion, or sympathy for whatever it was she imagined him to be feeling at this point – an empathy she could afford now that she'd dragged him there. It was misplaced. He felt nothing for these houses marooned in their little patches of grass.

Only one was brick, a two-storey affair decorated with concrete pillars and iron railings – the house Angelo Venditti's father had built on weekends, which for all the time Kelvin had lived next door to it had been a building site rendering up small stolen treasures: discarded nails, a couple of bolts, rusty reinforcing wire, the terrifying satisfaction of a deliberately broken windowpane. Now it was finished it was simply another house. They were all just houses.

The only surprise was that he had somehow forgotten the street's most obvious feature. Its name, Seaview Court, no matter how clichéd, was at least honest. The whole hillside was exposed to the ocean. The southern ellipse of Twofold Bay was spread out in front of them, deeply blue on this late summer day, lichen-covered rocks tumbling into the water, eucalyptus trees clinging to its shore. Across the wide expanse, on South Headland, the bright stab of the mill. Strange not to have remembered something of such enormity.

Jessica thought that if he saw where it was he had grown up he would feel driven to contact his family. She couldn't imagine knowing where her family lived and not going to see them. Or perhaps she just wanted proof that all this actually existed; needed emotional evidence, or to meet his mother, to be sure. Well his mother had once lived in that weatherboard house. Perhaps she still did, but even seeing it across the street did not provoke in him the need to go and find out. He wasn't sure what sort of person that made him. What he did know was that he'd left, and sworn never to return, for reasons that had been good solid reasons then and they still held true nine years later. If it was memories she wanted he could do them. They were coming in spades: bicycling down the hill into town; the track that led out of the top of the street into the back of the old timber mill; the internal walls made of sagging unpainted masonite and the little strips of wood that had framed the sheets, the same stuff on the ceilings, his bedroom

143

an entirely brown world except for the fine white watermarks on the ceiling left by storms which he made into maps of continents. The sound of his mum and dad's voices in the next room, their movements amplified, their words distorted. The silence and then the deep curt resonance of his father's voice saying something and his mother's monosyllabic reply. The scrape of a chair to put another log on the fire. The inevitable rise of his father's anger, at first not as sound, in the beginning as an absence of sound. He had never known what his father was angry about, only that somehow it had always been to do with him. Was that the kind of memories she wanted? They were there. But they were his. He could not articulate them. He had managed to tell her about Sydney, at least as much as he could bear to reveal to someone with her gender's special view of sex. He had managed that. Because he needed her. Perhaps that was why he was going along with Andy's plan. For her. But he would not cross that road.

'We're being watched,' she said.

He turned in time to see a curtain fall across a window.

'Let's go then.'

'Aren't you going to tell me anything about it?'

Andy and Jim might be going to do it as a demonstration of ideology, or as some sort of prank – for no other reason, perhaps, than that they'd been talking about it for so long and that making up stories has a strength in itself. He wasn't at all certain why they were involved. But Kelvin was going along because of Jessica, and because of Carl. It wasn't the scene with the horse that had done it, but it helped. Not the hitting. The staying. Kelvin had no capacity to stand his ground. None. Instead there were only justifications, an endless series of carefully worked philosophical and ethical positions for not standing up to forces which might hurt him. For shifting aside, dodging them. And this code of his, this philosophy that had led him to Sydney and Shelley and on to Brisbane and Darwin and then back to Melbourne and now here, this code had been developed at number five Seaview Court.

'There's nothing to say,' he said.

She put the car in gear, did a U-turn. At the end of the street she turned down into the town, took a left at the Ampol, towards the airport.

Out of the silence she said, 'You're a weird cove.' Smiling.

Something had shifted, or else she just wasn't any good at goodbyes.

'You will look after my place, won't you? And Suzy? I'm trusting you.'

'Of course,' he said, remembering what he had forgotten, that she wasn't going forever, that she was leaving him the car, the house, the dog to look after, and that this must mean something.

'You won't do anything stupid, will you?' she said.

For a moment he thought she knew.

'Like not be here when I get back?' Her hand had mysteriously found its way back onto his thigh, was squeezing it. 'This is really big for me, going to Sydney. But I want you here when I get home.'

He leaned over and kissed her on the neck, below the ear

where the skin was smooth, rich in the smell of her. He wanted to hold onto her, didn't want to get involved with the others at all. It *was* just a prank, a joke, a lark. There was no need to get too serious about it. After he'd dropped her off at the airport he'd buy a drum of diesel in Merimbula.

'I'll be here,' he said.

nineteen

The first shower came as they entered town, big drops slapping against the windscreen, the three men across the bench seat of the panel van, the heater on because of the cold but the windows down because of the fumes that leaked in through the rear gate. When the rain hit Jim's face he started, woken too quickly from dreams.

'Just what we fucking need,' he said.

'This is good,' Andy said. 'This I like.'

Kelvin, squashed between them, could not see much to approve of. He was relieved when it stopped as abruptly as it had begun.

All that day the weather had been poor, low cloud tearing itself to pieces on the mountain, the air damp and cold and full of the promise of rain. Bad omens. Andy, thinking otherwise, thinking, This'll keep the cops off the road, took the highway north, the road slick and shiny and deserted. A couple of kilometres after the Ampol he diverted into an industrial zone. Kelvin had passed by there with Jessica the day before, and again by himself on the way back. On neither occasion had he thought to check it out. He was, he thought, an amateur at this sort of thing. He should have left it as a joke.

The place must have been recently gazetted, for the road was new and black, neatly kerbed and guttered, the pale concrete strip holding back the vacant building sites. The Forestry offices were huddled together on the turning circle of a dead end, a few low buildings with a driveway passing between them blocked by a shiny red and white boom.

'There you go,' Andy said to Jim, slipping out from behind the wheel, leaving the engine running, pulling a small bag out of the back. He went through to the rear of the building. Kelvin took up his position in the driveway. Jim drove off. There were no lights in any of the buildings. Five beige Landcruisers were parked in the small tarred area behind the offices. Beyond them was a tall cyclone fence confining larger machinery. Kelvin checked the boom. Where it came down beside a metal post there was a welded box protecting the hardened steel padlock from tampering.

He slipped back through to where Andy was working on the door of one of the Toyotas.

'The boom's locked,' he said, whispering.

'Fuck the boom,' Andy said. 'Go back and keep lookout.'

Kelvin went back between the buildings. Even before he'd got to the point where he could see the street Andy had the door open and was twisting in underneath the steering column. Nothing was happening out the front. The single streetlight was reflected in the puddles on the road. Concern at what Andy was going to do to get the Toyota out took hold of Kelvin's mind. The boom wouldn't easily come apart, even if rammed with the roo bar of a Landcruiser, and the noise and the mess would draw all sorts of attention. The industrial area was desolate, with only one other building a hundred metres away, looming in the darkness. Over on the highway, a couple of blocks away, a truck went past, its orange lights blazing. There was nowhere to hide if someone came. On the office wall a sign in the shape of a shield announced the property was watched over by Easts of Eden Security.

He heard the Toyota start and ran back through.

'All clear out front,' he said, swinging in the door, Andy sliding into the passenger seat, saying, 'Gloves.'

'Right,' Kelvin extracting his from his jeans pocket, pulling them on. 'How do we get out of here?'

Andy looked at Kelvin as if he was some kind of a fool. 'We drive,' he said, pointing.

There was no fence around the parking lot. The only obstacle between them and the vacant block next door was a line of small natives planted in chip mulch. The blood rose to his face. He eased forward and then out onto the road, searching for the knob to pull on the headlights, Andy stuffing his hair up into a cap.

Jim was waiting at Quarantine Bay, the panel van tucked in under the casuarinas.

'Quickly now, and *quiet*,' Andy said.

They transferred the drums, and a chainsaw in case of fallen logs, managing it all with what might be said to be military precision, but Andy's instruction rankled. As if he had taken it upon himself to become their leader. It wasn't that Kelvin wanted the role, he just didn't want Andy to have it.

Out on the highway, Kelvin driving because of his short hair, wearing a beige work shirt bought the day before at St Vincent de Paul's, the white gloves abandoned as being just plain stupid, he tried to make conversation.

'You got the door open pretty quick.'

'Something I learned in Canberra,' Andy replied, 'when I was a kid. Come Saturday night we'd go joy-riding, pinch some cars and take them out in the woods near Cotter Dam. Drag-racing. It was what we did for recreation.' And he didn't say, 'not like some other kids,' but it was implicit: Andy's working-class roots were like a badge. But then he didn't mention, either, that it was through that business that he'd got into this whole thing. That was another story. Instead he fished around in his tobacco pouch and pulled out a ready-rolled number.

'You sure we ought to smoke?' Kelvin said. 'I mean, don't we need to be, like, focused?'

Andy wet the outside of the joint between his lips. He leaned forward so he could see past Jim. 'Nobody's forcing you,' he said. 'You'd like a smoke, wouldn't you Jimbo?'

'Just a little one,' Jim said. 'Can't see a little bit of smoke going down the wrong way.'

Twenty-five kilometres south of town they turned inland on the Forestry road, and started to climb. There had been little traffic on the highway at this time of night, and on this road there was none, just the wide easy curves, Kelvin's eyes fixed to the small section illuminated by the truck's lights, on the lookout for roos.

'Jesus!' he said. 'I never looked, there's hardly any fuel.'

Andy was holding in some smoke. 'Hey man, anyone ever told you you're a panic merchant? Take it easy. Plenty of fuel where we're going.' He blew out the smoke and shook his head. 'I mean. Fucking relax.'

They turned off on Taggarts Road, a broad dirt highway rolling along a ridge, a serious road, built for logging trucks, the trees tall and straight and wild on both sides, dark forest stretching forever. They'd been driving for almost an hour and they seemed only to be going deeper into the trees, there was no end to them. In the dark of the night it felt as though there was no possibility of humans being able to destroy such a forest, that maybe they were wrong and the loggers were right; except for the road itself, this extraordinary indifferent thing pushed directly into the heart of the place.

'Slow down, man,' Andy said. 'I need to get my bearings.'

A side road offered itself, the only sign being a piece of plywood tacked onto a picket with the numbers *18/20* painted on it in rude letters.

'Here,' Andy said.

This was a narrower road, winding down off the ridge. Now, occasionally, there were open spaces above or below them. As they swung around one corner the headlights picked out a bare burned scree bordered by a wall of distant pale trunks, the cut edge fragile in the white light. Other tracks peeled off to either side. They kept to the main route, this narrow scar cut sharply into the hill, twisting back on itself again and again so that they wondered how far it could go down, how logging trucks could make it up, until abruptly it ended, delivering them onto a broad flat circle complete with machinery, a loading ramp, a portaloo and a stack of peeled logs. On one side a couple of forty-fours and a ten-gallon drum stood in their own little patch of stained dirt. Kelvin did a turn-around. There was no one and nothing else, only several tall trees inexplicably left around the edge, their trunks excessively naked and, in the centre, the bright yellow dozer and snigger parked neatly side by side, like giant toys.

'Don't turn off the motor,' Andy said. 'I don't want to have to start her again.'

Kelvin backed over. He stayed in the cabin while Jim and Andy fiddled with a hand-pump that was fitted into the top of one of the drums. Andy was holding the torch, giving instructions to Jim now, whose job it apparently was to work the pump while Andy filled the tank on the Toyota. Then they unscrewed the pump and took it out of the forty-four, and replaced it with a plastic funnel. Jim hefted one of the five-gallon drums off the back of the truck. Andy held the funnel. In the torchlight the sugar and diesel showed hints of colour as it poured out in a smooth stream, slightly viscous. When they were done they put the pump back in the drum and screwed it up tight, put the empty on the back of the truck.

The heavy dark smell of the fuel came back into the cabin with them, like below decks on a trawler.

'Right,' Andy said.

Kelvin put the truck in gear and headed back up the hill. It was as simple as that. They hadn't even looked at the machines.

'How much do you reckon they're worth?' Jim said.

'Sweet fuck-all after they put that shit in them,' Andy said.

'If you had to buy one.'

'I don't reckon you'd get any change out of a hundred grand. Each.'

'Shit,' Kelvin said.

The ability to grasp what they'd just done, and were about to do again, came slowly. He could feel rather than see the flattened forest around. He imagined one of those machines down the hill preparing to pull a log back to the dump; the motor failing, spluttering, belching black smoke from the little spring-loaded exhaust cap, refusing to take up the strain. The men gathering around it, trying to isolate the problem, bringing the other machine down to snig it up the hill and then that one failing too. Both machines crippled in a gully, tied to each other, the workers scrambling over them in their yellow hard hats, earmuffs clipped up like vestigial ears. He imagined their rage when they figured it out, their hopeless, directionless rage, the terrible force of their hatred, and he laughed out loud, filled with a strange elation.

'They're not going to be happy campers when they work it out,' he said.

'There, my friend,' Andy said, 'you're not wrong.'

'It's not just the loggers is it?' Jim said. 'It's every bastard up and down the coast. The cops, the chipmill, the insurance agents . . .'

'Too late to back out now,' Andy said. He pointed at another side road. 'Take a right here. But listen, these bastards've had it coming for years. We asked them nicely, didn't we? We said, "Please stop." How many times did they think we were going to do that?'

He'd argued with Jessica about it, without actually saying what they had in mind.

'Are you saying you wouldn't be glad if someone fucked up a whole heap of machines out in the forest?'

'Of course I would –'

'See.'

'– on some level –'

'You know all this talking isn't going to make a bit of difference. You need to make them sit up and take notice,' Kelvin said, hoping to make both Andy's and Carl's arguments work against her.

'There's ways to go about these things and there's –'

'You just don't want to get your hands dirty. You'd be happy –'

'Will you let me finish! You've had your say, let me have mine.'

'I'm listening.'

'Like fuck you are, you've got that look on your face.'

'What look is that?'

'Your stubborn look. Your I'm-here-but-I'm-not-going-to-listen-to-you look, your nothing-can-touch-me look. If there's one thing that shits me about you, Kelvin, it's that look.'

'So speak. I'm listening.'

'I want to stop the logging of these forests. I don't want a war. You start blowing things to the shit and you're going to have guys shooting at each other.'

'Right.'

'You don't think so? Your trouble is you think everyone arrived here yesterday, like there's no past attached to this. You think that because the people who live here have nice white skins and drive Holdens they're less capable of killing people than Africans or South Americans or Asians. You're not even scared of them. You read books but you have no sense of history. It's precisely because they have nice white skins that they're more likely to. How do you think we got to be the winners here? D'you see any Aboriginals around here? Huh? You think this place was empty when whites came? You're living in a dream world.'

Furious with him. As if he didn't know the nature of the place; as if he wasn't the one who'd been born there.

At the fourth site the rain came back. There was one tall tree on the edge of the flat and the wind was whipping at its branches so hard that Kelvin could hear the leaves lashing against each other above the motor of the Toyota. A great orange Komatsu was pinioned in the headlights while the boys did their work. It had a blade the size of a house and a great steel rod sticking forward above it like a bowsprit, what they called a tree-pusher. Someone had welded extra bands of steel onto the blade, a criss-crossing of beads which served no clear purpose. He went over to look at it. The tracks were as high as his shoulder. He put his hand on the rectangular steel plates, feeling their cold hardness, their extraordinary weight, the polished surface already tinged with a patina of rust.

'What the fuck are you doing?' Andy called.

The machine was of such a different order to everything he knew, impressive not only in its size but also in its solidity. Jim wandered over to join him. He hauled himself up onto the tracks and into the cabin, ignoring the first spots of rain and Andy's calls. He sat himself on the single black plastic seat in the cabin and took the controls in his hands, leering down at Kelvin, a schoolboy playing engine driver. Except against the size and solidity of this machine he *was* a child. This ugly, brutal device was what humanity was really about. Kelvin did not know how any of it was made or how it did what it was supposed to do, or how to make it do it. Other men, more focused than he, were responsible for these things; they had devoted their lives to mining and purifying and forging steel, to shaping it into component parts and designing ways for them to go together to make this thing. Kelvin's contribution was to contaminate the fuel in a couple of forty-fours in a logging dump out the back of Woop Woop. As if such an activity would make the slightest difference. It was starting to rain properly. Sheets of it coming down silver in the headlights of the Toyota. Jim had found something up in the cabin, a shifting spanner built to match the machine, a chrome thing just like the one in everyone's toolbox, except this one was over a metre long. Kelvin ran back to the truck. He expected Jim to follow but he stayed on the machine, the wrench in his hands. Kelvin drove over next to it and yelled out the window through the rain, telling Jim to get the fuck off there, which he began to do, clambering down onto the tracks, still carrying the wrench like it was some sort of sword or axe.

'Leave that behind,' Kelvin said.

Jim ignored him, negotiating his way along the top of the slippery plates of steel, the rain pelting him.

Kelvin tried to open the door but he was too close to the dozer, 'Fucking leave it,' he said.

'It's mine,' Jim said. He stepped down onto the tray. He put his prize up against the cabin, behind the empty drums. Unencumbered he swung off the other side and into the passenger door, his clothes soaked through, his beard dripping. Kelvin didn't move. The windscreen wipers were crap. The headlights showed a patch of mud across which water was beginning to flow.

'What the fuck d'you take that for?' Kelvin said. 'We agreed, we take nothing, we leave nothing. This is serious fucking business, remember?'

Jim stared straight ahead.

'No one'll notice,' he said. 'It doesn't fucking matter. Let's get out of here.'

'Can we?' Andy said.

Kelvin looked at the other two. He was about to object again, to make a stand. It was nothing to do with being discovered. It was simply wrong. Bad karma to steal someone's

157

tools. But if it was bad karma to steal a wrench, what was it to fuck a dozer? That was too hard. He put the truck in gear. The logging dump was at the bottom of a steep road which proved to be badly drained; streams of water were already cutting channels into the debased granite. A couple of hundred metres up, at a narrow place between a high yellow bank on one side and a drop-off on the other, there was a seam of clay. As soon as the Toyota touched it the wheels began to spin, the rear end skittering out towards the edge. He dropped a gear, and then another, but it made no difference.

He stopped and backed down, allowing the weight of the machine to carry it across the slick surface. When he was on firm ground again he got out and locked the hubs. The rain had, if anything, increased. Little rivers were flowing through the channels the tyres had cut in the clay.

He put the truck in low.

'Gun the bastard,' Andy said. 'Take a run at it.'

Kelvin ignored him. He ground forward at less than walking pace. For a moment he thought they would make it but the seam must have been deep because the wheels just kept slithering.

'You know how to drive this bastard?' Andy said.

'Clearly a fucking lot more than you do.'

'You need to take a fucking run at it,' Andy said.

'It's all yours,' Kelvin said, letting the vehicle's weight take it back down a second time. The road was now revealed in the headlights as a mess of thick grooves. 'Come on Jim,' he said, getting out. 'When he gets stuck we'll give him a push.'

Andy slid across to the driver's seat.

'You in four-wheel drive?' he asked.

Kelvin just looked at him.

'I'm going back down a bit further, get up a bit of speed,' he said.

'Listen,' Kelvin said, 'keep away from that edge.'

They stood on the side of the track, their hair plastered against their heads. Andy came roaring up between them. When the wheels hit the clay they began to spin furiously, digging in, sending up great sprays of mud, the truck's rear sliding sideways. They could see Andy silhouetted against the headlights, fighting with the steering wheel, turning it this way and that.

'Come on,' Kelvin said.

They put their shoulders to the tray but it was less than useless, only covered them in great gouts of mud. Andy wouldn't let up until the vehicle was at right angles to the road. He stepped out, swearing. The three of them looked at each other, at the road, at the Toyota, at the earth wall lit by the headlights. The rain was cold. It was perhaps three in the morning.

'Let's have a look-see how wide this seam of clay is,' Kelvin said. 'Maybe it's not too long. We can get some bark and logs and corduroy it.'

He started up the hill. He was cloaked in mud, starting to shiver, but was propelled by, if nothing else, sheer terror. Andy turned to follow. The clay was like lead around his boots.

Jim called out, 'Hey, boys, it's all right, it's all right. There's a winch.'

He was standing between the headlights like a refugee from Moby Dick, pointing at the bullbar.

'Oh you sweet thing,' Andy said. 'Oh you sweet little bastard.'

It took two pulls to get across the seam. By the time they made it back onto the ridge road every part of the Toyota was covered in mud.

Kelvin was driving again. He pulled over, careful to keep on the hard surface. The three men stared out through the curved wedges of clarity provided by the windscreen wipers.

'Fuck, eh,' Jim said.

'Fucking fuck,' Andy replied.

Kelvin rested his forehead against the steering wheel. At least the rivalry had disappeared. For a moment they were just three men, together, giving thanks.

'Well, we fucking did it,' Andy said. 'We fucking did it.'

The windows were all misted up with the heater, but it was warm. Kelvin stepped out to release the hubs. It was still raining and he started to rub down the outside with his bare hand. Clods of clay were gathered in the wheel arches, sprays of the stuff across the mudguards. He stuck his head in the door. 'What are we going to do about this truck?'

'Well we're not taking it to a fucking car wash, that's for sure,' Andy said, and laughed, and then they all started laughing though it wasn't funny, Kelvin standing in the doorway, still in the rain, the other two in the damp musty filthy cabin.

When they were moving again Andy dug in his tobacco pouch. 'I reckon it must be time, gentlemen, for a celebratory number.'

'I thought we were fucked down there,' Jim said. 'I thought we were completely fucked.'

'You weren't on your Pat Malone,' Andy said.

He lit the joint and passed it along, without holding on for his customary age. Even Kelvin took a drag. He figured it couldn't hurt at this point even though it wasn't over yet, there was still the drive down the forest road, the twenty-five kilometres of highway, the town itself.

'You know,' Jim said. 'We could just tell them.'

'We could tell who?' Andy said.

'The loggers. We could warn them. We could call from a phone booth, anonymously, and tell them we've contaminated a whole heap of fuel. We wouldn't need to say where. It'd be just as effective, it'd stop work all over the coast –'

'But it wouldn't fuck up their machines,' Andy said.

'Exactly. The point is we want to stop them doing what they're doing, we're not trying to hurt –'

'Are you getting cold feet Jimbo?' Andy said.

Sometimes he had an ugly way of speaking to people.

'It's just the loggers are going to be pissed off, aren't they? I mean if they found out, if they even thought they knew who was responsible, they wouldn't go to the cops, would they? They'd just come after you. They'd break your legs, or worse.'

'That's why you got to keep your mouth shut Jimbo,' Andy said. 'So's no one does find out. No one finds out nothing about nothing, no one talks to no one, nobody claims responsibility, there's no fucking leads anywhere, that's why we've gone to all this trouble. I like my fucking legs.'

'When I was up on the dozer –' Jim said.

'What the fuck were you doing up on the dozer?' Andy said.

'I was having a look. I've never been on one before. I thought I'd take a look. While I was up there I thought, I don't know. I thought how insignificant it is what we're doing, in the big picture, you know. I mean, we think it's a big deal, but it's not. It's not going to stop anything. It's just going to piss people off.'

'Shut up Jim,' Kelvin said. 'Just shut the fuck up.'

They drove in silence, the dope making their thoughts palpable, clouds of ill colour heavy in the cabin's dank air. Andy was glad it was Kelvin who'd shut Jim up. Despite himself he liked the boy. Even if he was giving it to that bitch Jessica. It was almost a shame, he thought, to fuck him up so badly.

They dropped Jim off at the panel van, leaving him to take the drums to the tip while they put the Toyota back, however useless that was now.

It was later than they wanted it to be when they passed through town. If it wasn't for the rain, now a drizzle, there would have been the beginnings of light. Perhaps that was why no one was about. Also it was Sunday morning, the morning after Saturday night in a logging and fishing town. Kelvin backed the truck in again across the little trees.

'If they've got several drivers for each truck maybe they'll blame each other for the mess,' Kelvin said.

'Whatever you like to think,' Andy said. 'But I'll tell you this, it'll exercise their little minds.'

He got down under the dash and pushed the wires back up, wiped off the surfaces. Kelvin did his best to repair the damage to the seedlings. Then they stood together under the building's eaves, waiting. The Toyota dripped mud onto the tar. A big lump of clay fell off behind one of the back wheels and started to dissolve. Kelvin had started shaking again. Andy held onto his arm for a moment.

'You done good,' he said. 'We're almost there. Don't fucking lose it now. See, here comes Jim. We're fucking out of here.'

twenty

He couldn't sleep. He'd come back to her house and to Suzy, so pleased to see him in the early morning, crazy with happiness at his safe return. He'd lit the stove and made coffee and washed and put his clothes to soak and by that time his exhaustion had transformed itself into a frenetic restlessness of both body and mind. He was in her house with her dog amid her things, the boxes of papers in her office, the books, her kitchen with its graters and grinders and sieves and strainers, her stack of mismatched china, each plate and cup and saucer individually chosen from op shops and markets across the country, Jessica the collector of things, postcards tacked onto the walls, the pantry door a collage of photographs of people that, generally speaking, he did not know, had never seen, and he distracted himself by examining them, this pictorial of her, the snapshots of her and her women friends in ones and twos and threes, smiling out at the camera, arms around each other, testifying to good times having been had somewhere that he was not. He searched through them for evidence of the person he knew, the thoughtful, serious, sensitive, singular, intimate woman, the one whose face was so close to his in the bed that he could hardly focus on it, but he could find little in the photographs to suggest her, and in his beyond-exhaustion state he found himself condemning her for a shallowness of existence. There was probably a record of similar moments in his life captured on film, but not by him, and he had never gathered them together, never stuck them all higgledy-piggledy to a door in his house, and the point was she had, and this need of hers to have and to hold both attracted and repelled him; it seemed to demonstrate, for a start, an undue concentration on the material side of life, a personality controlled at least in part by *things*, as if objects or the possession of objects granted the owner some status and he, being the owner of nothing, had therefore no right to anything, especially her. There was one picture, a photograph of her in some cold place, with pale skin, red cheeks, the colours darker and richer, just Jessica alone, a lichen-covered wall as background, looking out at the camera with an expression suggesting sadness or isolation, he couldn't put a single name to it, fragility perhaps. In this photograph she was beautiful. He wanted her to be looking at him like that, he wanted to be the one behind the camera, the one who could take her in his arms and make it all right, because, if for no other reason, he *would* be able to do that, because he knew those feelings, knew that place. He took the photo off the door, its corners pierced by drawing pins, its back mysteriously empty of attribution, and slipped it between the pages of the novel he'd borrowed from her bookshelf.

★ ★ ★

Eventually, of course, he slept, sleeping through the afternoon and into the night, waking in the small hours, peeing, and then sleeping again until dawn. Monday. At certain logging dumps off in the bush, he thought, men would be turning up for work, refuelling their machines for another day, all trace of his presence washed away by the rain.

The air was sparkling clear. He took Suzy for a walk over to Jim's, the dog running ahead and back, circling wide, using him as a centre to return to, an independent force which had yet adopted him with extraordinary trust, another aspect of Jessica he had borrowed.

Jim was in bed. His filthy clothes, contrary to every agreement and every ounce of common sense, were in a damp pile beside the cold fire.

'I'm sick, man,' he said, 'sick as a dog.'

'You haven't washed your clothes,' Kelvin said.

'I know, man, I'm too fucked to move. I've got the flu, shit running down the back of my throat, fever, headaches, the whole shebang.'

He looked the part. The shack, too, was a mess, made worse by the dead fire. Kelvin went outside and found kindling, split a log, built a fire, swung the kettle over it. Suzy came in, tail between her legs, slinking, and lay down in front of it, ears back, looking at him out of the corner of her eyes, waiting to be told to shift. He picked up the putrid bundle of clothes, boots and all, and dumped them in a pair of concrete tubs outside and left the tap running even if it was tank water, poking them with a stick from time to time, more out of self-preservation than any sense of neighbourliness.

Jim manoeuvred himself off the bed, which for some reason was suspended on ropes from the ceiling.

'Bastard of a thing to be sick in,' he said. 'Starts rocking every time you roll over.'

He staggered outside wearing only a ragged grey T-shirt, his skinny legs and pale arse darkly hairy, his face swollen, peeing only a yard from the door. The very air around him infectious. Kelvin made him tea and a piece of toast.

'Thanks, man, I mean it, thanks, I need this and I couldn't make it out to the wood heap. My head's pounding. When I stand up it's excruciating.'

'Have you taken anything?'

'Like what?'

'Panadol, aspirin, I don't know, what have you got?'

'I'll just ride it out,' he said. 'I'm not into drugs.'

He crawled back into bed.

A sudden thought crossed Kelvin's mind. 'Where's that wrench?'

Jim looked, if possible, more sheepish. 'It's safe.'

'Where?'

'I tell you, I've put it somewhere safe.'

'Where?'

Jim put his hand under the covers.

'Jesus Christ, Jim, you'll get us fucking killed.'

He went over and took the thing, the steel unpleasantly warm from its time between the sheets. 'You fucking love the thing, don't you?'

'I don't, it was just . . .'

Kelvin examined it. A formidable tool. Like someone had simply scaled up one of the little ones but better, all the tolerances exact, the worm screw tight but easy to turn. Needing two hands to lift. He took it back to his chair and laid it across the arms in front of him.

'When I'm finished I'll bury it,' he said.

'It'll rust.'

'Give me a bit of oil, an old towel and a plastic bag and I'll take care of it.'

Jim sitting up in the bed, the cup of tea in both hands. 'It doesn't matter anyway. I'll take it with me, leave no trace.'

'Where you going?'

'Melbourne, stay with my parents for a while.'

'Right.'

The silence summoned up by this statement lying between the two men. An explanation was required, but it wasn't clear if Jim would care to give it, didn't want to submit his reasons to scrutiny.

'I've been thinking,' he said.

'And?'

'I thought I might quit the Farm. Maybe I'll go back to uni, finish my degree.'

'Saturday night really put the wind up you, eh?'

'It's been on my mind,' waving away the suggestion. 'The other night was like, just a catalyst. I'm not doing anything here, I haven't been doing anything for months.' Looking at Kelvin, his nose blocked, his eyes red. 'I don't reckon we did the right thing.'

Kelvin sat with his hand on the wrench in front of him, working the worm screw to make the jaws open and close. The fire could have done with more wood but he'd have needed to move the wrench to get up and fix it. Suzy checked him with one eye and then hunched herself into a tighter ball. Kelvin had no reservations about what they'd done. This in itself, was remarkable. For once he was convinced of the rightness of his actions.

What interested him more was Jim's mooted departure. In the last month he'd spoken three or four times about his feeling for place, going on about how this land was *his* land in almost an Aboriginal sense, how it had spoken to him so strongly when he first came there, like it was where he had been meant to live. Apparently it had just been more bullshit.

'What's your problem?'

Jim was having trouble saying it, either he didn't have the words, or else he was embarrassed.

'You frightened?'

Jim looked away, talking to the wall. 'I'm lying in bed here thinking they're going to come and get me. I'm listening for every noise, I've got a fever and in my dreams there's fucking murder and mayhem.'

For a moment Kelvin felt it too. He stood up and shook himself off, like a dog after a swim.

'You haven't even washed the clay off your clothes,' he said. 'You've got the only piece of evidence linking us with what's happening right now, right this moment off in the bush, and you've got it in the bed with you.'

'I know, man, I know.'

'Listen, once we're rid of this thing there's nothing to connect us with what happened, no witnesses, no fingerprints, no criminal records, we were at the main house all evening, everyone saw us there. The kind of thing that's going to get us busted is if you do something stupid, like run off. Aren't you supposed to be at work this week?'

'I couldn't work,' Jim said.

'Not today, but tomorrow, or the next day. You've got to act normal.'

'If I wasn't so sick I'd have left already.'

Kelvin thought about it. He had liked this man, really liked him, but everything he was saying offended him. Perhaps Jim was best out of the way. If he was that scared, then he was a liability.

Kelvin should have been working himself, but he didn't feel up to Carl just then. Later, maybe. He buried the wrench in Jim's pathetic little vegie garden and ambled down the valley to Andy's, to see if either of the same bugs had struck him. An hour earlier he had been feeling fine. The air was still pristine, with a coolness to it, as if the season was about to change; the colours were still vivid and bright, sharp-edged, but now he was blind to them. He'd caught some of the bastard's unease. What he wanted was to speak to Jessica. He couldn't see himself surviving another week without talking to her.

Andy's tent was on the east side of a small clearing about a hundred metres from the creek. Not so many years before the clearing would have been larger but wattle regrowth had crept in from the edges and now barely more than the damp ground was vacant. Even this had been colonised by lomandra and reeds. The tent was on higher ground, up amongst the trees, more a shack than a tent, having a raised floor and half-walls of timber, as well as a rough stone fireplace, a roof made out of ex-army canvas. The blue panel van was nowhere to be seen, but there was the faintest wisp of smoke coming from the chimney. A small deck had been attached at one end, up a couple of steps. Whoever had built it, and it hadn't been Andy, must have had a small child because a rail had been constructed around it using the sides of a couple of playpens. It reminded him of the little veranda on the end of the train from Alice Springs to Port Augusta, which, in turn, brought up Yvette, who he hadn't thought about for weeks. Yvette, Alice, the journey to Shelley. Another lifetime.

Kelvin called out but there was no reply. He stepped up. The canvas end flaps were pinned open but even then the inside was dark. He called again, stuck his head in, but no one was home. The place, particularly after the mess at Jim's, was surprisingly sparse and clean, almost, he thought, austere, not what he'd imagined at all. There were a couple of old chairs, one with a crocheted blanket over the back, a double bed, a rudimentary kitchen, a guitar leaning against the bench, some embers glowing in the fireplace. Listening carefully for motor noise he went in. On the table was a pile of books: Velikovsky's *Worlds in Collision*, a paperback entitled *Longinus: The Spear of*

Destiny, something on the Knights Templar, and another one called *Leviathan*, the kinds of books, he could hear Slattery's voice say, whose authors seek to save their readers the trouble of highlighting or underlining passages by doing it for them, putting every second or third sentence, sometimes whole paragraphs, into capitals or italics.

The other night, on the way into Eden, while Jim was sleeping, Andy had got into one of his raves, sitting behind the wheel spinning a convoluted story about the true rulers of the world, the secret ones, and the secret societies they had belonged to in previous centuries and their present incarnation as executives of multinational corporations.

'There's evil in the world, man,' he'd said. 'Don't be mistaken. Just remember this: everyone's corruptible when it comes down to it, and these guys, these CEOs, are offered wealth beyond imagination, fabulous wealth, the opportunity to have and to do anything they want with impunity. All they have to do is *its* bidding.'

Kelvin had had no way of knowing how much of what Andy had said was fantasy or otherwise. In the dark cabin of the panel van, setting out to destroy huge machines with sugar bought in the supermarket in Bega – like soldiers of some modern Resistance – the stories had had a certain power, Andy himself had had a certain power, as if rather than possessing secret knowledge the secrets had possessed him and were using him to reel off the lists of names and dates of arcane and obscure events that somehow tied in with known facts of history. Now, faced with this pile of books, Kelvin felt

172

freed from the spell. They were cheap paperbacks whose garish covers showed flaming swastikas, a pyramid with an eye in the middle; they were airport trash. He tried to memorise the titles, he'd ask Carl. Carl would know.

Suzy came bounding up onto the deck, looking for him. Together they headed back up the hill.

When he pulled up at Jessica's phone box in Coalwater the panel van was already there. Andy was in the booth and Kelvin went forward to greet him, tapping on the glass and smiling at this coincidence. Andy pushed open the door, his hand over the mouthpiece.

'What the fuck do you want?' he said.

Kelvin stepped back. 'I was just saying hello.'

'I'm on the phone, man, can't you see?' closing the door.

Kelvin stood where he was, shocked into inaction. Andy held the mouthpiece against his chest and glowered at him from inside the glass, waving him away. He went back to the car and leaned against the door, offended, hurt even, but at the same time struck by the memory of where he'd seen Andy before, before they were introduced at the main house. It had been at the Australasia, that first night in Eden. Andy had been the man talking on the phone in the lobby who had so resented his presence. Try as he might Kelvin couldn't give any significance to this sudden knowledge and yet it felt important. He was no longer sure what he was doing in Coalwater, at midday on a Monday. The chance of Jessica being near the phone was so slim.

When Andy emerged he was once again his affable self, coming over to chat.

'Whatcha up to?' he said, taking out his tobacco.

'Thought I'd give Jess a call, see how she's going. How 'bout you?'

'It's my mum,' Andy said, 'her sister, my auntie, she's real sick, see, cancer. I might have to go up there, Canberra.'

'Sorry to hear that, I didn't mean to interrupt.'

'S'all right.' As if nothing at all had happened, as if he hadn't just told Kelvin to fuck off. 'How're you holding up? You seen Jim-boy?'

'Have you? He's a fucking mess.'

Andy raised his eyes. 'How come?'

The strange thing was that Kelvin, being skilled in mendacity himself, could tell Andy was lying. He might well have an aunt who was dying of cancer but Kelvin knew, as sure as shit, that wasn't the issue this afternoon. He told him what he'd seen at Jim's, but Andy was unconcerned.

'He's no loss,' was all he said, lighting his smoke. 'But you, Kelvin, you've not lost your nerve, have you? You're not calling up your girl to tell her what you've done, are you?'

This, in the midday sun, on the hill overlooking the valley with the Coalwater meandering across its sandy bed. Kelvin just looked at him. Andy was under the impression that he still held him in some sway. He was not aware that there had been a shift in the order, and indeed, now he thought about it, Kelvin was not keen for Andy to know about that, not yet, any alteration in status that might have taken place being too small, too subtle for analysis.

174

'Right,' Andy said, 'that's good,' though Kelvin hadn't spoken. 'The waiting's the problem, see, the waiting's what gets everyone at a time like this.'

Kelvin thought to say, 'And you'd know about that,' but didn't.

Andy was still talking. 'I guess we'll be seeing you tonight then.'

'How come?'

'Where you been? It's Martin's thirtieth. He's an old man now,' laughing. 'He's having a party at the main house, you need to be there.'

'I'll try to make it, I've got to go over and see Carl. About work.' Still explaining himself, though.

'How's that going?' Andy was suddenly solicitous, asking about Carl as if he were an old friend. There was nothing of interest to say, though, or anything there might have been, like the way Carl had reacted when the Telecom man came, he wasn't about to tell Andy.

That was the thing about secrets. They bred. Someone keeps one, someone else keeps another, and suddenly there's no end to the things.

It was Jessica who picked up the phone. Just like that. Her voice so immediate and present while he was in the phone box, watching the panel van make the tight turn onto the bridge at the bottom of the hill below him, feeding coins into the machine so he could tell her he missed her.

She was full of questions: How was Suzy? What was he

175

doing in Coalwater at this time of day? Why wasn't he working? Had he watered the pot plants? Had he told Carl he wasn't working?

'I can't believe you just didn't turn up this morning. You don't think that might be a tiny bit inconvenient? That Carl might have had some plans? You don't think it might be a bit irresponsible?' Going on about it.

'How's Sydney?' he asked, not knowing quite what it was he'd wanted from this phone call, only that it hadn't been this.

She told him. The conference was due to start the next day. She was staying with Claire and her new man, a solicitor, it was great to see them, they'd been out to dinner both nights, and to a film, the Art Gallery. 'They eat out all the time, it's my sister's kind of thing, she always hated cooking, she's the only person I know who could burn a boiled egg. They have this amazing house right under the Bridge . . .' Talking, talking, filling in the electronic space between them with words.

He thought she sounded like the woman in the photographs on the fridge.

She said everything except, 'I miss you too, I think about you every minute.'

She didn't say anything like that. And desperate though he was, Kelvin wasn't going to beg. He watched the money go into the machine until all the change was gone and then said goodbye over the top of the beeps.

The day had started well but it wasn't getting any better. At least he still had the dog.

twenty-one

Andy drove back to the Farm in a cold fury, slewing the panel van out on the corners, lurching over the culverts and the ruts, driving as if there were no possibility of meeting anyone coming the other way. He'd only called McMahon because it was essential that he had at least mentioned the possible existence of a radical environmental cell before any news broke. Just to let him know he was on the case.

And then the bastard picks up the phone and says in his oh-so-precious accent, 'Hello Milo, I was hoping you would call,' as if he was some refined Brit sitting in a high-backed chair smoking a pipe instead of a tight-arsehole ex-cop in a crappy office in Canberra. He wasn't the least bit interested in anything Andy had to say. He listened, but that was all. McMahon had his own bit of news.

Andy had lived in places where a single wrong word, a glance in the wrong direction, could have killed him. And not only for an hour or a day, for weeks on end. The job in Sydney had been like that. It had taken six months to work his way in, sitting in shitty home units in Punchbowl watching daytime

TV, smoking dope and drinking rum and coke with a mob of psychopaths. It could take that long to build up something like the trust needed in order to do the cunts in. Not for the faint-hearted.

It wasn't his fault that particular job went wrong. He'd done his bit. He was the one who had put himself on the line. He was the one living right there with them. No room for sloppiness in his role. All *they'd* had to do was turn up at the right time and they couldn't even manage that. So what happens? There's an enquiry and he gets the blame, he gets sent to a place where no one even asks your name, where they don't give a shit what your story is. A place where you only have to have long hair and smoke dope and play a bit of guitar to be treated like a long-lost brother. The sort of thing he could do standing on his head. The sort of place where nothing is going to happen in a million years. Which is not to say he hadn't been taken in himself for a while, all the talk about New Societies, all those books, the music, the pretty women with their refreshing ideas about sex. As if there really was something extraordinary happening down on the Farm. It took even him a bit of time to figure out it was just a mob of middle-class kids smoking dope.

He pulled over at the top of the hill, took out his little tin and laid a bed of tobacco on a cigarette paper, then sprinkled some powdered heads along the top. That was the thing about dope, most people used it to get out of it, they had a smoke and they were gone. Andy used it to see clearly; when he took a smoke the fog dissolved and what was important was revealed.

Which was what he required right then. He sat behind the wheel looking out over Rosehill, the land all carved up for pines.

Several weeks ago, in a routine call, he'd given McMahon a list of names of everyone and anyone who could possibly be of interest. As you do. Then settled back to see out the summer with the hippies, watching, listening, playing a bit of music. Not with any hope but because it was his job. And this wasn't to say they were all wankers. Some of them were all right. Martin, for example, was okay, as was his wife. His wife was definitely all right. But they had no idea what was going on, Martin was too involved in his own little power games. A couple of times Andy had even hinted at the truth, because he liked the man, he'd as near as told him that there were larger forces at work, powerful energies that were not interested in the fate of individuals or how they might want to live their lives. But he wasn't listening. No one was. They had their own little dream and nothing was going to interfere with it. Well things were about to change. All this talk of love. Martin couldn't even see how much the locals despised them. All Andy had done was arrange for the hippies to do what they'd been talking about themselves, that was the beauty of his plan. If there was a comeback then that was the price you paid for saying things you didn't mean, for living in a dream world.

So he drove into town and called McMahon and told him he thought he was onto something, that he'd heard a rumour about a group of eco-terrorists planning something out in the forests, he didn't know what. But the bastard wasn't interested.

'Now, Milo,' he said. 'This is all very well, but we want you to keep your head down for a while. The thing is we went through that list you gave us and it looks like something might have come up. You might recall you mentioned a Vietnam veteran who lives nearby, an American?'

Andy had to think for a moment before he figured out who McMahon was talking about.

'We ran some checks on him. There was a Tadeuzs who fought in Vietnam. But he's dead, or at least we think he is; missing anyway. Now your American could be him. But he also could be someone else. We sent a man in to visit, take some photos –'

'You sent a man in without talking to me?'

'I know, I know, but then we couldn't really, could we? You weren't in contact, and you weren't calling us very often either . . .'

And right then, when he's just about exploding with this news, that they sent some bastard into his ground without letting him know, against all their own protocols, Kelvin comes tapping on the window of the phone box. He was barely able to contain himself. When he was able to get back to the phone McMahon said they'd sent the photos to the US by wire and now the Americans were interested too. What McMahon said was they were 'wetting themselves'.

'So you see,' he said, 'we might just have a little coupe on our hands. What we want you to do is sit tight. Stay in contact. At least once a day, doesn't matter what time of day or night. For heaven's sake keep low. Don't worry about the hippies right now. We've got bigger fish to fry.'

'But who is he?'

'We don't know. They're not telling us, of course, but we think he might be something to do with the underground from the sixties. The thing is we'd like to sort this out ourselves, we don't want a bunch of Yanks running around, do we?'

The thing is. That's what McMahon always says. The thing is, Andy thought, drawing the smoke into his lungs and holding it there, looking out over the rough-ploughed hills of Rosehill, The thing is he's just been party to the destruction of a million dollars worth of equipment on four different logging sites and he isn't ready for a whole lot of operatives running around the joint. He'd been sitting down in his dark little tent worrying about his prospects and there'd been this fucking American just over the hill the whole time.

And then there was Kelvin.

Andy was talking to McMahon and looking out the window at him leaning on the car and he thought, Can I use him? He put the phone down and went over to talk to him and he was still thinking it. But he kept quiet. Now, as he clamped the roach into the little clip he had hanging around his neck on a leather thong, feeling the smoke work in his brain, he was glad he had because another thought was coming to him. What if the bastard's already involved? What if he knows who Carl is? He's out there staying with him. What if Jessica knows too? Wasn't she involved with Carl before? Now she's involved with Kelvin.

What did he know about Kelvin? What if it was him, Andy, that'd been set up? Best to do what he was told for the moment, best to sit tight.

twenty-two

The difficulty for Carl was that he had nowhere else to go. He had come to this country and made of himself another person, *again*; not as easy as it sounds, not just in a practical sense – the practical details were perhaps the easiest to achieve – but also in a deeply emotional way. In this place he had allowed himself to do something different. He'd bought land, bred cows, built fences, fixed up a dam, a pump, an old house, cleared a bit of forest. All the time keeping an eye on the way out. There was an abandoned fire trail in the north-west corner and he'd made it his business to see it was always passable in the Toyota. And if he had reason to believe they were watching that route then he always had the horse, which had no necessity for trails at all. It was surprising how little a man needed in order to survive when put to it, or when the will was there. Although, equally, he had, on a number of occasions, observed how surprisingly little was required to defeat most people: a couple of days of hardship, of rain and cold without adequate food, and ninety percent of the human race is ready to roll over and die. At least in the west. And while he couldn't be counted in that number, neither, now the time had come, was he prepared to leave. He had made attachments. He had gained possessions and, in the way possessions do, they'd come to own him.

It was also quite possible there was no danger, but that wasn't the way it felt. According to everything he knew he should be gone. Yet he stayed.

He drove to Bega like any normal man and bought three galvanised steel gates, hinges and chains, a couple of blocks of salt-lick and tags for the calves, supplies for the house, coffee, sugar, flour, beer. It was the cattle, as much as anything, that held him. As a boy, learning to ride, to herd, to nut out a steer, to use a rope, they'd been no more than beasts, difficult ugly obstacles resistant to his will. Here, on his own farm, he'd found something out. The cattle were it. When the cattle did well, so did everything else. The whole business revolved around them, not him. That they were the ones going to end up on the table did not in any way alter this central fact: from the moment of conception until the moment of exchange in a sale yard in Bega his role was to anticipate their every need. It wasn't about money, or if it was, then only marginally; money was of the least importance in the process. It was about earth and water and sunlight, about the animals themselves, who were not stupid, were simply engaged in a different process to humans, but one which touched intimately with their lives. It was about being a man who could, given enough land, work it so that it provided for his needs. The most ancient of arrangements. He'd gone around the world running from his family, as much as from anything he'd ever done, and in the end he'd come back to where he came from. It was something he'd hoped Kelvin might come to understand.

The first time he had had to run was in 1967. It had begun with guiding draft dodgers into Canada, through the Glacier-Waterton National Park; hiking the high trails with young farm boys from Iowa.

No, it had begun with Cody.

Cody was working in a coffee shop in the rough part of Missoula, a venue favoured by students. He worked behind the counter, making the coffee, but he was really the star attraction. A former arts student who had dropped out because he claimed that literature was too important a thing to be left in the hands of academics. 'A book,' he said, and this was the way he spoke, 'a book is a sacred thing. You can't be told when to read one, they come to you when you need them. By tearing them apart, what *they* call analysis, you kill the magic in them as surely as you would a man.'

Cody had been organising poetry nights once a week throughout that long winter and Carl, the shy one, with his French novels under his arm, had taken to attending, sitting in the corner by himself. Cody singled him out. He came over to wipe the table and took the book out of Carl's hand, holding it up like it was a scroll from the Upanishads. 'Now this,' he announced. 'This is special.' Saying the name in French so that Carl didn't even know what it was, *La Nausée*. 'Have you read his other work? What's your name? I've seen you sitting here.' All his secret desires fulfilled in one embarrassing moment. 'What are you studying? Engineering! You're kidding, you sure you're in the right faculty?' Cody, the son of East Coast professionals who'd been obliged to move to Montana because his father was something in mining, it was never specified what, something high up. His mother educated at Wellesley; Cody, the sickly child, the bookish boy, grown tall and skinny and handsome, magnetic, managing to make of his difference an attribute.

He took Carl back to his apartment, a freezing loft in a building near the rail yards that had once been some sort of bond store, only half converted to a living space, talking all the way along the street and up the open wooden stairs, always talking. 'Have you read Yeats? You have to read Yeats, and Eliot, of course. People say he's passé but he's not, he's talking about what can't be spoken of and poetry is the only language which is available to us to do that.'

Barbara coming with them, curling up on the bed silently, the standard lamp next to it throwing down its pool of light and giving the impression, from a distance, that she occupied a room by herself.

Barbara.

She, as much as anything, had attracted him to the cafe. The student fashion was for clothes of no particular style, a jumble, a mixture, a distrust of fashion itself. Amongst this Barbara was always immaculate, favouring white boots and short skirts, her straight blonde hair framing a doll-like face.

185

But more individual than her physical appearance had been an aura of self-containment, some aspect of untouchability that drew him to her as directly as the opposite pole of a magnet. Cody's girl.

'I should go,' he said.

Cody following his eyes.

'Because of her? Don't worry about her. You're all right aren't you?' Raising his voice. Even the simplest act of speech was, for him, a performance, 'She likes literary talk. Hey! Isn't Carl a find? Who knows what lurks in the hearts of engineers.' Switching back and forth between them. 'You've found a home here. Barb likes you already. I can tell. You're her type,' pulling down books from his makeshift shelves, only in his early twenties but already having shelves and shelves of them. 'Just don't get any ideas, don't be confused by those long legs, by her being in my bed.' Pinning Carl with his eyes. 'I've seen the way you look at her, but don't be mistaken, whatever else Barb believes in it isn't free love. She won't even come across for me. Look at her, sweet as honey, lying there.'

'Stop it Cody,' she said.

'Stop what, honey?'

'You know . . .'

'I don't baby, I don't. I live with all your talk of love. She reads Christina Rossetti for fuck's sake, but she ties me up in knots, honestly I'm like a teenager around her, begging her for it.'

But Carl could take it no longer.

'Really,' he said. 'I have to go.'

Not that he was Carl in those days. He'd been Robert, the only one of the Cordale family ever to make it to university. Historically speaking the settlement of Montana was a giant nineteenth century con, railroad magnates selling land to poor easterners who came out west full of dreams, only to find the soil was poor, the lots weren't big enough to support even a small family, the winters harder than it was possible to imagine. But the Cordales – and this was the thing – Robert's grandfather, had survived. He and his Lutheran wife had pasted newspapers over the cracks in their timber shack against the temperatures of fifty below, and in the spring they'd ploughed the hard ground, and two generations later they had begun to prosper. Robert, the fruit of the fruit of their loins, a young man out of Bozeman, had been sent to Missoula to learn a useful trade but had taken to reading Sartre instead, had been seduced by Cody and his ideas, by the idea that the world was changing, that the old order was bound to give way to the new, not eventually but right then, within his lifetime, within his very youth. There had been no end to the dreams of his generation.

And if Cody brought culture to Robert, then Robert brought the natural world to Cody. Robert's escape from his family, and from those early signs of difference that had only grown larger in Missoula, had always been to walk in the woods. It happened that there were five separate mountain ranges within an hour of Missoula. He took Cody up into the Bitterroots, onto the Mission Range, up along the Clark Fork.

In those places Cody's imagination was fired. He stood on

187

the top of the ranges, looking out over the endless forests, the snow-capped peaks, the glaciers, the mountain lakes, the great torn scars of winter avalanches, the extraordinary unequivocal beauty, and announced that this was the true heartland of America, it was not in Washington or New York, not in any city or in any jerk-off national anthem, it was there in the wild places. This was what Whitman had been talking about, and Woody Guthrie, Jack Kerouac, Henry David Thoreau. Cody always had a host of names to back him up.

The strangest thing was that Cody had chosen Robert to be his friend. Cody, the most remarkable man in Montana. Robert had never known a friend before. He didn't know other men, had never known them, had always been on the outside. Cody took him as a friend and told him that in friendship there should be no barriers. That friendship meant talking about everything. Cody liked to discuss sex. For him talking about sex was almost as good as sex itself, to describe the wondrous crude detail of it was to revisit the act. That Robert wasn't having any didn't matter, perhaps even made it better for Cody. This, too, was something of their time, something magical which had been hidden from previous generations by the forces of repression. Hitching back from the woods one day the three of them took a ride in a pick-up. Robert rode in the front with the driver while Cody and Barbara sheltered under the tarp in the back. By that time she'd started fucking him, and that afternoon, in the back of the pick-up, she went down on him. When they got back to the loft, after Barbara had left, Cody told Robert about it, not to make him jealous, not to turn him on, simply because he was ecstatic. He'd been sitting on a pile of sacks, he said, the wind blowing his afro hair every which way, with Barbara sucking his cock, and he'd undergone a kind of secular epiphany. He described the mechanics of it to Robert, what it felt like, how she did it, but it was the revolutionary aspect he wanted to communicate.

Cody just had no idea, that was his problem. Every step towards a fatal act, when seen later, is so small that it seems impossible the players did not have the strength, the presence of mind to turn back. But then, because of the smallness of the steps, nothing at the time feels irrevocable.

All across America the sons and daughters of that great nation were rising up to oppose an unjust war and Cody, being at the forefront of everything, had managed to become the representative of an organisation, the nature of which, even the name of, he refused to specify. But it was through its influence that they started ferrying draft dodgers into Canada. Simple, honest, healthy work, doing something that counted.

Except it turned out that running occasional midwestern sons across the border into Canada wasn't enough for Cody or Barbara. They required some larger statement. Cody had taken to calling their little group of three a *cell*. He said that it was in the interest of the members of the cell that they didn't know the names of people in other cells so that if they were captured they wouldn't be able to give them away under torture. He loved secrets so much he could have been an agent himself. He had acquired a roneoed copy of *The Anarchist Cookbook*.

'Even the act of possession of this book is an offence,' he boasted, already fluent in the language of dissent.

The bigger thing, this larger statement, and this was Barbara's idea, involved a national service office in the old part of the city, a timber building not far from Cody's loft. The plan, much altered, much debated through long nights, was to fill the back of a pick-up with a mixture of fertiliser and diesel and park it under the office, which was up on stilts, then blow the whole thing in the small hours of a Sunday night, when no one was about, setting it off with a detonator stolen from a shed on Cody's father's ranch. Thus destroying every record of every draft-eligible young man in the north-west of Montana in one bold act of resistance. They would claim responsibility on behalf of the Dental Floss Tycoons. It would be a blow against the government, but one that involved humour and satire, a witty stab at the military-industrial complex.

In the event, however, things did not go quite so well. The liberated pick-up had a tendency to stall. It fell to Robert to drive the thing, an old monster stolen that afternoon from a mall outside of town. It had been easy to steal because the driver's window was open; indeed, it turned out, refused to close; so that later, close to midnight, the October rain that had set in fell on Robert as he coasted down the laneway behind the office, headlights off, full of the excitement and the terror of the task. On either side were high picket fences, beyond them the backs of old storehouses, their windows dark and lifeless. He stopped by the cyclone gates and Cody got out to cut the chain. The only light came from the next street over.

The rain was cold and hard. Robert pulled the hood of his parka tighter round his face and gripped the lower part of the steering wheel with both hands. He noticed that he was grinding his teeth. When the motor began to falter he gunned it gently. Even then it produced a deep-throated chortle. Cody was taking too long with the bolt cutters. As he rattled the chain past the hollow steel, too loud, the motor died. Cody swung around, the heavy tool dangling in one hand, the chain in the other, his face hidden within his parka but his feelings entirely evident. Robert turned the switch, pumping the pedal. The motor turned and turned, then caught, coughed, backfired like a rifle shot, then settled into its customary lolloping idle. Robert eased forward but could not make it through the gate in one turn. He needed to reverse back to straighten up, revving the motor with each crunching gear change. Without waiting for Cody he pulled in under the building and stopped.

It was dry amongst the concrete pylons and unnaturally quiet. Water dripped from the body of the pick-up. Cody slung the bolt cutters into the back. There was blood on his hand, running freely with the rainwater. It did not strike Robert as unusual. He was, however, unable to move from behind the steering wheel.

'C'mon, man,' Cody said. 'Let's go.'

'I have to check it.'

He managed the door. Climbed out, got in the back and took the cover off the fifty-gallon drum. The little remote-controlled device was sitting there, snug like it was supposed to be, in the reek of ammonia. He extended the aerial as far as it would go. Small actions were possible, but had to be taken slow, like in a dream.

Cody was pulling at him. Together they made it through the gates into the lane.

'What happened to your hand?' he asked, but those words, too, seemed to come from somewhere else.

'I got it caught in the thing when the link gave. Hurts like fuck. At the time I didn't feel it.'

Barbara was a block away in a rental car.

They were twenty miles north when their bomb went off, destroying the whole building. That wouldn't have been so bad, might even have been good, but a young man from the Army Reserve, woken by late-night calls from some central office and sent out to investigate, was standing beside the pick-up at the time.

On Monday morning Kelvin didn't show. Carl made breakfast and sat on the veranda, waiting. He'd left the gates tied on the back of the Toyota because they were heavy and fixing them was a two-man job and right then he had no other use for the vehicle. Hanging them was what he had planned to do that day.

Without Kelvin he was at a loss. Certain the arrangement had been clear, he could make no sense of the boy's absence and it disturbed him more than he was prepared to admit. Perhaps they had got to him. But for what reason, for what possible advantage? He went back inside, poured himself more coffee, then decided he didn't want it. His fragile equanimity was missing. He'd put the bloody gates on himself. He'd use rope where he would have employed Kelvin. What he couldn't do was sit still. The boy would show or he wouldn't, he certainly wasn't going to go looking.

He drove across to the new fence, the dogs racing beside him. The weekend's rain had cleared the air. In the rich colours of the day he could almost forget his problems. The grass along the fence line where he'd pushed aside the scrub was beginning to come through and the long silky green blades were heavy with drops of water, silver in the morning light. He parked beside the strainer Kelvin had dug and hauled one of the gates off the back and into position, lifting one end at a time. He measured everything to see it was right and connected the augur bit to the saw and drilled the holes, but when he went to fit the hinge he realised he'd read the tape wrong and put the top hole exactly twelve inches higher than it was meant to be. He couldn't believe he hadn't seen it at the time. It was only an extra hole in a strainer post in a paddock in the middle of nowhere but he was furious, as if he'd spoilt something valuable, irreplaceable. He stomped around the gateway calling himself names, mouthing obscenities. He drilled the hole again and wound the elbow hinges in with a pair of stilsons, then set about lining up the gate to drop it on. He slung a rope around the other post and tied up that end of the gate so it was level, but found this now interfered with the position of the hinge eyes. He abandoned the rope in favour of a lump of timber dragged in from the bush. By the time the gate was hung, swinging nicely, a job which should have taken half an hour had taken two. He was tired and sore. He went back to the house for coffee and took out a book.

The bombing achieved headline status in New York and Los Angeles. It received coverage in London, Paris and Tokyo.

In Montana there was no other news.

The reservist had been married, with children, of course. At midnight he had stood looking out of the bedroom window at the rain, the telephone in his hand. He would have resisted his duty of care for longer, might not have gone at all, but for his wife's insistence that it was nothing, that he should stay at home. Something about the way she spoke unmanned him. When he saw the cut chain on the gate and the strange vehicle, he called for back-up on the two-way radio, but then decided to look anyway. There were little enough opportunities for heroism in Missoula.

Each day the mainstream papers found a new angle from which to display the anguish of the bereaved family and the wider community. What they had suffered at the hands of these animals, these un-Americans. Certain organs of the underground press managed a different slant. The death of the reservist was regrettable but he was, after all, a volunteer; he had willingly put himself in the firing line of what was clearly a war. What was important was that a decisive statement had been made by courageous individuals, men who were, it was hinted, heroes in the struggle against conscription.

These latter comments cut no ice with Robert. He was no hero. He paced in rooms, walked the city at night, abandoned all pretence of lectures. He even visited the bombed building, which looked curiously undamaged from the front because the brick facade still remained, blackened by the flames. It was not a place pedestrians normally visited. He had no reason to be there. But that was where a man had died. Robert had never even seen a dead man. He had done wrong. He would be punished, if not on earth, then in heaven.

He wanted it right then. The weight of retribution, no, call it by its name, the terror of retribution was on him and he walked in the shadow of death with no rod and staff beside him, it was the rod and the staff he feared, they were what would bring him down. Soon enough the law would search him out. And when it did, despite their carefully planned stories, despite his own best interests, he would be unable to lie. He would tell the truth and then, when he did, it would happen: his father would find out. His anger would be worse than God's. No good to say, 'I'm sorry Dad, it was a mistake, I didn't mean to hurt anyone, I thought it was some kind of game, I thought that because the government was sending young men to die in Vietnam it was all right to destroy their paperwork . . .' Stupid to conceive of explaining that to his father, this simple man who was the son of his father and his father's father, this long line of simple men who might have been many things but were never traitors.

He was ashamed. That was the crux of it. Time and again he looked at the photograph of the man he had killed on the front page of the newspaper. This man in his army uniform, supposed to be one of the enemy, except it was Robert who was the criminal. He wanted them to come and find him. He would have been glad to confess.

It was not to be. Cody had been organising. They, the mysterious ones, had decided to get them out. At a meeting in his loft Cody told Robert and Barbara they were to take the northern route, to Canada, where safe houses would be waiting for them. He would go south. They were simply to leave, to get up and go and never come back to where or what they had been. Robert was stunned by the clarity and harshness of the decision. He didn't question it. Barbara, however, was more than simply furious. She accused Cody of having an affair. This, she said, was his way out. With Cody anything was possible, but he had indicated nothing of the kind to Robert. Barbara showed no restraint. She lashed out at Cody, crying and yelling, beating at him with her fists while he denied all her claims, defending himself with his one good hand.

Kelvin rolled up midafternoon, clattering up the steps onto the veranda with Suzy. He stopped in the doorway, his hand on the jamb, back-lit by the sun on the paddock.

'Where you been?' was all he could manage in response to the boy's greeting.

Kelvin waved the question aside, toeing the doorstep. 'Got a bit sidetracked.'

'Right.'

He came in. 'Sorry,' he said, but with his head down and to the side, mumbling.

Carl couldn't help himself. 'I thought you were working today.'

Kelvin said nothing.

'I thought we had an agreement you were coming here to work.'

'I said I was sorry.' Kelvin looked up for a moment and then back down again.

'Where did you get to?' he asked, as if he had a right to know. He sounded like his father.

Kelvin made this same sideways move with his hand. 'I went into town, to get some smokes, make a call.'

'To Jessica?'

'Yeah,' defiant.

'Already?' And suddenly he was off, lecturing Kelvin on how to handle a woman, as if he knew anything on the topic, as though he was giving advice when in fact he was telling the boy what a useless shit he was because he didn't turn up on time and wasn't there to help with the gate and because Carl had actually *worried* about his safety when he was probably off smoking dope with some of his other retread hippie mates, because this was who had replaced him with Jessica and he needed him to know her value.

'If you don't want me here I can go,' Kelvin said, and just

stood there, entirely defeating Carl with his sullen passivity, his lack of care. According to this, Carl was the one who needed him, there was no reciprocity. 'I just came over to see how things were. Last time I saw you we packed up kind of suddenly.'

'No, I could use a hand. I put one of the gates on this morning. There's two more to do.'

So back into the paddock with the tools, and this time it was easier because he'd done one already and because the boy was there, but the technical stuff was only part of it, the ease of being together was gone, the boy was present, helpful, necessary, but also withdrawn and resentful. Which pissed Carl off even more. If anyone had reason for resentment it was him.

At the end of the day, driving back up to the house, the work done, he invited him in for a meal, trying one more time.

'I have some meat, some beer I bought in Bega.'

'I'd like that,' Kelvin said, 'I was going back to Jess's, water the garden and all, but to tell the truth I'd as happy stay here. There's some sort of bash on at the main house and I'm not that keen.' Just the smallest smile at the corner of his mouth.

Robert and Barbara had not been in a position to argue with Cody. Just one day later they set off north across the border, taking the route they had used with draft dodgers earlier in the year, braving the snow on the high country, camping in the early dark below the peak where the idea had had its conception.

The walking in the cold air, pushing up the sides of hills through occasional banks of snow, relieved something in Robert. His mind, in conjunction with the altitude, sloughed off its despair and terror, opening itself to the simple healing of moss on a fallen log, the hearty conversation of a stream in spate, but also to the awareness of Barbara as a companion. All day he watched her, bounded in her fury and her hurt.

She had a simple broad face, with large eyes, a small nose, and a mouth whose tight cupid's bow ended with a tiny lift, a tremulous upward curl that destroyed its symmetry, whose one-eighth of an inch gave the whole an irresistible character. Out there, without her make-up, it had even more power over Robert. His relationship with Cody had meant a kind of vicarious relationship with Barbara. Sometimes he had felt as though he was already her lover, but it wasn't so. Cody was. Robert was her friend, brother, confidant. Over the months he had found himself wanting to do nothing but watch that mouth, to wait for it to break into a smile solely on his behalf.

As they climbed hardly a word passed between them. With the natural world all around it had not mattered, but at night, in the tiny tent, wrapped separately in their down bags, fed on packet soup warmed on a primus, not ready for sleep, it was unbearable.

'What are you thinking?' he asked.

'I don't want to talk about it,' she said.

Silence again.

'Are you scared?'

A sigh.

'I am,' he said. 'I'm frightened about what will happen to us. About what will happen next.'

'I don't want to talk about it. I want to sleep.'

'You miss him, don't you?'

'No,' she said. 'I don't.'

'Really?'

'Yes, really,' her anger directed at Robert. 'It's not enough that he's fucked off with this bitch. He's screwed up my entire life.'

'Things will get better.'

'They will? How do you know that, Robert? What is it that makes you say that? Is it just part of your down-home nature? I'm on my way to Canada. I'm wanted by the FBI and the CIA, the US Marshals, probably the fucking NSA and the National Guard. I have to change my name. I can't ever call home, never mind go there. I've lost my family – not much fucking loss there – but to top it all off it turns out my man's been fucking someone else. And why am I in this mess, Robert? Because you guys couldn't get it together to break into an empty yard in a downpour, you couldn't even steal a fucking working truck.'

Silence.

'I'm sorry, Barbara.'

Again the darkness, the rustle of the nylon sleeping bag, the cold of the night outside the thin sheath of tent, the vast and empty night.

'It's not your fault, Robert.'

He fumbled with the zip of his bag, undoing it to his waist.

'Let me hold you,' he said, not expecting she would, but without answering she came to him, a cocoon of a person within his arms, resting against him, all hard and tight inside her sleeping bag. And little. She was such a forceful person that she had, in his mind, grown in stature physically. In his arms she was small, fragile. After a time she started to cry. She made no sound but he could feel her shaking with a constant small motion, hardly more than a vibration, like a machine winding down. He was cold but said nothing. A feeling began to grow in him which at first he did not even recognise, having nothing to compare it with. There was simply a warmth inside him and it was lighting up every portion of his body, radiating out into the person beside him. He was aware of every sound in the night, a distant fall of water, the movement of branches in a tree. He imagined the pad of a passing animal on the forest floor.

It was a long time before she stopped. He thought she had fallen asleep but he still did not move. He lay on his back looking up at the opaque lines of the tent, the tiny triangle of lightness which must have been the window. A moon was rising, coming clear of the treetops. Barbara was in his arms, her head on his shoulder, he could feel her breathing.

'You must be getting cold,' she said.

'I'm fine.'

'No you're not. I'm sorry, sometimes I'm so selfish.'

She rolled away and began the complex ritual of undoing her bag, extracting an arm and feeling his exposed chest.

'You're freezing. Come here, let me warm you.'

She unzipped further and dragged the open flap of her bag over him, inviting him within her warmth, her smell. 'You're very sweet, Robert.'

She put a hand to his face and kissed him on the cheek, their bodies, as far as their waists, touching. 'You make me feel safe.'

She pulled his face around and kissed him on the lips.

He was twenty-one years old. He had been kissed before but until that night had been a virgin, able but almost unwilling to imagine what might happen; certainly unable to envisage what transposed in the tent, which never seemed to occur again though they slept together night after night for six months, through the days of their walking into Canada to their lodging on various alternative farms in the backwoods, through the long Canadian winter and into the spring, when she went away. That night it seemed that she opened herself, that, through some deep yearning, possibly not even for him, doors inside her fell apart so that they arrived at a place, together, where nothing else mattered except that they were there, with the wild country all around them singing their meeting. Many times later, making love, having sex, in beds in handmade houses under different names, he would apply all the skills he learned so eagerly to please her. Often he found himself perched above her, looking down at her beautiful face with extreme longing; inside her, yes, but still shut out; pushing into her gently, pushing into her hard, reading the signs and giving pleasure but never gaining entry, watching as she shut herself down to him and the world. That night he had been released from everything, thrown up into a new world, a land-bound creature suddenly become a being of the air.

It was only years later, with Jessica, that he had known again that level of intimacy. And that time he had been the one who had lain beside her without speaking, without declaring his love. She had had to do it for both of them.

It wasn't that there had been no other women in between. Of course there had. But Jessica had come at a time when he had permitted himself to think connection was possible, no longer forbidden. On their last night together she had said she wanted normality, an intimacy that was founded on the day-to-day experience of another person, not their absence, not on the reasons they couldn't be together.

'I'm not interested in Romeo and Juliet,' she had said, 'I know that might sound cold and mundane to you, domestic even. But I want someone to share my bed with, to wake up beside. I want a life with someone. It feels like every time I meet a man I care for there's some impediment to this: a wife, or a job, or a dream, or a past. What is it with you, Carl? What's your excuse?'

He'd opted for the latter. The easy way out, this history of Vietnam, an unhappy childhood, some such shit, while the bed grew cold between them, her body tremulous beside him but already lost because he wouldn't take her in his arms and say, 'This is also my dream.' Staring at the ceiling while she became angry, unwilling to let him go, pushing him. 'What's the matter, Carl? Are you afraid to love? Is that it? When a woman lies next to you and says, "I love you" then you have to

203

run away because it's too fucking real? Is that it? You can only love someone when they're unavailable? I can't do this, Carl. I've done it for too long. I hurt inside. Listen. Are you listening to me? Carl, I love you,' spelling it out. 'But not enough to be used again. I won't take it.' The dawn creeping into morning. The currawongs calling like echoes of each other. The kooka-burras in the big gums near the dam going on and on, and him saying nothing. He had held onto the belief that real love meant not involving her in his life.

Jessica had undermined such certainties. What if she was right and he was free but clinging onto fear as a protection against loving and being loved? Wasn't that the ultimate goal? To love another, to love oneself, to *forgive*, whatever that might mean? Garbage. The leftovers from psychotherapy, from cheap, mass-produced western interpretations of eastern philosophy. To which he was not immune. He lacked the resolve to believe anything. He had yearned for her so, he thought he'd die of it; he'd never known such pain, his own home, look you, this goodly farm, become a prison.

But there had been other arguments.

If he wasn't at that time, then he had been once, a card-carrying citizen of a different world in which there had been an imperative of blood-letting, where blood was held as currency, where pints or litres of the stuff could be measured against such ideas as Justice, or Rights, or the big one, Freedom. For a time he had lived amongst people who talked like that. For a brief time, if honesty was required, he had become convinced that humanity's ritual spilling could be brought to an end by just one more death here, or perhaps another there: surgical strikes, strategic removals of key personnel. It would have been impossible to speak to her of such things. It was hard enough for him to reconcile that the two worlds could exist side by side, that they still did, that somewhere, right at that moment, it was still going on; to admit how wrong he had been in thinking it would ever end. To speak would have been to lose her, never mind that to be silent was to do the same. She was not part of that world, these things had no possible connection with her. They were real but they were also a kind of madness. If she knew of his part in them she would have hated him. Perhaps the hippies weren't so stupid with their dope and LSD and dreams of peace. *He* had joined with people made mad by history and he had been stained by it; no, that was the wrong word, because when he had lain next to Jessica watching the dawn come he had been horribly cold in his body, separate and alone, but also safe, watching her do the feeling for both of them. He had not been stained, he'd been drained of the vital capacity to act in the most important field of human endeavour.

It was surprising he did not simply roll over and die.

A couple of hours after dark the dogs went stupid, only being cowed into submission with a greater aggression than their own, resorting to low growls and half-barks, the little yellow bitch the worst of the lot. From the veranda they could see the lights of a car, moving slowly; and once again there was the anxiety, even though he knew no cop would come like that, not after dark, not alone.

The car, something low-slung by the sound of its belly on the road, came right up to the house. Only when it stopped did he turn on the big torch, pinning it in its beam, a Trans-Am with a wide stripe running from the front to the rear. Gazza stepped out, one arm raised against the light, in the other a polystyrene stubby holder.

'Jesus Carl, is that you?'

He inclined the light, went down the steps. 'Gazza,' he said.

'Fucken hell but you take some finding.'

'That's the idea,' Carl said. As if he needed more trouble. He wondered what it would take to make Gazza simply turn around and leave.

'I had to ask a couple of places. Found Coalwater and the store all right, had to knock the bastards up to get some info, but then I ended up back down the road at some hippie place. I got out of there real quick.'

'What brings you out here, Gaz?'

'In a tick,' he said, intuiting rather than seeing the figure of Kelvin on the veranda. 'Who's this?'

Carl swung the torch around. 'A friend.'

'Here, you want a beer?' Reaching into the car for his smokes and the soft plastic rack of a sixpack.

They went up into the house, there was no help for it. He sat him at the table, accepted one of his beers. Kelvin and he had finished eating and the greasy plates were stacked by the sink. He didn't offer food. He took up his place by the stove.

'What's the story then, Gazza?' he said.

Gazza nodded to Kelvin, who made to rise. 'I'll go out for a smoke.'

'Sit down,' Carl said, and to Gazza. 'He's all right.'

'If you say so.' He didn't look too happy, but then looking happy wasn't Gazza's way. He'd grown his sideburns down along his chin and back up again so they met the opposite downward curve of his moustache. The spaces in between were filled with three days' growth. His hair was cut short on the crown, long at the back. He had tatts on his shoulders and upper arms. It seemed to Carl that people adopted different uniforms for different reasons – businessmen, blue-collar work-ers, housewives, priests, hippies or criminals. It was a choice they made. It was a mystery why Gazza should have chosen this one. As if he deliberately sought attention.

'It's like this,' he said. 'I got in a spot of trouble back in Melbourne, thought I'd better lay low a bit. See if I could raise some of the ready.'

'What sort of trouble?'

Gazza looked at him, took another drink.

'Remember a couple of months ago I was doing a run through these parts? Well, see, on the way back I had a load of cash to deliver and some of it went missing – it wasn't my fault . . .'

'Jesus Christ.'

'Hey! I got screwed. I wasn't going to hurt no one. I know my business. I didn't use it all. I come out of it orright, just not ahead. I owe some people.'

207

'So now you want to hang out for a while. With who knows who the fuck after you.'

'I might,' letting that sit for a minute. 'But then I might not. You got your own problems.'

'I have?'

'You growing a crop out here?'

'No.'

'C'mon, I've come square with you. We go back, remember?'

'Not a plant.'

Gazza took another drink.

'All this space and not a plant? Yer shittin me, aren't you?'

Carl said nothing.

'Well some bloke is,' Gazza said. 'Otherwise I can't see no reason for having a narc over the hill.'

Gazza looked from Carl to Kelvin, then back again.

'There's a narc over in hippiesville,' he said, and waved his hand vaguely in the direction he'd come from. 'I stopped at a house over there to ask directions, some sort of party going on. I knock on the door and a chick opens it, vague as fuck. I asked if she knew where youse was. While she's thinking about it I took a squizz. A whole bunch of people inside. Couldn't believe my fucken eyes. I stepped back out quick smart. Over in the kitchen was our Barry. He's probably not called that now, but that was his name up the Cross. A narc.'

Gazza looked from one of them to the other and back again. It took him a while to realise this was news. At which knowledge he could barely mask his delight. 'You didn't know, didya? Didya?' he laughed. 'There's a few wouldn't mind knowing where he is, I'll tell ya.'

'What's he look like?' Carl said.

He glanced at Kelvin. He was sitting across the table, breaking matches with his fingernails. He'd stopped when he heard the news. He was still holding one little ellipse of wood between his thumb and forefinger, frozen.

'About yea high. Good-looker, never pick him. He's grown his hair for this gig, has it in a ponytail. He plays guitar, sings a bit. Thinks he's the best fucken thing in the world, god's gift to women. He hung around with us for months, setting us up for a bust. We must have sold him thousands of dollars of shit. This was a couple of years ago. The bastard would have done us.'

'You know who he's talking about?' Carl said to Kelvin.

'Could be any number of people,' Kelvin replied.

'But it's not, is it?'

'This guy,' Kelvin said, 'does he have a beard?'

'Scrappy thing.'

'What's he wearing?'

'Didn't get to see.'

'He look like a local?'

'What's a fucken local look like? I was just in the door. He was in the kitchen, talking to a sheila. Looked like he belonged. That's his knack, see. Except one day he let something slip. He likes the dope himself, always smoking, that's what made us believe him. But this thing he said got us thinking. We set him up and he walked straight into it. Trouble was he'd fucken set us up at the same time, fucken cops everywhere, his big bust. Disappeared after that. Otherwise we'd have topped him.'

Carl had that low emptiness in his belly which comes when the pieces start to fall into place, when all the little inklings and assumptions and fantasies run together into one thing.

'Well now you know where he went, don't you?' Carl said.

'Could be anyone,' Kelvin said.

'But you think you know, don't you?' Carl said.

'Could be Andy.'

'So what's that to you, Kelvin?'

'What do you mean?'

'What I mean is, if you think it's Andy, and you do, then how come it matters to you?'

'If it's Andy then it means there's a narc on the farm. That's bad news.'

He was lying.

'Listen, I know where this guy lives,' Kelvin said. 'If it's him. You can get a view of his place from across the creek. I could take you there, to make sure.'

Not only had Carl been living next to a fucking cop for months he'd let one come and live in his house. All this shit about the Cross and prostitution, second-hand bookshops, Shelley. A fucking story. For which he'd fallen. The whole fucking thing. What to do now? Jessica too. Jessica involved with the bastard.

'You got telescopic sights on yer rifle?' Gazza asked.

'I've got binoculars,' Carl said.

'I wasn't thinking of birdwatching.'

'No,' Carl said.

'Fuck you, no,' Gazza said. 'The man's a cop, a pig. I bin waiting for this.'

'Not on my watch. You've only been here ten minutes and already you're killing cops. Give us a break.'

'I ain't just going to leave him there.'

Carl sighed, 'Gazza, would you hold off a moment? We have to figure what he's doing. He's been here for months.'

'Who gives a fuck. We just do him. You got plenty of paddocks round here.'

'You want cops walking in lines across them? Just between you and me there are some people whose attention I want to avoid.'

Carl pushed himself away from the bench. The emptiness had spread into his chest. All day, ever since the boy hadn't showed, he'd been angry. That feeling had now been replaced by something else. The blood flow to his brain seemed to be affected. He could feel each heartbeat individually, as if he was standing amongst waves at the point where they break on a shore, being buffeted by them, the rip pulling at his legs.

'Kelvin,' he said, 'I need some help down at the yards. I forgot to slide the rails through.'

'Sure,' Kelvin said, standing.

He had liked the boy. That was the problem. For years he hadn't allowed anyone close – not simply out of policy, no one had presented themselves – at least no other man. There'd been Jessica of course, but women were both easier and harder to separate from. A woman required something in return for sex which he could never supply, and sooner or later they figured that out and either threw themselves at him or stalked off, both options equally disagreeable but at least in some way final, the situation resolved. Men were different. In the moments when he had permitted himself the luxury of a future not directly related to cattle and fences he had never even considered friendship, as if it was outside the bounds of possibility. Then along came the boy. Sometimes when they'd been working he'd found himself watching him, the way his body moved, the muscles under his skin, the freshness, the aliveness of him, and he'd felt a burst of such intense pleasure, nothing to do with sex, just a kind of admiration, a sense of privilege that Kelvin could have chosen to work with him, to be his friend. Whatever could have possessed him to think that someone Kelvin's age would want to hang out with him?

He took the torch, a long thing like a night stick, and headed outside, telling the dogs to stay. The night was clear and already cooling off, no sign of a moon. He pushed ahead towards the yards and the shed.

'Hang on, Carl,' Kelvin said, behind him.

He kept going. He heard Kelvin increase his pace and he stepped out a bit faster. He rounded the corner of the shed and dropped the torch. When the boy appeared he caught his arm. He pulled him forward, tripping him, using his own motion to propel him, turning him like he might a steer, slamming him into the corrugated iron with a great crash.

He brought the boy's arm up between his shoulderblades,

kicked his feet out to the side. The anger was still there all right. It took less time than you could count.

'Now, you little cunt,' he said, chest heaving, his face in the boy's hair, in the smell of him. 'Start talking.'

He pushed the arm up further and Kelvin gave a short electric yelp, like an injured dog.

'You bastard,' Carl said. 'You fucking fucking bastard.'

The boy was quivering. 'You're hurting me,' he said.

Carl jerked the arm again. Again the yelp.

'Talk,' he said.

'About what?'

'Who do you work for? Who sent you? Why?'

'Nobody. I work for you, Carl.'

'You're lying.'

'I'm not, I swear it.'

'When we were inside I asked you about Andy and you lied.'

'That has nothing to do with you.'

'Everything you do around Andy has to do with me. Are you a cop?'

'No.'

'So help me god you better not be. You heard what Gazza wants to do to him.'

'That's bullshit.'

'Don't count on it,' he said, although he was fairly certain it was. Whatever else Gazza was he didn't take him for a killer. But then in this field you never knew.

He let the boy go. His heart wasn't in it. He stepped back

a pace and picked up the torch. Shone it on Kelvin. The boy half turned, sliding down the corrugated iron, his arm limp. He made to roll over. His nose was bleeding and there was rust on his cheek. With his good hand he pulled his hurt arm around in front of him. He didn't look up.

'Who are you?'

'None of your fucking business,' Carl said.

The blood from Kelvin's nose was running into his mouth and off his chin. The front of his T-shirt was soaking it up in a broad stain. He wiped his forearm across his mouth and in doing so spread a smear of blood and snot down its length.

How easy it is to reduce a man.

'Are you finished? Can I go now?'

'No. Tell me about Andy.'

'Kill the light.'

He shone the torch onto the ground between them.

'I'm waiting.'

'It's a long story.'

'Not another one.'

Kelvin clammed up.

'Go on then.'

Kelvin told him. He told him about Jim's place and the diesel and the fire at Nadgee and their plan and how they had executed it. Carl listened.

When Kelvin was finished he said, 'Whose idea was this?'

'I don't know. Andy's I guess. I came in late.'

'Does Jessica know?'

'Shit, no.'

Carl turned the torch off.

'You are such a stupid fuck. Did you think about her before you did this?' He turned away, slapping the torch into the palm of his hand.

'Don't fucking move,' he said over his shoulder. Kelvin said nothing. Now he was sorry for hitting the little shit. Even if he deserved every bit, and more. It seemed like it was a day for regrets. He looked up at the stars. There were billions of them. As usual. It was cold. He turned back to the boy.

'Anything broken?' he said.

'I don't think so.'

'Well come up the house and we'll get you clean.'

Kelvin made no move to get up.

'Get up,' Carl said.

'Not until you tell what this is about.'

Carl turned away again. He switched on the torch and shone the beam at Arcturus. At least the boy had some guts. He gave it an instant's thought. Such things were niceties.

'I've told you who Andy is to me. Who is he to you?' Kelvin said.

'It doesn't concern you.'

'Like fuck it doesn't. I'm bleeding here.'

'Let's just say there are several reasons an undercover cop might be interested in me.'

'To do with Gazza?'

'No. That's nothing. When I first came to Australia we grew a crop together, him and another bloke. That's how I bought this place. There's another connection. Now get up.'

'No.'

'You want to stay here all night?'

'I want you to explain.'

Carl laughed. 'I don't think you're in a position to tell me what to do. You've just fucked up millions of bucks worth of logging equipment in the company of an undercover cop.'

'You're a bastard, Carl.'

'It's true. Now get up. We'll see if we can sort this out. Gaz and I are probably your best bet.'

'Be fucked,' Kelvin said. But he stood up. Carl offered him his arm but he pushed him away. 'Don't touch me,' he said.

They went up the hill towards the house, slowly. When they were almost within the arc of the veranda light Carl stopped.

'I'll tell you what,' he said. 'If you still want to know after this is finished I'll tell you.'

The blood had clotted around Kelvin's nose. It was smeared across his cheek.

'I thought you'd be proud of me,' Kelvin said.

Jesus fucking wept.

'What the fuck did I ever say to make you think that?'

Carl started walking again. For some reason tears were streaming down his cheeks.

twenty-three

Carl's bathroom was rudimentary, built into a section of closed-in veranda as an afterthought, the old floor still sloping outwards, the walls bare timber, the ceiling unlined so you could see the corrugated iron where it was nailed onto the rough-sawn battens, you could see where the nail points had come through, splitting the wood, now smoky from lamp-black, each one a narrow scaffolding for cobwebs. There was a table and chair, a tin bath and an old ceramic basin with a cold tap. A mirror hung above the basin but age and exposure had caused its silver to buckle and tarnish, and in the yellow light the images it reflected were bilious, like a cinema screen at the moment when the projector fails and the film begins to melt.

Kelvin splashed the water on his face, trying to find a way to clean himself without causing more pain. The contents of the basin were already red. Through the half-closed door he could hear Carl telling his story to Gazza, and told in that accent, as if someone was imitating a cowboy, it sounded both foolish and as if it belonged entirely to somebody else. Kelvin had ceased to notice that Carl was a foreigner, but his inflection confirmed that he came from a country radically different from his own, one with a different history and culture, different rules.

He ran a fresh basin and soaped up a facecloth. Most of the blood was gone but one cheek was rust-grazed and his nose was swollen, the nostrils plugged with dark clots, a bruise forming above the right eye. His hands were shaking and when he touched the cloth to his face it hurt so much that he had to stop and hold the sides of the basin. His mind registered that he was in shock, but this information seemed to offer little help. He was taken with a shameful desire to cry, as if he were a little boy who had been pushed over in the playground, crying not simply because it hurt but also out of the indignity of it, of being forced to recognise that the world was not necessarily a nice place, something Kelvin thought he had known, but had clearly forgotten or ignored, or both. Jessica had insisted that the world was benevolent, that when she went into the forest it was to reassert this awareness. At the time he had had no idea what she meant. Now he would simply tell her that she was wrong.

Maybe it wasn't the world, just people. Certainly he seemed to know very little about them. Without, it appeared, due consideration, he had taken action, and that action was already having its effect. Policemen, angry loggers, their wives, their children, were starting to seek him out. Tame, innocent, midwestern backwoodsmen whom he'd regarded with a sort of homely affection, as if they were slightly stupid or slow, but endearingly so, had proved to be effective employers of violence, players in some much bigger game. Misguided, drug-addled, ill-appointed hippies of no account, fantasists whom he'd thought to turn to his own advantage, had shown themselves to be the ones in control. He'd been making up stories for himself. This was what he saw in the mirror.

Back in the kitchen Gazza was, outrageously, unimaginably, serious. He wanted to kill Andy. Kelvin had never knowingly met anyone who had killed a man, or thought about it as a solution to a problem.

And what was even more disconcerting was that Carl was sympathetic, only opposing the idea because he thought it inefficient. 'I'm as keen as you to be rid of him,' he said. 'But we've got Kelvin with his Save the Forests program. We've got the problem of what Andy was doing on the Farm.'

'Fuck the forests,' Gazza said.

'Maybe we can just stop it,' Kelvin said. 'I mean, I . . . I could ring them up and tell them what we've done, then there'd be no damage. There's still time, they only went back to work today.'

Gazza, with his drooping moustaches, gave him a look of terrible disdain. 'This isn't just about you,' he said.

'It's too late, there'll be some of that fuel in the machines by now,' Carl said. 'Besides, I don't reckon what you did will hurt. Might even make them think.'

'I doubt it,' Gazza said. 'They're going to be mighty pissed.'

'The insurance will cover them,' Kelvin said.

The two men turned to him, incredulous.

'You what?'

'The insurance'll pay. That's why we did it this way. All the machines are insured. We're not hurting *people*, just big money. It's like you said, Carl, this industry is owned –'

'Insurance companies don't pay,' Carl said. His tone was full of derision. 'Not in the long run. They're not in the business of paying. It's the timberworkers who'll be hurt by this. I thought you'd figured that. I thought that's why you did it.'

'What do you mean?'

Gazza glanced from one to the other, trying to parse the meaning of this exchange. Kelvin could see the pattern of Carl's thoughts, all the different ideas coming together in the same way that the spinning icons on a slot machine come to rest, but it wasn't right, nothing to win on this pull, he thought, except he couldn't fail to recognise it was the same lack of pattern he had felt in Eden with Jessica. Why, he wondered, were things that were so obvious to other people so difficult for him?

'It wasn't like that,' he said.

'Now,' Gazza said, 'here's a thing. If you could hand this narc to the loggers, they'd sort him out.'

'Gazza, my man,' Carl said, 'now you are talking. There's what you might call a certain elegance in that.'

twenty-four

The function room they have been assigned for the committee's social evening is long and broad. It's part of the new building but manages to maintain some of the grandeur of the old. High windows look out over the Domain to where the fig trees on the art gallery road cast long shadows. There are perhaps fifty people present, although, Jessica thinks, the numbers have thinned now that the Premier, a smaller, plumper man than she had expected from his photographs, has been in and shaken a few hands, offered them all his smile.

Norton Rawlings, the Independent Member for Eden-Monaro, has her pinioned against a wall near the bar. His hand is spread against the plaster beside her; he rests the bulk of his weight on it, the other arm stuck out behind him so the smoke from the cigarette lodged between his fingers blows the other way. Courteous to a fault, she thinks. But nonetheless predatory. He would, she thinks, be courteous in bed. It is not an irrelevant thought; it is implicit in his pose and the accompanying flattery. They are talking business but the language is sexual.

'You should consider politics,' he says. 'We need more of your sort up here, and not just because you're young and pretty. Politics is about style as much as anything, it's about getting your words out where people can hear them. The media love anything that's different. What they don't want is the humdrum. They'd love you. You're every bit a woman *and* you can speak.'

Norton is a big man, not overweight, just large in every way, well presented. He's loosened his tie and the top button of his shirt and the whiteness of the cotton and the blueness of his tie and the quality of his suit heighten the colour of his eyes. He is pleased at his own success, it has brought him a confidence which is in itself desirable. She doesn't want him but it's fascinating to be desired by him, to have the opportunity to take him if she so chose. He's interesting and he knows it. In another circumstance she might have seen it as demeaning to be wanted in this way, but he doesn't make her feel like a sex object, he makes out that he's interested in her; perhaps, even mildly, he actually is.

'Don't get me wrong,' he says. 'I'm not suggesting you're only about style, I'm just saying you could do well here. Me, I sympathise with your position. The problem is you're way ahead of your time. This country isn't ready for you. Anyone with any intelligence can see these issues have legs. But it's not there yet, it's not on people's minds yet.'

Jessica has never been in receipt of the individual focus of a skilled parliamentarian. Norton is something of a wunderkind, the honest independent, a brandisher of private member's bills, uncoverer of corruption in places both high and low. In the glow of his attention she is, for a moment, alive. She's almost persuaded to consider a career in politics. For too long she's been accustomed to the sloppy thinking on the Farm, where the dominant ideas have emerged from the Californian social laboratories of the seventies, suggesting that the western mind is too much in control, an argument for which she has some sympathy; except on the Farm such a belief has been taken as an excuse to leave the brain at the door.

'If the government moves too fast the people affected get left behind,' Norton says. 'You get a backlash. If we did what you want us to do we'd be up to our necks in logging trucks in Macquarie Street, the government would be out on its ear. You'd have the other mob to deal with, and I'll tell you what, if you think this lot are difficult . . .'

She is tempted by the suggestion that she might fit in. That she could be part of something important. She thinks only rarely of Kelvin. On the first night in town she and Claire and Michael had ducked across the Bridge to Surry Hills for dinner, the car weaving in and out of streams of tail-lights while the buildings reared above them, driving towards a restaurant where they ate bolognaise at long bench tables in a loft along with hordes of strangers, while up the end of the room unlikely middle-aged Italians produced huge vats of spaghetti; everyone talking at once, drinking red wine, everything interesting and exciting and, above all, new, as though out there in the bush she'd forgotten what was happening in the world, this great experiment, Humanity, and all its works.

Amongst the clatter and noise Claire had leaned across the table to her and said, 'So. How's your love life?' and she had waved the question aside, as if to say, it does not exist. This to Claire, her little sister, with whom she shared houses when they were at university, who has witnessed everything, and those events she hasn't actually seen, which have occurred at too great a distance, she has heard about in detail, has commented on. Claire, who has listened patiently while Jessica outlined the advantages and disadvantages of a relationship with not just one married man but two, Jessica being not a serial monogamist but a serial adulterer, although she is never sure whether or not it is adultery when you are the other party, or if it is only the married one who adulterates, the other being just the foreign body disturbing the purity of the marriage. To Claire she denied the existence of Kelvin.

She had had enough of him right then, she thinks, the whole business with his past, with all the conflicting stories. Before Nadgee, before she uncovered the lies, she was diving into some sort of dream romance where connectivity was assumed on the basis of similar backgrounds. But then Kelvin had proved not to be what he appeared. Lovers perhaps never are, but he was even less so. Something had changed for her that last day, on the way to the airport. She doesn't even want to consider what it might be. She doesn't like it that he was raised in Eden. She can admit that. Almost every person on the Farm comes from somewhere else and they each wear their journey to it like a badge, or a pedigree. It is important that they chose to uproot themselves from wherever it was, be it

Hunters Hill or Birmingham or Perth. They have turned their backs on society. They have actively gone out and sought to make another one. They have, in one way or another, put their lives on the line for the idea of a different world. But the local people, well, they have stayed at home, they are country bumpkins, yokels, rednecks, they are the scions of the culture which her generation wants to replace. The difficulty is that Kelvin can't be included in their number. He left too. The problem, clearly, is elsewhere. She had thought he was the son of a bookseller and it had turned out he was the son of a logger, of a logger from Eden, someone who lived in one of those old falling-down wooden houses whose wife, Kelvin's mother, looked like Alice in Coalwater with that tired beaten face. This is what troubles her, this is what she doesn't want to see, that and the thought of his cloying need, which only days before she had shared so profoundly.

The committee meets in another room in the same building, although this time it is windowless, low-ceilinged, the walls panelled with timber veneer. The so-called stakeholders of the southern forests sit around a long table on soft swivelling chairs. Glasses of water, pens and paper are provided. Jessica and a girl from the Conservation Foundation are the only women. They sit down one end, together, sidelined for being both women and conservationists. To belong to this particular club you have to be a man and have an economic interest in the forests. The conservationists are tolerated only because they have become an effective lobby group, not because of, but despite, their opinions.

At lunch Jack Mullen comes over to their table. He's from the Timber Workers' Union. He's heavy-jowled, wheezing, fingers stained with nicotine, thin grey hair on a liver-spotted skull, belly over the belt, cheap tie, a man of embarrassing humanity amongst all this sophistication, alongside the polished Norton Rawlings. But keen, like a knife.

His target is Jessica. He, too, is full of flattery. 'Let me tell you something,' he says. 'I like youse. You've got your head screwed on, which is more'n I can say for most of them around here,' and by the sweep of his arm it is clear he means not only the people in the room but the whole of the parliament. 'You're a breath of fresh air, that's what you are. But you're wrong about these forests. Wanting to lock them up in national parks.'

She raises her eyes to her companion, who meets them and rolls her own. If Mullen catches the glance it only encourages him.

'You think that way you're going to get to keep them. But I tell you this, you'll kill 'em by doing that just as sure as any clearfeller will.' Pausing for effect. 'Land isn't something separate. You need to have a stake in it. Like your Aboriginal. I think I can tell you this, you're a smart one. Your hippies down there, they're just playing games – hear me now – they're children of the upper class, too much education for their own good. All this back-to-the-land rubbish. It's so much cow dung. I've seen 'em. They don't know nothing about it. To know land you gotta work it. You have to get it to give up its bounty by the sweat of your own labour. Put one of your hippies out there in the forest and ask him to survive, I mean *live*, on what he can get from it and he'll have it all cut down as soon as look at it. The rest is just sentimental shit. Pardon my French. You gotta be dependent on land. Making these forests into a national park will turn 'em into a museum. It'll kill them.'

She should have an answer for him but it is not so simple. She begins to see why those engaged in armed struggle resist coming to the table to talk to their opponents (at least until they are in a position of such strength that they can get what they want). It is much harder to hate the other with quite so much zeal when the other is a person sitting across the room. Which is not to say she has developed affection for any of them, or even sympathy for their opinions, it is simply that they exist as people, holding points of view which, regardless of their validity, they believe in and are determined to defend. Their arguments require attention and she finds herself brought up by their acuity, has found herself fumbling for words, for the simple names of things. Besides, the arguments to counter this sort of thing never seem to be available or in the right currency for men like Jack Mullen, especially when he is voicing thoughts she might have had herself. It is only later, *esprit d'escalier*, that the illogic shows up and the words present themselves with the due amount of anger: Yes, but *you* don't *know* this land either, you're not dependent on it. That's the lie at the centre of it all. You survive simply by killing everything on one piece of land and then moving onto the next bit and killing everything on that; until it is all used up.

On the third morning the news about damage to equipment in the forests breaks. All other agendas are suspended to allow the members to express their opinions on this development. One by one the representatives of the Forestry Commission, the union, Norton Rawlings, the spokesman for the Minister for Mines and Recreation, the manager of the chipmill (visiting for the day) express their contempt and outrage. It is, they say, an indication of the need for greater security – clearly select areas of forest need to be off limits to all but contractors. Calls are made to have harvest allocations confirmed immediately for the next decade. 'Uncertainty is the single most damaging force in our business,' the manager of the mill explains. 'It locks us into unsustainable patterns. We need security of timber supply, not just for the next six months, or the next year, but for the next ten years, otherwise there is no incentive for investment.'

Jessica has never felt so small. If the fuckwits who'd done this could hear these guys, she thinks, they'd regret . . . no, they wouldn't . . . the kind of people who do this sort of thing don't listen, don't see, they have their own agendas.

When it's her turn to speak she says that the suggestion this damage was the work of radical conservationists is not, as yet, backed up by the facts, no one has claimed responsibility, and that the time for apportioning blame will be when they know exactly what has happened, not before. To assume the problem has come as an act of sabotage is to pre-empt an enquiry, or even an analysis of fuel supplies. It is possible, she manages to imply, that it could be the owners of the machinery themselves trying to get the insurance. 'This incident could not have come at a worse time for the conservation movement,' she says, marvelling at her capacity to spout words she does not believe. 'We have only just arrived at the negotiating table. One might be forgiven for seeing what has happened as an attempt to sabotage *this* process. We give no support to the action whatsoever, either implicit or real. What it does highlight, however, are the problems of continued exploitation of the forests, which are not owned by the timber industry but by the people of New South Wales, who have a right to determine whether or not they will be cut down, and who do not feel they are being listened to.' But even then, speaking as stridently as this, she thinks there is, in her tone, too great an edge of frailty, too much emotion.

Norton takes her aside, invites her to join him for lunch in the members' room. He makes sure she chooses the best food on the menu, has her delivered a glass of white wine so chilled that condensation runs down the side of the glass. She thinks he is still playing the same game as the other night, but she has misread his intentions.

'Tell me,' he says over the dessert, leaning close. 'D'you have any inkling as to who might be doing this in the bush? There can't be that many who are radical enough to act like that, it takes a certain, how shall I say, dedication . . .'

She sips her wine.

'It's just I had a little bird tell me that there might be an international connection . . .'

'A little bird?'

'Come now, Jessica,' he says. 'We can speak frankly to each other. We're on the same side. But I can't reveal my sources any more than you can.'

'But I don't have any sources.'

'How much I'd like to believe that. My work with certain government agencies has given me a reputation as, how can I say, a safe leak . . .'

Jack Mullen lumbers towards them between the white tables. Jessica wonders how he managed to get in here, but Norton welcomes him.

'Jack,' he says, shaking the older man's hand as if he's glad to see him, the switch so immediate and automatic she can't help but admire it. 'You know Jessica, don't you Jack?'

'We've met,' he says from a throat full of phlegm. 'I was over there with Paddy and I saw youse two having a palaver and I thought I better come and break it up. Protect the interests of my constituency.' He laughs, and Norton joins in, but Jessica only smiles.

'We were only talking about the trouble in the forests, Jack,' Norton says.

'Bad business that.'

'It does nobody good,' Jessica says, for want of another cliché.

'Nor does saying it was my workers done it theyselves,' Jack says.

'That wasn't quite what I said, I just mentioned there were some teams who're finding the terms of trade a bit hard, what with more regulation coming in.'

'It's called deflection, Jack,' Norton says.

Jack moves on. They sip their coffee. Norton leans forward again. 'This was a professional job,' he says. 'Efficient, clever, effective. No one on that farm of yours has been talking about this sort of thing, have they?'

She thinks of the Farm, and the evenings in the main house with Martin and Jim and all the others. Of Andy, of the dope, and it seems, at best, unlikely that anyone from there might have got themselves together into something resembling an efficient organisation. She thinks, too, that Norton already knew something about this when he cornered her at the social evening, that his interest in her has always been only for how it can serve him, for nothing else.

Suddenly she would like to speak to Kelvin. Kelvin is who she wants.

twenty-five

Carl thought of all the things that had been forgotten. There had been little enough time for reflection. Not that in Andy's van in the forest in the dark with what could best be described as unstable cargo in the back was an appropriate moment for it. But there was little else for the mind to do.

Gazza had had no time for his plan. 'Just fucken leave, man. It's not so hard. You've been sprung, it's time to go. This,' and by this he included Kelvin, the farm, the cattle, the dogs, the whole enterprise, demonstrating an unusual grasp of the wider picture, 'all this won't count for shit when you're in jail. Or dead. Me, I'm off.'

When he was young, Carl thought, he had suffered from a kind of failure of imagination. He had believed himself immune to misfortune. Things happened, but to other people. The passage of years had brought, if nothing else, the realisation that he was a person too, just another human like every other one. He, too, was susceptible. He felt for the door handle, locating it in the dark as the car swerved on a tight bend. If there was trouble he could always run. In this sort of forest a hundred yards would be enough, they'd never find you if you could put a hundred yards behind you. How long does it take to run a hundred yards? An athlete can do it in nine seconds, with the threat of death and in these clothes he could probably manage thirteen. Fifteen. Too long. Just possibly with the dark and the trees thirty yards would be far enough. But a hundred would be better. Running straight, head down, not thinking, let the body do the thinking. The body would find its way between the trees for itself. Unless they had dogs of course. But why would they have dogs? Was this the best he could do? Was this the updated version of the never-to-be-forgotten rule, to always have a way out?

Andy had been nothing short of apoplectic when Carl and Kelvin had visited him. He'd come out onto this funny little deck and stood there, keeping the higher ground, looking down at them. Gazza's description had been right, he was sort of handsome, thick dark eyebrows and an angular jaw, a Roman nose. They'd never met before but Carl could see nothing too complex in the man: he could see the curiosity in his face transform itself into incredulity, and then, when he'd worked out that Kelvin had told Carl what they'd done, absolute, pure rage. You couldn't fake that. He could hardly get the words out, just this long string of expletives.

'I figured it out,' Carl said, inserting himself between the two of them.

Andy turning to him, 'You can shut the fuck up, just shut the fuck up.'

233

That was how angry he had been, the words slipping out before he'd even thought them. Once they'd been said, and he realised who he was talking to, he backed off. There was an awkward moment while he took a deep breath. 'No offence, mate.'

'None taken.'

No, the man was transparent, lacking in guile. Even for a cop. Like a sheet of glass. Vicious though.

'Then you won't mind if Kelvin and I have some words, will you, alone?'

'I'd sooner speak with you myself,' Carl said.

You could see him struggling with it.

Carl tried to make it easier for him. 'I was watching Kel here when it came on the radio and I saw the blood drop out of him. I put it to him he had something to do with it and he lied,' holding Andy's eye; it was necessary to keep the pressure on him, they didn't want to give him a chance to think too hard about anything. 'I was in Nam, see, and I learned a few things there. I know when someone's lying.' Offering the challenge. He held up the bottle of Scotch he'd had in his hand the whole time. 'But listen, I'm not after trouble. I've a proposition.'

Andy looking backwards and forwards between them. 'So that'd be the cause of his face then?' he said.

Kelvin with this bruise to his forehead and nose, a scab on his cheek. 'You might say that,' he said.

'So what's it to you?'

'I thought we might come in and talk about that.'

Did Andy know who he was? That was the question that was exercising his mind in the van. If Andy had had any idea who he was, then why was he fucking around with the hippies? Setting up all this stuff in the forest? It didn't make sense. If Andy's superiors knew who he was, if they'd sicked Andy onto him in the first place, wouldn't they have pulled him in a long time ago? There was no need for all this nonsense.

The thoughts going around in his head. Rationalisations. He was tired, that was the real problem. He was not used to this sort of thing, being up most of the previous night, driving down forest trails to drop off the bike, unable to sleep when he got back, and now being up again near midnight. These things never used to bother him, he has gone soft, he's become used to nine o'clock bedtime and rising with the dawn. Which is bullshit, of course, because it has always been like this, always and every time before an event the mind works like a terrier, gnawing at a bone from all sides; that's its job, to find the weak point, the one which would kill him. The trouble is it doesn't know when to stop; one part of the mind has to instruct the other to be quiet before it becomes the weakness itself, and that part has gone missing.

'I spoke to Jess this morning,' Kelvin said, apropos of nothing.

Nobody took him up on this comment. The van barrelled on into the night. The trouble Carl and Kelvin had arranging that: when they had turned up in Jessica's car a couple of hours earlier and announced they'd broken a tie-rod in his, Carl's, truck, Andy had wanted to take Jessica's car. 'It's perfect,' he said. 'She's not here. She's got the perfect alibi.' Kelvin had said he wouldn't be in it, he had to protect his girlfriend. Then Andy said if they were going to argue with everything he said the whole thing was off. All sorts of shit. But eventually he'd given in. But still pissed off, which was why, no doubt, he was driving like a crazy man, throwing the Holden into the corners, braking too late and too sudden, skidding out the other side.

'She's all done in Sydney,' Kelvin said, still talking to himself, his voice cracking with anxiety. 'I've got to meet her at the airport, she says she's had –'

'Kelvin,' Carl said, 'd'you have to?'

But Andy wanted to keep him going, 'She say anything about this stuff?'

'She says it's all over the papers.'

Andy had taken them inside the tent and sat them down at the small table with the canvas brushing the tops of their heads. He'd hung the lantern on a piece of rope dangling from the ridgepole designed for that purpose but it meant that his face was in semi-darkness while theirs were lit up. Something about the whole setup reminding Carl of South America. Andy accepted a glass of the Scotch and listened while Carl spun his tale about the plans the Forestry had for near his property, about farming and land and all the rest. He said he thought he could bring some special skills to the endeavour, '. . . as bone fides of my intention I thought we could –'

'Who's we?'

'Why, Kelvin and I. You, if you wanted to join us; Jim.'

'Jim's out of it.'

'He is?'

'Fucking hopeless,' Andy said. 'Worse than fucking Kelvin here.'

At least, Carl thought, having a particular task in mind for Jim, something was going according to plan.

'Go on then,' Andy said.

'I thought we could do something this weekend, hit them while it's still hot, then lie low. They won't be expecting anything more right now. If we do something a bit different it'll confuse the hell out of them.'

'What sort of thing?'

'It happens I have some skill in munitions . . .'

Andy holding back, staying in the darkness, asking the questions. But after a time he rolled a joint, passed it around, and the subject changed. They started in on World War II and the betrayal of the Russian POWs by the Allies, the way they just handed them back to Stalin after the fall of Berlin, after which the Man of Steel had simply sent them to the gulags. All of them. Meanwhile the Nazis were being shipped out to Argentina. From there it was an easy step to the Americans and their secret services. That was when Carl knew he had him. Andy was self-educated, having his own particular historiographical perspective that had developed out of marijuana and acid and stoned raves; you could see his mind working and it wasn't slow or stupid, just in the wrong gear.

'So where's the stuff come from?' Andy said.

'There's a stack of gelignite out my place. For blowing

stumps. It's a bit old, predates me, you'd have to be careful with it, but I reckon we could manage it.'

In the end Andy couldn't let his little project be taken over by someone else, he had to be there, he had to be the one in charge.

Carl bunched up against the door of the van. Hand on the handle. South America had been on his mind a lot recently. His meeting with Cody there close to the end. Carl had never been any good as a revolutionary. There had been too much of a requirement to see things in black and white. All those months with Evelyn in the flat in Toronto waiting for her husband to pay up had worn him down. They'd wanted to convert the young, beautiful wife of the industrialist to their way of thinking. There had been a complex routine. Always one person in the room with her, always one outside, six people in rolling shifts, three men, three women, in what appeared from the outside to be a student flat. It was supposed to be over in a fortnight but dragged on for six months. Carl had been the one converted. The others hadn't seemed to share his concern for her. To them she always remained the enemy – rich, educated, well spoken, privileged, the wife of a man who was manufacturing, amongst other things, napalm – no matter how vulnerable she was in their little room. It wasn't her beauty that got to him either. After not too long in their hands she had been anything but beautiful. She became just another person, all her vanities revealed as the try-hards of a little girl, the constant picking at herself, playing with her hair, touching her face, biting her nails till they bled; the construct falling away, just another person, suffering, begging them on the basis of their common humanity to let her go.

'You've picked the wrong girl,' she told them. 'You've probably figured that out by now. Alec couldn't give a shit about me, nor me him. You want me to go back out there and *change* him? Some hope. He'll be glad to be rid of me. This is convenient. It's a suitably dramatic way for him to lose a wife. Think of the sympathy it will engender. So much more pleasing than the mess of a divorce. Catholic, you know. If you kill me he'll be the darling of the world. He'll build the biggest bomb you can imagine and drop it on anyone he wants and everyone will love him.'

But to Carl she told the intricate details of a failed society marriage, the union of an older man and a younger woman, knowing, instinctively, Carl's weakness. And he listened, because that was his nature, but remained strong, if that's what it was called. He watched her slow destruction and the others' indifference. If this was the way the world was changed he wanted no part in its new form. Better all humanity disappear.

It was in South America, a year later, that he saw Cody again. Less than two years after they had parted his friend was already much older. Cody had become a soldier, with a soldier's intensity and concerns. Nor did not he seem especially pleased to see Carl. They had spent a single night in an old pueblo, left alone by the locals on the basis of their shared nationality to drink the local wine, to smoke the hand-rolled cigars. Carl had wanted to talk about Missoula but Cody passed it off.

'We were so naive,' he said. 'I was so busy that year I couldn't think, juggling all those different groups. But there *was* a passion, you know, a sense we could win.'

Carl should have left it there.

'Different groups?'

Cody still couldn't resist the opportunity to boast. 'I had a big organisation going there. I left some good friends behind.'

'Who?'

'Oh, it doesn't matter now, I don't know if you even knew them.' He gave some descriptions anyway, no names of course, but ending up with, as a kind of add-on, 'And you, of course.'

It shouldn't have hurt, it was self-indulgent to let it. It was old stuff. Even then. But it had always been one of Cody's attributes, to be able to make Carl feel like a child, a younger brother, too eager for appreciation and affection, getting hurt but always coming back for more.

'How did you go with that girl?' Cody said. 'The blonde one. What was her name? A tight shiny creature. You were desperately in love with her if I remember. I left you two to walk into Canada. I often wondered what became of you.'

He never saw Cody again. In November that year there was the debacle in Santiago. That event, much more bloody and less successful than the one with Evelyn, in theory more painful to be part of, had hardly touched him at all. There had been nothing personal about it. Afterwards they had all been required to disappear in their own ways and Carl took it as a chance to be completely gone. Not that such a thing would ever be simple, he knew too much about too many people to ever be forgotten, no matter how small part he'd ever played. It took him another five years to reach Australia.

Somewhere in the seventies he came across Evelyn di Lorenzo's book about her experiences, *In The Belly of the Fanatic*. There was a quote in big type on the back page: 'It was my love for Alec which sustained me. My love for him and his love for me. I would sit in that bare room and concentrate on him and a kind of peace would flow through me . . . the money was never an issue for Alec, he just wanted me back.'

Everything, it seemed, was a lie.

The car was the problem. The terrier in his mind had found the crack which would allow it into the marrow of his fear. Andy had been too easily persuaded about the van. It wasn't that Andy didn't care. He wanted them to go that night, he had his own agenda. Carl's fingers tightened on the chrome handle.

He could always run.

twenty-six

Stevo's idea was to make a party out of the thing. Get some blokes together, go out there, sink a few beers, then, when the greenies showed up, do 'em over in such a ways as they'd never touch another fucking machine, but not so bad they couldn't tell their friends. That was his idea. He's that sort of bloke. No reason it couldn't have been a bit of fun.

Jim comes up beside him in the pub Thursday night while he's at the bar. A face like a wild man, hair all around it, straight out of fucking Hippiedom.

Here, he thinks, what's this? He's never had much time for the bastard, never said more'n two words to him.

'You got a minute, Stevo?' he says, and you can see he's all worked up about something. Nothing unusual there, he's always nervous this bloke; when he starts to speak you think he's about to stutter or burst into tears or something.

'Sure mate,' he says, 'but it'll cost you,' then he laughs, to show he's joking, but the cunt doesn't notice. He's not even looking at him straight, only in the mirror behind the bar, pretending it isn't happening.

Makes a fellow curious.

'Pretend you're taking a leak,' Jim says. 'I'll meet you out the back, in the car park. Don't tell anyone.'

So he takes the beers over to the table and then goes off to the gents and slips out the back. Jim's waiting for him and they go to his car, which wouldn't you know is a fucking Kombi.

'What's all this about?' he says. 'I don't want to buy any fucking maridgeawana.'

'It's not about dope,' Jim says.

So they get in and the bloke says he knows who done the machines out in the dumps last week.

So he asks who. As you would.

He can't say names, he says. He says he doesn't even know 'em. They're from up Sydney. But he's heard tell they're planning to do some more. They figure no one will expect that. Jim says he'll tell Stevo what he knows, but only if he swears not to tell where he heard it. They'd kill him if they found out. He asks him to swear, and he asks him on what and Jim says on whatever he thinks is sacred. Now there's a fucking laugh. They're sitting in his Kombi in a car park behind the Australasia and this cunt is asking him what he thinks is sacred. Not a fucking lot. You couldn't swear on a can of beer could you? So he swears. But first he asks him how come he's telling *him* and he says these Sydney cunts are greenies who want to make out it's the hippies doing it. The hippies even put them up out their way for a couple of weeks. It's about Coolantippy. They come down here to stir things up. The Forestry's allocated coupes out Coolantippy way and there's been this shit fight about it in the papers and all. The greenies want to make it national park. Bastards would lock everything up if they could. Used to be you could go fishing up the beach north of Tanja. They made that a national park. His family's been going there for generations, his father's fucking father, then these cunts come along and block the road off. There's not a bastard up and down the coast doesn't hate their guts. He asks Jim how come he knows about it? That's none of Stevo's business, he says, and won't be pushed on it. Fair enough, he thinks. The story is they're planning to do in another couple of dozers on the weekend, does Stevo know who to talk to?

Does he know?

He goes to see Bill Polson. His being one of the machines that got fucked last week. They reckon it's sugar and the motor's rooted. Bill not being the sort of bloke you want to get the wrong side of. He's got a family, a house, a mortgage, the whole catastrophe. He's a big bloke, can carry a truck tyre under each arm, he's seen him do it, seen him pick up a forty-four and put it in the back of a ute.

He runs Jim's story past Bill and Bill goes quiet.

'I'll handle this,' he says.

So now they're heading out there in the dark, eight blokes in two Toyotas, and he hopes Jim wasn't bullshitting because otherwise he's in deep shit. He should have made the bastard come with them, then if it went wrong there'd be some come-back. Too fucking late now. Bill's got it organised, no alcohol, just a couple of truckloads of blokes with pick handles, not a fucking laugh amongst them. You wouldn't want to be a greenie, that's for sure. He managed to get Anthill along and Anthill's slipped in a hip flask of his friend Jack Daniels, which is just plain sense isn't it? You can't be out there in the forest at this time of night without a nip or two.

Besides, in the dark no one can hear you drink.

twenty-seven

Felling had not yet commenced in that particular area and the weight of the trees was heavy around the dump. The machines were there, though, two of them, parked in the centre of a clearing of their own design, standing a little apart, dull yellow in the dark, the churned earth caught in between the tracks and in the grooves of the giant tyres.

McMahon walked around them with a torch. The great slabs of cast steel brooded above him, the handrails and footholds for access to the cabin welded on like afterthoughts. He noted their type and manufacture in a pocketbook, and then, taking up a position as near as he could see to equidistant between them, called the men around. He asked Barnes, the senior federal man, to provide light and then proceeded to draw a map in the dirt with a length of eucalyptus.

'Gentlemen,' he said.

He liked to be correct, it was one of his things, and on this occasion it was all the more important because the men referred to came from three different departments, Federal, local and Special Branch, with McMahon being the nominal head of operations. There were understandable tensions. The local man, Sergeant Bragg, was a stout redhead, all freckles and cracked lips, accustomed to keeping the peace in a logging and fishing community. He resented the Federal boys, Barnes, Leuwin and Boyd, and they, kitted out with their boots and automatic weapons and little leather patches on their shoulders, looked down on him. Both groups regarded Masters and himself with customary suspicion. Everyone was keen for something to happen. This was not necessarily a good thing.

'Gentlemen, this is the field of action. Here's the road we came down. Barnes, you and Leuwin will take up a position on either side where it enters the clearing. Sergeant Bragg, if you and Boyd would be so good as to take the opposite end of the clearing, here, on the uphill side. Masters and I will bivouac up here on this slope. We'll maintain radio contact with each other at all times. Use, however, will be confined to emergencies. Until such time as our guests arrive we'll do a half-hour check-in.

'Our man will be travelling with two others. Cordale is the older one. It is essential to keep in mind that Cordale, whatever else he might be, is also an experienced soldier. He is not to be underestimated. He may well be armed. It is our intelligence that he will certainly be carrying explosives which he and the other man will be intending to stow aboard one or both of these machines. Our intention is to allow him to at least begin to deploy them before acting. While Cordale is thus occupied our man will move away from his machine and seek cover in the forest. When he is safe he will blow a whistle. This will be the signal for Barnes to let off a flare.

'It is imperative that we apprehend Cordale and his companion at this time. Should they make a run for it, a warning shot may be fired. If they persist in trying to leave the area you have permission to use whatever force is required to restrain them. Remember, however, that we want, if at all possible, and I will repeat that, if at all possible, to avoid casualties. Position yourselves – this applies primarily to you, Boyd and Bragg – so that if it comes to it there will be no damage through inadvertent crossfire. No accidents please. If by some unforeseen circumstance they do attain cover, Boyd and Masters may give chase. Leuwin and Barnes, you will maintain your positions next to the road and stop any vehicle attempting to depart. Any questions?'

He glanced around the group but without lingering long enough to encourage discussion.

'No? Right then, let's do the thing with the watches. I have 2247. We don't expect any activity until after 2400. Take your positions. Radio check on the hour and half-hour.'

McMahon rubbed out the diagram with the toe of his boot then accompanied Masters to the edge of the clearing. The understorey was thick on the uphill slope. They had to push through it in order to gain the necessary elevation.

'Could be a problem if we want to get down at all smartly,' he said to Masters. 'You better stay close. I'll go up.'

He climbed until he had what was probably the best possible overall view, looking down through the tall trees to the clearing. The moon was still young but it spread a little light, glinting on the machines.

It was up to Andrew Weiss, also known as Milo Cermic, to provide the guests. McMahon was not altogether happy about that. Cermic had long been aware of his antipathy and saw it as evidence of snobbery on McMahon's part, but this was far from the reason. There were plenty of working-class people in the service, some of them good men. McMahon disliked Cermic because he distrusted him. He was a man with no allegiance to anyone but himself; clever, but in some way profoundly ignorant at the same time. There had been much hoo-ha in the media during the previous months about members of the intelligence services nurturing political beliefs at odds with the democratic and multicultural nature of the society they were supposed to serve. And while McMahon was of the opinion that the public, by definition, should have as little knowledge as possible of the workings of any intelligence agency, he had thought of Cermic when he read the inter-office memo. Cermic, he was certain, would screw whoever it suited him to achieve what he wanted; he was not a man whose principles were at odds with the government's, he was a man of no principle whatsoever. It had never been entirely clear what had happened in Kings Cross a couple of years before, but McMahon thought of it as Cermic's fault. He blamed him for the months of wasted time. If he could have arranged to have him dismissed he would have done so, but the enquiry had cleared him of any wrongdoing, and anyway, dismissal is rarely simple from government departments. His postings as an operative amongst various groups of new alternatives was as good a compromise as he could manage. It got him out of the way, which is where he had conveniently stayed. Budget cuts would eliminate him eventually.

But if Cermic really could provide this forgotten American terrorist, *and* some sort of environmental conspiracy, it would benefit them both. Another cock-up, on the other hand, would have the opposite effect, and another cock-up, now that he was settled in the deeps of Coolantippy State Forest, did not seem outside the bounds of possibility. The location was not good, there were too many variables, not enough visibility, radio contact with base impossible. Typical Cermic stuff. He would never have agreed to go along with the arrangement if it hadn't been that the department wanted to sort it out before the Americans arrived.

At 23.26 there was the sound of a motor.

'Alert,' he said quietly, his voice breaking into the silence of the headsets on the five other men.

There was an alarming amount of noise. More than one vehicle was coming down the hill. He watched the headlights follow each other around the curves, flicking in between the trees.

'We have two vehicles, repeat, two vehicles,' he said. 'Await instructions.'

A pair of four-wheel drives entered the clearing. They pulled alongside each other and disgorged a group of men. In the beam of the headlights he could see they were civilians, rugged up against the cold. Carrying lengths of timber.

Several wearing woollen berets. One of them went directly to the dozer and played a torch over and under it. McMahon couldn't see him carrying anything else. The others stayed by the vehicles. The man looking at the machine paid special attention to the padlock on the fuel tank. He climbed up and inspected the cabin. Then he called something back to the group. He jumped back down and went to the snigger. McMahon counted seven men, possibly another in the cab of one of the vehicles. He could see no sign of Cermic, but then it was dark and he had only their torches to go by. Cermic had said there would be only three men and one vehicle. There seemed to be something of a leader who was giving instructions, but he couldn't hear him over the noise of the motors. The man who had inspected the machines returned to the group. The leader pointed his length of wood to various locations around the clearing, apparently directing men to go to them.

'Hold still,' McMahon said into the radio. 'Do not engage. Bragg and Boyd, you may have men approaching, avoid contact, repeat, avoid contact.'

The men had divided into several groups of two. Each man had a torch and some of them were shining them around, into the trees, onto the ground. The leader went back to the unmanned vehicle and climbed behind the wheel. He made a sweeping turn around the machines and headed back towards the road with the other vehicle in tow.

'Barnes, Leuwin. Let the vehicles pass,' McMahon said.

They wound away up the hill. His guess was that the drivers

would be back. His immediate fear was that they would discover his own vehicles. Bragg had insisted that he drive the police four-wheel drive out of Eden. The damn thing was covered in reflective signs, the smallest amount of light would show them up. However, in some excess of care, he had made them drive several hundred metres along the side track. Perhaps it would be far enough. There was enough to think about as it was. It appeared these were not his saboteurs, the best guess was that they were some sort of vigilante group hoping to arrange an ambush. The situation was clearly out of hand.

The men left behind were calling to each other, swinging their lumps of wood about, six of them, which meant at least eight altogether. They were apparently reluctant to head into the scrub. One of them was shining his torch into the ti-tree close to Bragg, calling out.

'Something in the bush here, I heard it move.'

'Be a fucking wallaby.'

'No way I'm going in there in the dark.'

'Reckon I'd rather go in there than argue with Bill,' another man said. Two of the men began a mock fight.

The sound of the vehicles was fading. McMahon had to make a decision. There were too many civilians around. Should he call it off? But if he announced their presence all hell might break loose.

He looked at his watch. 2351.

The fight had distracted the other men; taking advantage of the noise, he spoke into the radio. 'So, gentlemen, we have company. It appears they are not a threat to us but to our expected guests. Just for the moment we'll keep our own counsel.' At least until he could think of something better.

'Permission to speak, sir.'

It was Bragg.

'Yes, Sergeant, go ahead.'

But before he had time to speak McMahon heard another motor.

'Hold it,' he said, his voice cutting across the other man's transmission.

He assumed it was the vigilantes returning. But the men in the clearing had heard it too. The torches went out. There was a great crashing as they pushed into the scrub.

twenty-eight

A ndy drives the panel van with what he likes to think of as a certain finality. As if the need for games is over, which clearly it isn't, yet, Kelvin beside him in the beige work shirt with the epaulettes that's supposed to make him look like Forestry, and this *Carl* over by the door, all in black from neck to toe like he was the fucking pink panther, wearing a belt with more gadgets on it than a Swiss Army knife, including one of them, too, of course, or his own version of it, bigger and better, being American, with a fucking pair of pliers on it.

He needs to relax.

No one's talking, but Andy doesn't mind that, he doesn't want anything interfering with his train of thought. He's thinking how this is the last time he'll do this, that this evening is not just the end of this particular operation, it's also the end of Andrew Weiss, and he won't miss him one bit, he can't believe how long he's put up with him. Tonight a new life begins, one that includes hot and cold running water, flyscreens, television sets, supermarkets, a pub. He'll take a holiday, that's what he'll do, he'll go to fucking Thailand and get a room in a hotel in

Phuket with a view of beaches and palm trees and women, a proper room with a big bed and white sheets and a fan overhead, a bar fridge, he's owed that. He'll stay there for weeks and just unwind, he'll swim and he'll stand in the shower with the hot water running over him until Andy has been completely washed away. He no longer knows who he is, he's been so many different people for so long. He needs to stand under that shower for days. He needs time to find himself. That's what hanging around with the hippies has done for him. He's started thinking like them.

Kelvin begins talking some shit. Jessica and the airport. The American tells him to shut up but Andy asks him another question to keep him going. People let things slip when they're nervous. You can't have too much information.

Say what you like, the American knows his stuff, he knows what's important. If he wasn't his ticket out of there, his gift from the gods, he could almost like the bloke. He's got class. The other night in the tent. Talking for hours. All sorts of stuff. By the end of it Andy had his books out on the table. The American understood what he was on about and that's rare, there's not many who've even heard of Tesla, or Thomas Aquinas, or the problem of evil. Carl getting worked up about it, what he called the modern face of evil, Andy liked that, the modern face, Carl saying that language was the problem, the way that the owners of money had distorted words, making out they were the good guys and that anyone who opposed them was evil, when it was the other way around, and Andy had had to agree with him because it was true, but at the same time he was thinking, it's all very well mate, but you're not it, you're fucked, you're my passage out of here if I can only figure some way to hand you to McMahon. And now he's got that. The man gave it to him himself. On a plate.

Kelvin thinks he's meeting Jessica at the airport. Dream on, cunt.

He pulls out a joint, ready rolled. He wets it between his lips so that the paper doesn't burn too quick, so it burns even, and then, holding the steering wheel with his knees he lights it and takes a couple of tokes before offering it along the line, but nobody wants it. Carl winds down the fucking window.

The first drag hits him hard. He smokes all day, most every day, and it's rare to get a hit like that. Must be the combination of the new heads and the adrenalin. He feels powerfully present in the car, the wheel under his hands, the pedals at his feet, the rough surface of the Forestry road coming up through them. But at the same time it's like he's in a film. The headlights contribute to that, making a movie screen of the road, but there's more to it than that, because right then he sees himself from further back, from the point of view of Milo Cermic, as if he's sitting behind Andy, but he can also see Milo Cermic from somewhere behind him; he's not sure where that is. Which is interesting in itself, but that's not the point. The idea that's grabbed him is that he, Andy, isn't really Andy, and Carl's not who *he* is either, and, now he thinks about it, he's got no fucking idea who Kelvin is, which makes the three of them nothing but figments of their own imaginations, which is something like a definition of the present moment.

People aren't *things* at all, they're just collections of information, nothing exists the way we think it does . . .

In the midst of that thought he gets this terrible shaft of paranoia. What if McMahon's not there? The dope is so strong that he has a hard time holding onto what he knows to be true – that the paranoia is part of the dope – that he spoke to McMahon just that afternoon, that it's all in place. He tries to bring himself back to where he was before, driving the car with the other guys beside him. There was another thought in there. Yes, that's it, he, Andy, took an idea he got from Kelvin's girl and built it into a plan which has now manifest itself as these two being driven into a trap they suggested themselves. There's a symmetry there. It would have been better if they'd been driving their truck, the way he'd planned it, but that can't be helped. He gets lost for a moment in the picture of Jessica arriving at the airport and Kelvin not being there, and the perfection of that, the justice of it. This is the sort of thing Martin is always on about, *You do less and less every day and in the end there is nothing left undone.* Taoism. He never understood what it meant before, but now he sees it, and it's very beautiful.

'Here's the turn,' Carl says.

As if Andy doesn't know where they're going.

'Okay,' Carl says. 'Does everyone know what they're doing?'

And Andy thinks that Carl seems to think he's in charge, and he's thinking he could almost get upset about that, except that in some way it's true, Carl *is* in charge. This is his gig. Andy, or Milo, or whoever the person is who is always, and always has been, watching, right from the very beginning, is

257

only a conduit, he's not doing anything, he's just the agent of Carl's demise, and that's the way it's supposed to be: not doing, letting happen.

twenty-nine

'Here Anthill, you bastard!' Stevo says, and raises his mattock handle like it's a broadsword, swinging it at him.

Anthill's got a torch in his hand and he only just sees Stevo in time to block the blow, dropping the torch and bringing up his lump of wood. So they go at it, whacking each other's sticks, hitting hard, growling and yelling, circling around each other with their feet wide apart and their knees bent; and all the other blokes turn their torches on them and for a moment it's like the circus, like gladiators. He's had a few sips and he's happy, he can feel the spirits working in him. This is what he wanted, a bit of fucking fun, it's not too much to ask is it?

Howard isn't happy though.

'Quit it youse two,' he says. 'That's enough.'

So they put up their sticks and get the torches again and point them at the scrub. He shines his up in the trees, it's a good one, one of them as floats, he bought a new battery this morning and the beam's solid, lighting up the trees, only there's nothing to see except branches, no birds or nothing, there never is. Where do all the birds go at night, that's what he wants to know. All day long they're flying round but come night-time you shine your torch in the trees and you see nothing. Anthill comes up and mimes having a sip, so he mimes not understanding back at him. Then they have one. They're all still standing about. No one wants to go in the scrub. Anthill tips the flask up, you can see he's sculling it, the bastard.

'Here,' he says, and takes it from him, and just then they hear another motor coming down the hill.

He and Anthill dive into the scrub but it's fucking dogwood, all vines and shit. They get in a couple of metres and turn around, crouch down. You can hear the other blokes rustling about, then it goes quiet except for the motor which you can hear real clear. They've got bits of leaf litter and tree in their faces, there's probably fucking bull ants coming for them right now. Then he remembers Bill and Matt never come back to the clearing. This might be them now, else they're still up the road with the vehicles. If they are then they'll have to do without them. He's still got the flask in his hand so he takes a swig and passes it to Anthill, beautiful fucking stuff it is too. The motor's coming into the clearing. It's a car by the looks, a van or something. It drives in and circles around, shining its headlights into the bush. Fucking miracle if they don't see some bastard. It parks so the lights are shining on the dozers. Three blokes get out and go around the back and take out a box. One of them all in black, balaclava and all. This is them. They put the box on the ground. It's something fucking amazing is what it is. Three blokes in a clearing in the middle of the bush. Bill said they had to follow his lead but Bill's not fucking there. They're handing out something to each other. Two of them go the other way, towards the snigger, one of them comes this way, over to the dozer. When do we fucking do it? Stevo's got Anthill by the arm. This bloke by himself, he gets to the dozer. He looks around to see the other two but they're behind the light, you can't see them any more. The bloke walks, casual like, around to their side. He puts down what he's carrying. What the fuck's he doing? He's coming for the scrub. He's coming right at them. He must have seen someone. That's what it is. He must have seen something and now he's doing a bunk. The bastard's started running. Stevo jumps up.

'They're doing a bunk!' he yells.

He pushes his way out of the scrub, his stick raised. The bloke stops in his tracks, looks behind him, then swings back to face Stevo. The bloke can hear someone coming towards him but he can't see him. He puts his arms out, he says something, a name maybe. Stevo gets to him and gives him the fucking mattock handle straight, but the bloke must have sensed him 'cos he puts up his arm and he gets him right on it. You can hear the bone break. The bastard kind of crumples. He makes a noise like the wind's gone out of him, like surprise, fucking surprise is what it is. He can hear Anthill coming up behind him but this cunt's his, he'll have this one. He takes another swing at him before he can get up again, whack, fair on the fucking head, like hitting a melon. Then there's a sound like a gun, and the lights come on, but it's quiet, real quiet and he can see all the branches of the tall trees and they're white and red, red and white against the black sky, not a bird in sight.

thirty

McMahon watched the car circle the dump. It stopped a little way from the two machines, the headlights shining on them. Three men went around the back and unloaded something, the exhaust fumes blowing around and getting caught in the cones of the headlights. It was a disaster. These must be his guests. A complete fuck up. Time to call it off, but how? Best to announce their presence. Fuck Cermic's cover. It was out of control. He spoke into the radio. 'I'm going to call this. Barnes, on my word we'll have that flare. When the lights come on I want you to advance, everyone, weapons ready.'

'Now, sir?'

But Cermic had already separated from the others. He'd reached the dozer. He assumed it was Cermic, hard to tell in the dark. He was alone, that was something. Whoever he was he put a parcel down next to the machine, turned to look behind him, then started towards the hill, the light behind him. McMahon couldn't see the others.

'Now, Barnes,' he said. He paused for the count of one. 'Okay, all units, advance.'

There was a moment in which, by the peripheral glow of the headlights, McMahon could see the man he thought was Cermic running towards them. Then another man stood up out of the scrub and ran towards him. The other man was shouting. McMahon raised the loudhailer to his lips, but as he did so, as he opened his mouth to speak, the second man hit Cermic. Then there was the bang of the flare gun, the three second wait, the pop and the red light. By that time Cermic was down and if he was not mistaken someone had fired a weapon. Did they have guns? There were men all over the place, running. Everyone was shouting, swinging the lumps of wood. There *was* a gunshot. Someone was firing.

'This is the police,' he said into the loudhailer. 'Put down your weapons.'

His voice sounded peculiarly distant, impotent, in this natural environment. The loudhailer was designed to be used amongst buildings. Here, in the woods, the words went out and simply died, absorbed in the leaves.

But it froze the locals. In the purple light they were caught mid-action. Two men were running down the road. Barnes had stepped out of the wood to intercept them. He had his gun to his shoulder. Leuwin, Bragg and Boyd were moving onto the site, their vision of the other men hampered by the machines. The van's motor was still running. Masters was below him standing over what appeared to be two casualties. Beside him was another man, possibly injured.

Less than two minutes had passed since the van had entered the clearing.

thirty-one

The road down was narrow, running into tall forest, past trees with bark made silver by the headlights, ripped out of context. There were still some fine stands in these parts, messmate and stringybark, silver-top ash. There'd only ever been sleeper cutters into this stuff and that was years ago. Pockets of rainforest remained in the gullies, keeping their secrets and their dreams. Carl wouldn't have minded taking the time to actually blow the machines while they were here. The bastards had no business coming into places like this.

Andy took the van for a turn around the perimeter of the site, but all was quiet. If the timber boys were there then they were well hidden. And if they weren't? He'd cross that bridge when he came to it.

'Let's do it then,' Carl said. Andy gave him one of his looks, but said nothing.

No love lost there.

They went round the back. Kelvin following, but slowly, scared half to death. No time to worry about that either. Carl held the end of his little torch in his mouth and opened the crate, folding back the waxed paper. He passed out the sticks of nitro, sweaty and cold, handed them each a roll of tape. Andy's hands were shaking. Carl tilted his head back so the torch shone on his face. Perhaps it was the brightness of the light but his eyes seemed infused with a peculiar excitement, his lips pulled back from his teeth in a kind rictus.

'Set it like I showed you,' Carl said. 'Then I'll come and sort out the detonators,' looking at him one more time. 'But careful. I mean it.'

Andy leaving, walking into the dark towards the dozer with the package and his torch held out in front of him like something fragile. Which it was. Carl glanced at Kelvin standing there like a stuffed chook. He took out his knife and drove it once, hard, into the rear offside tyre. Just in case. He walked over to the snigging machine pinioned in the headlights. Kelvin like a weight, like dead meat, behind him. He indicated to him to put the nitro down. He took him by the arm, ducked under the machine, into its shadow. Then he began to run. Before he'd gone ten paces someone behind him shouted.

That wasn't in the script.

Eyes not yet adjusted to the dark, Carl ran straight off the edge of the platform. Whoever had made the pad had simply pushed the subsoil out in a great mound. Rocks and dirt had piled up against the trunks of the trees. He stumbled down them in a sickening unbalanced gait, crashing into a stand of ti-tree. Kelvin coming down beside him.

Somewhere in amongst the tumble was the sound of a shot, perhaps more than one. Then everything lit up. A flare. Kelvin was lying on the ground, in foetal position, all the wind gone from his belly. He put a finger over his mouth to silence him. He could hear someone talking through a loudhailer.

'It's a trap,' Carl whispered. 'Can you move?'

Kelvin rolled onto his belly. He stood. Carl didn't wait any longer. He took off into the forest, running, crouching low, heedless of noise.

They were on a steep slope, going down, going fast, his feet heavy on the dried bark and leaves, allowing the weight of his body to carry him, allowing his body to make the decisions for itself, not looking, not even trying to see. His mind had let go at last. The pale red light receded and went out. It made no difference. It occurred to him that this was madness, to run like this in the dark in a forest, but he did not stop. He ran with his arms pushed forward, fingers spread wide, his head down, like a blind man might walk in an unknown room, except he was running, brushing past branches and tree trunks, whipped by undergrowth. This was it, then, the way out. Plan B. The act had, strangely, a familiar feel to it. As if he'd done it as a child, or in a dream. Perhaps that was it. In a dream in Montana in a pine forest, moss heavy on the ground. Strange how you can dream something before it happens, as if time, like some people suggest, is not such a straight line after all. He hoped Kelvin was following. If they got separated now that would be the end.

He turned his head to listen. He felt, as he did so, the air on his face change. Cold. Registering it but not noticing it, not responding to it, not acting on it, not soon enough. His

267

momentum carrying him out, past the last tree, out into the air, into the darkness.

Had this emptiness, this weightlessness, this sense of falling been in his dream too? He didn't think so.

All he knew was that it extended for long enough for him to think.

I'm falling.

Which was all the time in the world.

thirty-two

Kelvin ran. One moment he had been crouched on the ground, the air stolen from his body, and the next he was up and running, following Carl through the trees in a purple glow. He could not think what the glow was or why the glow was, he only ran, running down, running into the darkness and the trees, past dogwood and wattle, past stringybark and grey box. The deadness in his body which had made it so difficult to move in the logging dump having found life in him, the deadness had been his terror and the terror which had been on him like a cold hand had found in him this strange new automatic life. He could no longer see Carl, he could only hear him. The light was gone, they were running together in the darkness, stumbling, he was stumbling, he lost his footing and ran faster to catch himself. He was right on top of Carl. He managed to regain some sort of balance but had to stop, had to catch his breath, could no longer run headlong into the darkness with so little knowledge, a mind needs reference points; he held out his hand and his fingers found a tree trunk, smooth-barked, a hand's width in diameter, and he grasped it, pulled himself up on it, swinging up around it, the tree bending with his weight, this smooth hand's-widthed tree wrenching his arm and shoulder, darkness in front of him, suddenly silent. He was hearing Carl's crashing and then he was hearing nothing, nothing at all, nothing for much longer than it should have been possible to hear nothing.

'Carl,' he said, softly.

There was no reply.

He repeated it but still there was nothing. No voices, no disturbance of leaf or bark, nothing, only the rasp of air in and out of his mouth, down his throat and into his lungs, an enormous, heaving, broken noise. He tried to exert control but it was beyond him.

He looked back along the way they had come. He expected to see torches. All was blackness. He turned back around. He saw stars ahead of him instead of trees. He was alone. He had lost Carl. Without Carl, he was lost. He had no idea where the bike was. Without Carl there was no hope. The terror which had driven him to run had nevertheless been diminished by the movement. Now it came back, as if from outside, settling on him. It shook his body. Made him weak. Where was Carl? He felt about him on the ground. He was standing on bare rock. He felt further out. He was close to the edge of some sort of fall. His breathing was starting to subside. He thought he could hear water trickling.

Carl must have gone over.

He looked back again. Still no sign. He wondered if he had heard the fall. There had been a strange sound, distant. But perhaps he imagined that he had heard that. He had no idea how far they had come but it must have been a little way. Perhaps he was not even being pursued. Or not yet. Somewhere in his mind were the words, 'It's the police' and Carl's voice saying, 'It's a trap,' but they were confused, as if they were part of a dream, a glowing purple nightmare.

'Carl,' he said again.

Still no reply.

He wondered if he dare risk a light. They would be looking for that. If someone was looking for him then they would be looking for light. Unless they were using torches themselves. In which case they wouldn't be able to see.

Strapped at his waist were the knife and the little steel torch Carl had made him wear. Andy laughing at their preparations.

'Quite the little terrorists.'

Andy.

It's a trap.

Kelvin had thought Carl was talking about their trap, the one they had set. At the time that was the only way he could make sense of it. He had thought he was running away from the loggers. If he had thought about it he would have wondered why they were not moving according to plan.

He unclipped the torch. Cupping it in his hand he risked a small light, pointed in the opposite direction from which they had come. There was nothing. Empty air. Even downwards there was only darkness, the top of some eucalypts.

He had to move, but without Carl he was unable. He put out the light and then turned it on again immediately, panicked by the complete darkness. He made himself breathe slowly then turned it off again and sat, waiting for his eyes to adjust, until he could see the stars again, see the absence and presence of forest along the cliff edge, see the outline of hills, far distant, indistinct, lit by some source he could not see. Then, reluctantly, he began to make his way along the cliff edge, searching with his hands and feet for a way down.

He moved slowly. To his left was the empty space which had taken Carl. To his right and behind him were police and loggers. Only the possibility that Carl was alive kept him moving.

The cliff edge became a steep curve downwards. Small hardened trees clung to the bare rock. He passed from the trunk of one to another, finding the next before letting go of the last, descending in a series of terrible lurches, never sure there would be another, needing to trust but lacking the will. After a time the vegetation became thicker, the air damp and cold. Once again trees were above him on all sides.

Beside the creek there were moss-covered rocks and rotting branches, slippery underfoot. He could see in a very minimal kind of way. The light from the stars where it penetrated the trees seemed to be gathered by the presence of the water, creating an image of the path described by the creek. He wondered if this was an illusion. Crouching on his knees he drank deeply from a pool, then began a fumbling journey upstream.

He was brought up by the sound of voices. Powerful electric light shone out above him. He curled down into himself, making a little ball, another rock in the creek. Beams of light played in the tops of the trees. The men were only a hundred metres above him. Two of them. They spoke into a radio, he could hear the crackled noise when it replied. He heard their voices but few words, none intelligible.

Then they were gone. He stayed huddled for another ten, maybe fifteen minutes. He had always wondered at the capacity of animals to stay still, now he understood. He determined to risk his light. He shone it along the creek. Nothing happened. No gunfire, no answering light. No sound. He picked his way upstream until he came to a waterfall. At another time it would have been a pretty place, delicate ferns where the small rivulet spread itself over rocks, a larger tree fern leaning precariously over the dark pool. There was a broad-leafed tree on the other side. On a low branch which jutted out above the water four or five leaves were shuddering. The falling water made the air very cold.

He turned back.

Between the base of the cliff and the creek was a steeply sloping fall of mossy boulders. A few large trees grew out of it, bracken fern around their trunks. At the base of one, perhaps the one he had looked down on from above, Carl was lying. He must have run straight off the cliff, in much the same way as Kelvin had at the platform earlier. Except there had been nothing to catch him. He lay with his head below his body, but in an unusual relationship to his shoulders. One leg in completely the wrong position. Even by the light of his torch he could see that the black clothes were bloody. He played the beam over the whole of the body, lingering on the face. Then he vomited. A visceral, unexpected reaction. He crouched over in the bracken fern and brought up whatever was in his stomach. He had always hated to vomit. As soon as the bile rose in his throat he became like he had been as a child, vomiting and crying, the two inseparable, except that this time he did not cry, could not let himself. Whether it was from fear or exhaustion, or the climb down the cliff, he did not know, but his legs, his whole body was utterly weak, loose, hopeless. He collapsed back against a rock, his head in his hands.

It was then Carl spoke.

Just one word. Something unintelligible. Kelvin, startled out of his misery, involuntarily shrank back. He found the torch and played the light over him again. His eyes were open. Had they been open before? They were looking at him.

'Carl,' he said. 'Can you hear me?'

There was no response. He was close enough to touch Carl's body but he couldn't quite make himself. The sensation that had produced the automatic vomiting was still working in his mind as a kind of disgust, a horror of this bloody body in the darkness of the forest. He said his name again. Eventually he approached, leaned over with his ear next to Carl's lips. He was breathing. There was a short, shallow, uneven, moist movement through his mouth.

Kelvin sat back. Everything had become a bit remote, happening right there but at the same time at a remove, not to him, to someone else, and by that he didn't mean to Carl, of course Carl was someone else, Carl was the one who was injured, but the watching, that was happening to someone else too. He was relieved that Carl was alive. He had thought Carl was dead but now he was alive and this released him from something. At the same time it was no better than him being dead. It was worse for him to be like this, upside down, broken across the rocks.

He thought that he should move him, and then that he should not. Wasn't there some rule about waiting for the professionals? Except there would be none, nobody was coming to where they were. Or perhaps they were, but not to help, not doctors and nurses anyway. The implications of what had occurred began to insert itself into his mind in little pieces. Andy had got the better of them. The plan had gone wrong. Now Andy was out there, searching for him. When he found Kelvin, he would kill him. Kelvin had known it was wrong to try to get him killed. It didn't matter that it would have been a demonstration of some sort of natural justice. It had been wrong for purely practical reasons. When he'd lived in the Cross Spic had told him never to pick up a knife in a fight unless you knew how to use it. The other person would take it from you and use it against you.

Carl made another sound, a kind of half-cough. A thin line of blood spilled from the corner of his mouth. Lying in that position, with his head below his body, the blood in his throat or his lungs would drown him. Kelvin knew that much. The least he could do was to turn him around. Perhaps if he turned him around he could leave him for someone to find him. Was that cowardice? Would it help to stay? He was sorely confused. It seemed he could feel the consciousness which searched for him and it was not kind. It was relentless and cruel. He stood up, shining the light down on Carl's body, trying to work out how he could go about it, then sat back down again in the dark. He tried to bring his mind to the problem of where he was, of Carl and the night and the forest, but it kept skittering away. After a time he could hear the water where it fell over the rocks.

'Right,' he said, and came up the slope and tried to get into a position to lift Carl's body. He put his arms under his shoulders, stretching himself across the man's chest, balancing on the rocks. But when he lifted Carl's body his head flopped back. The muscles of the neck seemed to be no longer working. He put his other hand behind Carl's head, as if he was cradling a child, except for the weight of him, the stubble of his short hair. He tried to lift. But could only move him a couple of inches, there was some obstacle. He put him back down and took the torch from his pocket again, shone it around. He had his knee on Carl's arm. He'd thought it was a mossy log. Carl had not seemed to notice. This fact alone was in danger of pulling Kelvin back out of wherever it was he had gone. He changed position and made another attempt. He draped Carl's arm over his shoulder and slid his own arm under the man's back, holding his head again with the other hand. He was right up against him then, against the maleness of him, the smell of him, the sheer size of him. He held him against his chest with an awful intimacy. He managed to raise him, but the process was clumsy, awkward. As he lifted him Carl began talking, saying words that barely registered in Kelvin's mind, names, he was saying someone's name, not Kelvin's. Then he stopped speaking again, his breath coming in strange rasping bursts. Some awful burbling in the chest. None of his body seemed to be connected to itself anymore.

He had, Carl thought, been wrong about a number of things. Not just Andy.

There was Cody, for example. During that five days he and Barbara had spent walking across the high country into Canada, there had been moments when he had thought that life would never be more perfect. That was the thing about the meeting with Cody. Carl should not have been hurt when he said that stuff, because what Cody had or had not felt towards him was of no consequence. Cody was the one who had made it happen. Something had been given to Carl in the mountains that he had never considered applied to him, had never even looked for: the possibility of happiness; not just the possibility, the actuality of happiness had been delivered wholesale, complete in all its mystery. The rules changed. Not just for those days but for always. As if the rarity of the atmosphere was also a rarity of spirit which allowed for new interpretations of law, both man-made and natural, as if, had they taken the notion, he and Barbara could have stepped off their mountain trail into thin air and kept walking, across glaciers, over fields of wildflowers, past evergreen trees and rivers, separated from the hard-edged rock, outside of time.

That had been the important thing, not the other stuff.

Such a difficult lesson to learn, that one; that sometimes you have to be happy with people for what they are to you, not what you are to them.

Kelvin propped Carl against a rock. He searched for something with which to wipe the stream of blood that had run from the corner of Carl's mouth but found nothing. He settled on Carl's T-shirt, pulling it up from his belly to reach his chin, exposing the white skin of his stomach, the dark curling hair, an awful purple contusion. He wiped the blood carefully, talking into the silence, Kelvin doing the talking now, telling Carl what he was doing, keeping up this strange, stupid running commentary for which there was no audience, none at all.

thirty-three

McMahon pushed down through the scrub into the clearing, the loudhailer in one hand, service revolver in the other, ignoring Masters and what some part of his mind was registering as casualties, going straight to the tight little knot that Bragg, Leuwin and Boyd had rounded up within the van's headlights. The civilians had their hands on their heads. Various lumps of wood and metal were scattered around.

'Detective Senior Constable Boyd,' he said, 'search these men, then collect those weapons. When you're done do me the favour of turning off the motor.'

'Permission to speak, sir,' Masters said from behind.

'A moment,' he said, holding up his hand. The flare was dwindling.

'Boyd,' he said.

'Sir.'

'Leave the headlights on. Yes, Masters.'

'As near as I can tell, sir, I have one man dead and another injured, possibly critical.'

McMahon drew breath, engaged in a kind of operational

triage, attempting to find, within his rage, the most efficient next move.

'Leuwin, Bragg, keep those men under guard. Cover Boyd. Barnes will join you in a moment. If any of them so much as speaks, shoot him. Show me, Masters.'

As they walked over, his assistant kept one pace behind him.

'I'm afraid I'm responsible for one, sir,' he said.

'So that was you?'

'Yes, sir.'

'I don't recall giving the order to shoot.'

'No, sir.'

He looked down at the bodies. One was Cermic. He was dead, or if not exactly, would be soon. The skull on one side had collapsed under the force of a blow, probably from a mattock handle. Perhaps it was just the torchlight but McMahon felt the instinctive disgust which head injuries always inspire, a too graphic display of our animal nature. He turned his attention to the other man, who was lying curled around his stomach. A pool of blood was forming behind him on the dirt, dark and shining and viscous against the slick slabs of stirred-up clay. He was blond, tousle-haired. What he could see of his face was deathly white. McMahon had never seen him before. In his hurry to hold his belly the man had apparently been unable to release the mattock handle which now, curiously, was sticking up in the air, swaying like a demented metronome. At least it showed the man was still alive.

'This is Cermic, sir,' Masters said. 'I don't know the other man. He is the one I shot. It appears I have wounded him in the abdomen, sir.'

Boyd turned off the motor. A deep silence descended over the clearing. McMahon looked up at the trees overhanging the place. He turned back to Masters.

'Quite correct. I think we can safely diagnosis Mr Cermic as deceased. See what you can do for the other chap. We'll do our best to get medical help. I'll arrange for someone to assist.'

He went back to the group of men.

'Numbers, Barnes,' he said.

'Seven, sir.'

'Seven?'

'Sir.'

For the first time he addressed the group of men who had come in the four-wheel drives.

'Which of you is the leader?'

A heavy-set individual released his arm from above his head, a narrow wristwatch band cutting into the flesh. He was wearing dark pants and a blue anorak, unzipped; a man with a protruding belly, in his thirties. It would be a mistake to think any of this was fat.

'Name.'

'Bill,' he said. 'Who are you?'

'I'll ask the questions. Surname?'

'I said, who are you?' Bill said.

'Boyd,' McMahon said.

'Sir.'

'Would you do me the service of using one of those lumps of wood to break Bill's left leg.'

'Sir.'

Boyd bent down to pick up one of the handles and came over.

'Permission to speak,' Bragg said.

'Not granted. Go ahead, Boyd.'

'Polson,' the man called Bill said.

'That's better,' McMahon said. 'You can hold off for a moment, Boyd. How many in your party, Mr Polson?'

'Eight.'

McMahon looked around the clearing. 'Reports please, gentlemen.'

All his men were present. No one else was injured.

'We appear to have something of a problem. According to my calculations there should be eleven men, including our two unfortunates over there. I can only see nine. What did you say your name was?' He pointed at Polson, who repeated his name. 'Are all your men accounted for?'

This seemed to be a novel question. Polson counted his companions.

'All except Stevo,' he said.

'And these men here. Are these the ones you came with?'

The man seemed to have trouble with this question.

'What I mean is, are these the men who accompanied you tonight?'

'Yes.'

'I thought as much. Well thanks to your efforts I have one

dead man, another injured and it seems we have lost two of our guests, including, possibly, a terrorist wanted by every agency in the western world. I hope you are well pleased. Barnes, go and see if you can assist Masters. Boyd, you and Leuwin can do a recce around the clearing. Sergeant Bragg, you had something to say?'

'I know some of these men, they're locals.'

'Thank you, Sergeant. So,' coming back to Polson, 'explain. Who are you and what are you doing here?'

'We're timber workers, out of Eden. I had a dozer and a snigging machine rooted by these cunts. Over behind me is Howard Tench. He owns the dozer. Owen Rogers here owns the snigger.'

'Sergeant?'

'That's right.'

'So. Where are your vehicles?'

'About half a mile back up the road, on a side track.'

'No doubt obstructing our own.'

He paused briefly, considering the options. He would have liked to know how they knew to come here but pushed it aside, it could wait.

'Mr Polson, I assume that at this point you and your men will do everything you can to assist us in our operation?'

'Whatever you reckon.'

He looked at the man, waited the ten seconds required for him to raise his head and meet his eyes.

'You don't sound convincing,' he said.

'We'll help,' Polson said.

'You may lower your arms. Sergeant, take Mr Polson and one other man with you in the truck, I want our vehicles down here as soon as possible. Get Polson to drive.'

'Sir.' It was Bragg.

'Yes.'

'The van has a flat tyre, sir.'

'It does?'

'Yes sir, deliberately damaged.'

He looked at the sergeant with his extra kilos. 'Then you'll have to go on foot,' he said.

The logistics were only getting harder. They would need to get someone up on the ridge to achieve radio contact. He needed helicopter support immediately and right then he didn't even have a fucking jeep. They would have to start a manhunt in the morning, although his fugitives, if they had any sense, would already be miles away. He needed a roadblock set up. If this cretinous logger had not killed Cermic he'd probably have done it himself.

thirty-four

The forest moved around him. A wind came up along the creek and gently stirred the tops of the trees, moved on. Something with large wings flapped; he could hear the movement of its pinions against the dispersed invisible molecules of air, those same molecules which went, also, in and out of him, but not of Carl, because Carl was dead in this dark place.

Kelvin crouched on damp rocks next to the body, arms wrapped around his knees, hearing the night. After the flying thing had gone, the sound of the creek came in again, a small incessant noise, the splay of water falling on black rock. He wished that they would come for him, come and get him, because what he knew of this place he did not like and he wanted to be relieved of it.

It was the cold which stirred him. The adrenalin which had sustained him thus far was being diluted and he began, by parts, to be returned to his senses. In the rush of events it seemed that a deeper part of his psyche had taken over, deciding with primal ruthlessness which parts of his body it required to keep functioning, and discarding the rest. It had been dark and he had been moving so it had dispensed with sight, taste and smell, giving all his attention to sound and touch. Now that he was at rest the other bits returned, clamouring for attention, and with them an acute bodily awareness. He was cold and there was a smell of shit. Had he shat himself? He had heard that people do when terrified. But a quick check showed it wasn't him, which meant it must be Carl.

Abruptly he stood and went to the creek, suddenly keen to wash his hands. He crouched over the water, the end of the little torch in his mouth the way he had seen Carl do, so as to point its light at his hands, tasting the metal on his tongue. His hands were covered in blood, sticky with it. He rubbed them in the water and clouds of the stuff puffed away, but it wasn't just his hands, his arms where they had been under Carl's body were caked in it, cold, hard, congealing in the fibres of his shirt. Carl must have had injuries on his back. Then the realisation penetrated. There would be blood, too, on the torch, where he had been holding it. Carl's blood was in his mouth. That taste of metal. He spat, he gagged and spat. If there had been more food in his stomach he would have brought it up. He took a couple of paces upstream and rinsed his mouth again and then again. Then went back to cleaning his hands. The blood had gathered itself in the cracks and pores, beneath the fingernails, the water was icy and he was shivering and the blood would not be removed. Carl was dead and it was his fault. With the dissipation of the adrenalin his mind, too, was beginning to work. He had wanted Carl dead. When Carl had proved himself to be alive Kelvin had wanted him dead so he wouldn't have to stay with him and now he was dead and the weight of his absence and his own part in that loss was too much for his mind to bear. He started to wander away, down the creek, without direction, he simply did not want to be cold anymore, did not want to be there anymore; moving for the sake of movement in the same way as before he had sat, simply to be sitting. A hundred metres further down a tree had fallen across the gully, blocking the way. If he wanted to continue he would have to climb out. He sat. A cigarette would have been good, or some food, a cup of coffee, but he had none of these, not even the cigarette which was strange because he had had some, and matches, and he could not remember leaving them anywhere. By then he was shaking uncontrollably, teeth chattering. The torch, too, was fading. He had been using it too much. He banged it on his palm. It brightened and then immediately went dull again. Carl had another torch. More than anything, more even than Carl's body, he was frightened of the darkness. He began to make his way back up the creek.

Carl had food too; as they were leaving he had put a plastic bag of nuts and raisins in one of the pockets of his trousers, 'You never know when you might be hungry,' he'd said.

'Fucking Americans,' Andy had said when he saw Carl's equipment. Andy had got the better of them. Death, that thing which happened in films and books, was no longer abstract.

Carl was where he had left him. A crumpled body in bloody shitty black army pants. Had he expected him to have moved? In the pockets he found the food, the complex folding knife, a map, a compass, the torch, some string, matches, some tobacco, his own, he must have given it to Carl, the keys, his watch which was still, quietly, improperly, ticking away to itself. Three am. He lit a smoke and pulled on it heavily, drawing the tobacco into his lungs, drinking the calm that came with the first hit of the drug. He unfolded the map and tried to locate his position. They had stowed the bike in scrub a couple of ridges across to the west. If he climbed back up the cliff and crossed the creek he might be able to find his way over the next ridge and then across the next valley after that. If he was in the right place and going in the right direction.

A helicopter came over the hill.

It came from behind him, beating the air, the great search-light attached to its underbelly shining down in white radiant shafts, lighting up the tops of the trees, its motor filling every atom of the night with noise, a machine of extraordinary power, invincible. Kelvin curled in against the base of the tree.

When it was passed he looked at the map again but found it meant even less. He tried to think but the machine had made his hands shake, it had addled his brain. They had not forgotten him. They wanted him. He remembered the compass and took it out, laid it on the map and spent several moments turning it, or turning the map, until eventually he had them both aligned in roughly the same direction.

Carl had drawn the new road's path along the ridge in red biro. Kelvin was delivered, momentarily, of a clear picture of the map on Carl's wooden table, the milky plastic stem of the old biro, Carl's attempt to teach him about maps. They would be watching the roads, that's what the helicopter said. The bike was out. That's what the helicopter said. Kelvin had no idea where he was. Jessica had said to go downstream when you're lost. When they were in the bush together and he asked her what happened if you got lost she said you find a creek and follow it down. Eventually you'll come out somewhere.

He located a creek on the map, somewhere near the logging dump. But there were lots of them, lots of little blue threads on the green map running at right angles to the red contour lines where they wriggled tightly together. At least, he thought, the creeks go in the same direction, all running to one river, shown on the map as wide and sandy, even he could see that. And what was this river called? Cooral Creek, flowing in slow, wide meanders towards the Coalwater, miles away.

In the distance he could still hear the helicopter, hovering.

He stuffed Carl's belongings into his pockets as best he could. He went to Carl's feet, took the heavy boots in his hands and set about dragging the body down through the bracken to the creek.

'I'm sorry,' he said.

The slope was steep. Once he had him moving it wasn't so hard. He tried not to think about the effect it was having on his body. There were some flat rocks next to the stream and he laid him out on them, putting his arms on his chest like they do in coffins, the skin already cold, the head, when he straightened it, both impossibly large and at the same time smaller than it was when it had belonged to Carl.

He stood beside the body searching for some appropriate words, but could think of nothing.

At the fallen tree he climbed up and out, keeping towards the right, leaving the creek bed, taking the contour towards the ridge, warmed by the exertion, but stumbling and awkward. When he thought he had found the back of the ridge he began to follow it down. All his movements were contained within the small circle of light provided by Carl's torch, tree trunks passing on both sides, walls of scrub looming up, logs and rocks to be clambered over, branches of fallen trees negotiated. The larger direction was invisible, given only as down. His path defined by the relative inclination of the ground. When it became too steep he assumed he had turned too far to the left or right and sought to retrace his steps, managing to maintain his course by a kind of exhausting intuition. Jessica would have been proud of him.

Jessica would be asleep in Sydney. He looked at Carl's watch. He was supposed to meet her at the airport in seven and a half hours. He doubted that would be possible. Jim would have to go. At least he had thought to arrange that. But his failure stung him further. Now he would never see her again. That thought was too difficult to deal with. It needed to be filed somewhere else, along with Carl being dead, somewhere behind him.

After a time he heard birds, tiny chinks of sound around him. Then the kookaburras began calling in the day. He stopped and looked outside the small fading area illuminated by the beam of the torch. There was a greyness in the east. He turned off the torch, it would be easier without it.

He found he was tracing a course down the spine of some great mountain. Out of the fading night ridges began to appear on both sides, paralleling his route. To his left, perhaps in the gully he started from, there was now the rush of falling water. Somewhere below he could begin to sense the valley floor, but his legs were like jelly, refusing simple commands. The slope had become so sharp that he had to hang onto trees to stop himself from hurtling down.

The gathering light had come just when it was needed because the further down he went the thicker the scrub became. The rough-barked eucalypts gave way to spreading trees with smooth white and grey trunks, their branches draped with long tresses of bark, the dry mustard-smelling dogwood thick beneath them. The slope levelled out some- what and then presented, remarkably, an area of grass, heavy with dew. A mob of wallabies occupied its lower half. They looked up, ears turning like radar dishes, then leapt away. At the lower edge of the clearing the undergrowth was particu- larly thick. He had to crawl under vine-covered bushes to get through. On the other side, down a short and vertical drop, was the riverbed.

He stepped out onto the wide corridor of sand, shaken and empty. The night was gone, he was off the mountain, out of the bush, the way now clear. Looking up to the hills in the distance he could see the sun begin to touch their tops. He found the stream, not a big run of water, most of it under the sand, but a definite flow, meandering from one side of the sandy bed to the other, gathering itself in long shallow pools where it encountered the smooth granite boulders.

He sat in the very centre of the expanse of sand, as far from the forest on either side as could be achieved, and searched out the packet of nuts and raisins. He ate a few, then was unable to stop pushing them into his mouth until they were gone. Afterwards he lay face down on a boulder and scooped the water up into his mouth. There were old cow pats on the riverbed but he didn't care. He washed his face and his hands, scrubbing the grooves in his skin until every last skerrick of blood was gone. He could do nothing about the clothes. He went back to his seat and smoked a cigarette, studied the map.

It was all guesswork, but it seemed to him that he was probably only six or seven of the map's squares from the boundary to Carl's property, which was to say six or seven kilometres as the crow flies, but the creek meandered, so it was probably closer to twelve kilometres. He could do that in three or four hours, another half up to the house. Then he could get the Toyota and drive over to the Farm, get Jessica's car from the main house, even drive the Toyota all the way to Eden, Carl didn't need it anymore. It was only six in the morning, which meant the airport at Merimbula was still possible by lunchtime. He was taken by this idea, this strange assumption that the night, which had lasted years, should have simply deposited him back into the world. That, by getting to Merimbula on time, he might make it all right again.

He started walking, hopeful; filled, in fact, with exhilaration. The sun was sweeping down the sides of the hills and everywhere it touched was radiant with its light. He was alive. He was not the one who was dead. The boy who had survived his family in Eden, who had survived living in a squat in Sydney, Daz, Brisbane, Cairns, Darwin, was still going. He'd been out all night in the forest and he was still alive and within cooee of home, or rescue, or something. He paced out, stepping large on the soft riverbed. He would make the meeting with his lover, he would explain all, he would ask for forgiveness; he would do, he had no idea what he would do, but it would be all right, he would escape.

Except the sand was difficult under his feet, large-grained, dry, granting no purchase for his feet. When he had begun walking after his breakfast there had been a distinct corner perhaps a kilometre away, marked by tall white gums standing out of the darker forest behind. He had walked towards it for what seemed hours without it getting any closer. When he eventually reached this landmark he was faced only with another stretch looking exactly the same. He could measure the passing of time but there seemed to be no way to judge the passage of distance.

Then the helicopter came again.

He was standing in the middle of the creek when he heard it. He had been walking like that all the way. As if he had wanted to be found. The noise of the rotors echoed off the mountains, shock waves of air preceding them. He ran for the bank, diving into the forest and crawling under the scrub.

Looking back he could see his footprints in the sand, like a long signpost, pointing directly at him.

Eventually the machine arrived, after more time than seemed proper. It came whopping down the valley within the ambit of the mountains but still quite high, following the course of the river. Then careered off to the east.

He went back out into the open with the compass and opened the map again, desperate for a reference point. He was on a long straight section of riverbed. Steep forested hills rose on both sides, obscuring the view to the north or south, but to the east, captured in the V of the river's course, there was one broad hill with shoulders like the arms of massive chair, a blue haze cradled in the shadows between them. If indeed he had started back up in the hills where Carl's biro marks indicated, then it was possible by a process of elimination to guess where he was.

The problem with the map, if he was correct in his reading, was that it showed him as being on the other side of a mountain from the Farm. If he was to take an abrupt right turn and start climbing he would come out on the top of the mountain on whose opposite slopes he and Jessica had walked the day they made love in the grove. He had been walking towards Cooral Dooral because it was a destination he didn't have to think too much about. There was a vehicle there, and the dogs needing to be let off their chains. He would have been able to get to Merimbula by twelve going that way, except hours had passed and it was after nine, the sun was out and helicopters were scanning the hills. It was all bullshit, he'd gone nowhere.

The problem with the map was that it suggested it would be better for him to go back into the forest, and he did not want to do that. The trees frightened him. He had wanted to locate himself and now he had and he liked it even less. Be careful what you wish for, Carl had been in the habit of saying. Carl had been in the habit of saying a lot of things and Kelvin had been in the habit of not listening to them, of regarding them as no more than words used to fill the empty spaces between people. Kelvin had not been in the habit of listening to anyone, of letting anyone get through to him. The only people he had ever known who had wanted to get close to him had always turned out to want something. Except for here, in these backwoods, where he had encountered two people who had seemed to require very little from him. It was he who had wanted something from them. So what had he done? He had taken what they offered and betrayed them; because, well, because that was all he seemed to know how to do. It had happened with his mother, and with Yvette, and then in Melbourne with Shelley, and then again here. It would have been nice to think it was someone else's fault, Andy's perhaps. Except Andy hadn't been in Melbourne, or Darwin. Kelvin was the common factor.

He had had no idea how to find Shelley in a city of several million but had never doubted for a moment that he would. As if the sheer momentum of the journey from Darwin, down through the Alice to Port Augusta, then by road, hitching to Adelaide, across to Melbourne, had granted him special powers. Nor had he given much thought to what might happen when he did find her, the idea had been simply to get there. Except Melbourne was other than he had anticipated. Despite being summer it was cold and wet and excessively green, stately and solid after the frailty of tropical Darwin and the brittle sparse vegetation of the Centre. He went looking for her in the St Kilda clubs, as if it was inevitable that she would still be on the game, but without considering what that might mean. One of the girls said it was possible she had heard of her, who was he?

'She's my sister,' he said.

He found her living in a small flat behind a row of tenements. He had to go through a kind of tunnel, an archway into the back of the building, to get there. It had probably once been the stables of some grander establishment which had long since disappeared. There were stone buildings around a cobbled courtyard. Several painted doors giving onto it, one open, from which came the sound of a television. He knocked and someone within the dim interior moved and said, 'Yes,' and, 'Is that you Jimmy?'

He said, 'It's Kelvin, I'm looking for Shelley.'

And the voice said, 'Kelvin?'

And the certainty which had carried him all those miles suddenly broke. He hadn't seen her yet, she had only said six words, but already he could tell what was going on by the slowness in her voice and the smell of damp and of unwashed nappies and stale cigarette smoke laid over the top of some older, even more profound reek.

His inclination had been to turn around there and then.

But what was left of the momentum forced him on. It wasn't as dark inside as he had expected. The flat had been made by dividing up a larger room with fibro partitions. There was a plastic-topped table bearing a litter of mugs and breakfast plates, open cereal packets and a small carton of milk, an overful ashtray. There was an old couch against one wall and a television badly tuned to a commercial station showing daytime programming; a tiny kitchen, a half-closed door to another room. Shelley was sitting at the table, smoking, her back to the screen. A child asleep on the couch.

It was Shelley but she had changed. She was both heavier and thinner at the same time, as if she had lost weight and then put it back on but in all the wrong places, fluid retained in legs and wrists, in her neck and face. Her skin was pale and soft, her hair lank, the same grey colour as the rings under her eyes. It took several awkward moments to pull herself back from wherever she had been.

'Kelvin,' she said. 'Come in, come in. Well, look at the place. Look at me. What you must think. Where have you come from like that, all of a sudden? I heard someone was looking for me, I didn't think it'd be you.'

She stood, she fussed, cleared dishes to the sink, put the kettle on, tied up her hair, but in a drawn-out way, not slow motion but not at quite the right speed either. She was wearing track pants and furry slippers, a sweatshirt with a faded picture of Mickey Mouse on the front. She came over and put her arm around him, laid her head on his shoulder.

'You've become such a man,' she said.

He did not want her body against his.

He sat at the table while she wiped it with a cloth that left a wet swirl of drops behind it. She lit a cigarette, leaned against the sink.

'It's so good to see you,' she said. 'You've no idea.'

'You too,' he said.

She spoke, she told him things, but they were just words. She was still somewhere else, she was acting, making up things to say that she thought were the proper things for old friends to say to each other.

'Where have you been?' she said. 'Darwin? Really? I keep meaning to get up there. I was going last winter, I could have gone, but there were Sophie to think of. I couldn't leave her. Can't wait for her to wake up. She knows all about you, Kelvin. I told her about our times together in the Cross, catching the train to Brissie.'

As if she had conjured him up from her past for the sake of her daughter. He wanted to escape before the child woke. He didn't want to be an honorary uncle.

She became sentimental. She touched his hand when it was on the table and then his leg when he withdrew his hand. There was in her touch a closeness, a cloying lover's need that made him withdraw, pulling into himself, like a mollusc in a tidal pool. He was not her lover, never had been. The drug in her was confusing even this relationship. He said that he had some people to see, that he had to go.

She tried to tie him down to another visit. Later that night, or the next day. 'We could do lunch,' she said, as if she were living in Toorak and not some squalid boarding house with a habit and a child.

He said, 'I'll give you a call. No, you don't have the phone. Listen, I'll come around tomorrow, in the morning.'

He stood to go, but then couldn't quite leave. She was watching him and when he met her eyes he could see that she, too, knew that he was acting.

'It was nice of you to come, Kelvin,' she said.

The only other time he'd been quite as alone as he was next to Cooral Creek was during those days in Sydney, before he met Shelley, when he was a kid, fossicking in bins for old food. After that everything he'd ever done had been, in some way, done within the cradle of Shelley's love – as if, even in Darwin, even out in a trawler in the Arafura Sea, he'd had a special force around him. It had been there for so long he'd forgotten it existed. Shelley had been family and he had simply abandoned her when it didn't suit him. Just walked away, packed his bags and stuck out his thumb on the Princes Highway. The wrong road as it happened.

According to the map the hill rose steeply for almost a thousand metres. If he reached the top he could then continue east and eventually he would come down into Gubra Creek. Almost any ridge would take him there.

'Climbing mountains seems a pretty pointless activity to most people,' Jessica said. 'A lot of sweat for little reward. But if you stand on the top of one you find that a couple of paces in either direction will take you to a completely different world. There's a kind of power in that. You stand in a place like that and you feel it's possible to make decisions. Although,' she laughed, 'it's probably just the oxygen deprivation, all that heavy breathing to get you there.'

On the map it didn't look particularly far, or even difficult; steep up for a time, then a long slow down.

He took a drink from the river and started climbing. By now it was probable that men would be out combing the forests for him. A dangerous man on the loose. The men would have guns; for all he knew, they might have dogs. He couldn't believe he had left tracks in the riverbed, he should have walked in the water in order to lose his trail. He laughed at that idea – like the ideas of a child in a game of hide-and-seek. They didn't need dogs to find him. Andy would have told them who he was. It would have been better with Carl beside him. Carl would have known what to do, how to survive. The only thing Kelvin knew how to do was run.

Once he had climbed a hundred metres the forest was clearer, the country similar to that he had seen with Jessica. If he hadn't known better he would have said he'd been there before. It all looked the same on these ridges, endless grey-barked trees, silent, with no opportunity to see out, just miles of trees. The only thing which distinguished the one he was on from any other was its steepness. At times it seemed impossible that trees could grow at such an angle. The sun was well up and it was hot. A little cloud of March flies had found him. Whenever he stopped to take a breath, which was every few paces, they landed, settling on his clothes, producing a thin whine as they searched for blood. His or Carl's.

The hill defeated him. His legs simply would not do the job. His lungs could not provide enough air. He had had no way of carrying water and his mouth was parched. He sat, listlessly swatting the flies. When he got his breath back he dug around for Carl's watch. Ten fifty-seven. Every minute of the day a calculation, a reworking of where he had been, where he was going, when he would get there. It was a way of covering for the fear of where he was and the fear of what would happen next.

He looked about him. There was nothing but trees. Avenues of grey-barked trunks spreading out in every direction, labyrinthine. The air was still, thick with the scent of eucalyptus. That strange sense of distance he'd had beside Carl was completely gone. He was utterly present, trapped within the mountain, imprisoned by the trees. Men who wanted to kill him could be at that moment hiding amongst them, they could be there, watching. The terror of it stole his senses. He wanted to breathe. He wanted to be away from there. He hated the encroaching forest, this endless indifferent wilderness. He wanted the trees gone. Jessica talking about the crimes against nature committed by the first settlers. 'They took it all,' she said. 'They didn't leave even a single bit, that's what I can't forgive.' But Kelvin understood. The forest enveloped him, he was trapped within it, hopeless within its vastness. It was not benevolent, not some earth mother who would suckle its favoured child, holding him against her breast. It was foreign and gigantic, utterly indifferent; if there was any benevolence then it was only that the forest made no judgement at all, would not help him to live, would not help him to die. It would not even fight back if it was threatened with its own destruction.

On the slopes of the mountain Kelvin was subject to larger time frames than Carl's watch. He recognised that he was invisible, and always had been. This was what he had never seen before, which had begun to penetrate his consciousness the night he looked in Carl's mirror, Carl who was dead, don't forget that, don't for a moment forget that, Kelvin. He had been living in a fantasy world in which he, Kelvin, had occupied the central role; but there was, in actuality, another one, a real one, separate from him, one which had existed before he was born and would go on after he died. When he was dead this mountain would still exist. This was not a point of debate. Nor was it a thought he welcomed, alone in the forest, unknown, unaccounted for. He had lived, but he had made no impression, none at all.

He started climbing again.

When he reached the top he could hardly stand. There was no sign that he had attained the summit, just more forest, but he knew it must be the top because there was nowhere further up to go. He sat with his back to the trunk of an old and blasted tree and closed his eyes, just for a moment. Even the March flies, feeding on his hands and ankles and face, could not wake him.

thirty-five

It's Jim who is there to meet her, standing outside the little shed which serves as an airport in Merimbula, and she can see immediately, even when he's still in amongst the jostling bunch of tourists in their aloha shirts and panama hats, that he's got something going.

'Where's Kelvin?' she says.

'He couldn't make it.'

'How come?'

He does this little shuffle, as if to kiss or hug her, but then, when she's in his arms, whispers something in her ear. Except he speaks so quickly and quietly that she misses it and has to ask him say it again.

'I'll tell you in the car,' he says and she is instantly, unreasonably, furious. It's probably just disappointment at Kelvin's absence and all that might mean, but Jim's secrecy, his clumsiness, suddenly seem to represent everything she hates about the Farm. They stand on the tarmac waiting for the tractor with the baggage cart. She has only been on the ground five minutes and already she's being dragged into some pathetic intrigue.

As soon as they're in the Kombi he starts.

'There's big things happening out our way,' he says. 'Have you heard the news?'

'No.'

She has been at Claire's all morning, their last morning together, sitting in the sun in the front garden with its view across the Harbour to Circular Quay and the Opera House and, even if it was a rented house and about to be demolished for flats, and the noise from the trains meant they had to pause every now and then in order to hear each other, it was still extraordinary to be drinking coffee and eating croissants with the great steel curve of the Bridge over the top of them. To be there with her sister at the end of a week in Sydney during which she had met important people, discussed important things. No matter that little had come out of it.

'We should be able to get it on the local station,' Jim says, fiddling with the dial.

'Just tell me.'

'It'll be on in a moment,' he says, 'it's just coming up to the hour – I want to hear it too – someone's gone missing out in the forest. There's helicopters, search and rescue, police. It's something to do with the trouble in the forests, the cops are everywhere, I've never seen so many of them – I had to go through a roadblock out near the Farm, they're searching every car.' Jim has always been a talker but there's an added nervousness to this speech. 'I was terrified they'd find some seeds or an old can of dope I'd forgotten about, but they weren't interested in that, they were looking for whoever's missing. Not much chance of finding anyone in that country.'

The topic of conversation at Claire's was, of course, Kelvin. During the week she had come clean about his existence. It would have been hard to deny with the phone calls. Claire wanted to know what she was going to do about him when she got back and Jessica said she didn't know, she was confused.

'Yes, but do you like him?'

'I don't know.'

'Hey, I'm not asking you if you want to marry him.'

'You'd have to meet him to understand,' she said, 'I miss him. He's like, beautiful, but unknown, as if he's never really been *put on*,' using this odd Shakespearean phrase, surprised to hear it coming from her own lips. She thought she should explain what she meant but she saw that Claire, in the way of sisters, had somehow understood completely and was able, in an instant, to turn it around into some comment on her.

'You like a man who knows who he is, don't you?'

A vast square ship, tesselated with containers, was emerging from under the Bridge. It let out a wonderful long blast on its horn. Claire's statement might have been quite innocent but Jessica didn't choose to take it that way, 'Whereas you?' she said.

'I just like a *man*,' Claire said, dissolving the tension with her wonderful coarse laugh. 'Don't look at me for advice. You know me, as soon as I open my legs my brain falls out. I'm just lucky with Michael, we're stupid about the same things. But listen. You like him, he likes you. What's the problem?' Just a momentary pause. 'Or is that it? He actually likes you?'

Sisters.

Jim pulls the van out onto the highway and works his way up through its gears.

Her annoyance has blinded her to the content of what Jim is saying.

'Kelvin's involved in this, isn't he?' she says.

'I don't know. He just told me that if he didn't turn up by ten o'clock I was to go and get you, so I did.'

She looks at him.

'Really, I don't know any more than that.' He meets her eyes for a moment and then his mouth forms itself into a little smile that is stupid and nervous and supercilious all at once.

'I hate things like roadblocks,' he says. 'Not that I get to go through them very often, you know, but customs, things like that, I feel guilty as soon as they look at me. It doesn't matter that I've done nothing wrong . . .'

The radio announcer is doing his lead-up to the hour and Jim turns up the volume.

'. . . I was shitting myself, I still am, see, my hands are all sweaty, listen here it comes now.'

'Police have confirmed two men are dead and a third is critically injured in the southern forests of New South Wales. The fatalities occurred in the early hours of the morning when officers of the Federal Police and Special Branch attempted to apprehend a group of men allegedly engaged in sabotage of logging equipment.

'The injured man has been flown to Nowra Base Hospital

where he is in a critical condition. Police fear for the safety of a fourth man, now the subject of a search-and-rescue effort in the region.

'Several incidents of contaminated fuel at logging sites have been reported in the last week and while no group has yet claimed responsibility it is thought the incidents are connected. Allegations have been made to the effect that the perpetrators belong to a group of international terrorists. At this stage police have refused to comment, although it is apparent that one of the men involved is American.

'Police and emergency service crews are searching the surrounding areas for the missing man. They hope he will be able to assist them with their enquiries. They have not yet released the names of any of those involved.'

She leans forward and turns it off.

'They didn't say that before,' Jim says. 'They just said someone was missing. There were helicopters —' and he's off again, prattling, and immediately her anger resurfaces.

'Just shut up for a minute, would you.'

Jim breaks off midsentence. She stares out of the windscreen, the cabin of the van abruptly, rudely, silent.

'Now listen, Jim,' she says, 'I need you to tell me everything you know about this.'

'I don't know anything,' he says. 'Honest, Kelvin just came to me last night, we were at the main house and he came to me and he said if he couldn't make —'

'And you just said, sure, Kelvin, I'll do that for you. You didn't ask any questions?'

'Of course I did, but he said he was going to Carl's and if something came up could I do it and I said yes.'

'Where's my car?'

'At the main house.'

'Are the keys in it?'

'I don't know, I don't think so. Why?'

She's not sure. Her level of anxiety is suddenly rising. According to some weird logic she thinks that if the keys are in the car it means he's done a bunk on her, that he didn't intend to come and get her – she hasn't ruled that out yet – all this stuff on the news, it doesn't sound like Kelvin. Unless that was the bit of the story he wouldn't tell her. Had that whole thing been another concoction? Which is stupid because he's too young to be wanted by the Federal Police. Isn't he? But then another thought slips in amongst the others, overriding the emotions connected with them and rendering them obsolete. He is one of the ones who is dead.

She had felt so cramped by him. It had been a relief to be in Sydney, to be in committee – that word which so often fails to live up to all its promising doubles, and which had done so again on this occasion. Days were spent wrangling over small points of order. She'd thought they were winning, that alliances had been made, but once outside of that low-ceilinged room it transpired that nothing had changed. It was all words; the forests remained utterly compromised. In that context Kelvin had seemed more and more attractive. There might be some confusion about his history, but when he was with her he was direct, present, there. He brought her alive.

She, however, had spurned him. She had had the opportunity to be with him and she had refused it and now it's too late. She wonders if she should be praying. Dear God. What? Dear God, please let him be alive. If he's alive she'll, she'll, what? Is there some formula appropriate for petitioning the Lord in such circumstances? If he's alive she will love him for ever and ever. Is that it? Is he dead because she didn't love him when he was in front of her. Is it her fault? Does she love him at all? Is he even dead? He's probably not dead, the little shit has probably just run off because he couldn't handle a relationship with her, because he's a cheapskate shit, a liar, a bullshit artist, she never loved him and never would even if he is dead, she's so fucking angry with him for not being at the airport like he said he was going to be and for going out into the forest to sabotage machines like Andy wanted to.

Andy.

Andy has been talking about this sort of thing for weeks. If you're serious about this come up and see me sometime.

Bullshit. The man's loopy, he's a fruitcake, a fruit loop, he couldn't organise a cake stall.

'Have you seen Andy?' she says, the words coming out abruptly in the silence.

'Not since last night, he was at the main house – Saturday night, you know, everyone was there. Kelvin was there too. They left around the same time, now I think about it.'

He's right about the cops, though, their new Holdens with their blue and red lights are everywhere, waving them through at the entrance to Cooral Road. Jim's arms cross over each other on the Kombi's big steering wheel as they follow the tight corners down into the Farm.

'Let's go and see Andy when we get home,' she says. 'See what he knows.'

'I don't think we should do that,' Jim says.

'Why not?'

'I don't think he'll be there.'

'Well let's go see,' she says and he doesn't reply, just goes pale before her eyes, his mane of black hair stark against the skin. She can smell the fear. Sometimes she's so gullible. 'What's the matter, Jim?'

'It's nothing.'

'Bullshit. You do know something about this, don't you?'

'No, it's nothing, I just don't want to go and see Andy, that's all. But we can, it doesn't matter.'

'Okay, let's.'

She's not convinced, but the stupid fuck apparently isn't going to talk. She can't exactly torture it out of him.

The road over to Andy's place was once a fire trail and has never been graded since. The mound of grass down the centre brushes against the underside of the van. The trees have grown too close to the sides, their roots extending into the tracks. When they come around the last corner, getting a view of the clearing and the tent, they see the police are already there. A big Landcruiser out of Eden with lights on the top and bullbars is parked beside the tent, and the nose of some other vehicle is poking out from behind it.

'Oh shit,' Jim says. He actually stops the van. He turns to

Jessica with an expression which says, See, I told you, but which might also be saying simply, Help, please. To her astonishment he puts the engine in reverse and swings his head round to see out the back window, as if he fully intends to back out of there.

'What are you doing?'

'I don't know.'

'You can't do that.'

She puts a hand on his arm. 'They're probably just asking questions. You can't turn around, they'll have seen us by now.'

He looks back into the clearing.

'I guess so,' he says.

He puts the van in first again.

'You shouldn't have lied to me, Jim,' she says. 'Now I don't know what's going on, do I?' She swallows hard. 'Listen, just follow my lead, okay?'

'Okay.'

A man emerges from the tent. He's in khaki, loose army pants and a polo-neck jumper with leather patches on the shoulder despite the heat of the day. Jessica steps down out of the van and goes to meet him, brushing off her skirt, offering her hand.

'Can I help you?' he says. He has a soldier's bearing, a pommie accent.

'We're just dropping round to see Andy. Is he home? If it's inconvenient we can come back another time.' Smiling, innocent.

'You'll excuse me if I ask your relationship with Mr Weiss?'

'Has something happened to him?'

'I am sorry but that's classified information at this time. I repeat my question –'

'We're neighbours. I'm Jessica, I live up on top of the hill, over there, and this is Jim, he lives –'

'That would be Cohen then, wouldn't it? And you'd be Hadley, Jim Hadley?' He doesn't even make the pretence of consulting a notebook.

'That's correct,' she says. 'And you?'

'McMahon,' he says, as if that was enough for anyone, no rank, no job description, no Christian name. 'Unfortunately Mr Weiss is unreachable at this time. We are in the process of conducting an investigation. I wonder if you would be prepared to answer some questions yourselves?'

Polite, to the point. But not to mess with. To Jessica it's as if she's shifting from one world to the other and back again. This is like talking to Norton Rawlings, without the sex. She's glad she's been in Sydney all week, it will take more than this cop to intimidate her.

'Certainly, Officer. It is officer, isn't it?'

A uniformed policeman comes out of the tent carrying a load of books and papers. He stops on the little deck and looks at the trio. A third man follows him out, dressed in a similar fashion to McMahon.

They go through the rigmarole. What's their business there, what's her mother's maiden name? He asks the same things of Jim, but more pointedly. When did he last see Weiss, who was he with? Jim has the sense to leave Kelvin out of it, except to add his name to the list of those who were at the main house until late. In order to deflect his attention Jessica reminds him that she's been in Sydney for a week so she can't really be expected to account for Andy's movements. She can't help boasting a little, she doesn't think it will hurt, perhaps even impress the man.

'I've been in committee in Macquarie Street.'

But he's onto her almost before the words are out. 'I know that Ms Cohen. What interests me is that you're on your way back from Sydney and you've come straight here. How is that?'

'Andy's a good friend,' she says, straight out, no hesitation. 'To both of us. Isn't that right, Jim?'

'Sure,' Jim says.

But McMahon's eyeing Jim again, a hawk assessing its prey,

'Has something happened to Andy?' she asks. 'We heard some reports on the radio. He's not one of the people who's dead, is he?'

'Why would you think that?' McMahon says.

'He is, isn't he? I can see it in your face. How awful! How absolutely awful.'

'I cannot reveal any information about Mr Weiss at this time,' he says.

She puts her hand on Jim's arm, turning her face in against his chest.

'Oh God,' she says, mustering tears. She never thought she'd cry for Andy. Jim embraces her and from within his protection, the frail woman, she turns back to McMahon. 'I think we should go now, Mr McMahon. I'm tired from my journey. This is horrible news.'

The uniformed cop has come over.

'I haven't given you any news,' McMahon says. He holds up a hand to the uniformed man to indicate he should wait. 'One last question before you go.'

'Certainly, anything we can do to help,' wiping her tears.

'Jim, you mentioned a Kelvin. Do you know of his whereabouts?'

'Kelvin,' she says before Jim can speak, measuring her words as evenly as possible, slipping her arm around Jim's back and squeezing. 'Didn't you say you saw him this morning, Jim? Trying to get my car started at the main house?'

'Excuse me?' McMahon says.

'I lent him my car while I was away. He would have come to the airport to get me, but the muffler keeps falling off.'

'He asked me to go instead,' Jim says. 'To pick up Jessica. He wanted to borrow the van, but I don't lend it.'

'When was this?'

'This morning, while I was milking the cows. Kelvin headed back down the road, to Cooral Dooral. He lives out there, see. Or he has for the last few weeks.'

'That would be with Mr Tadeuzs?' McMahon says.

'With Carl, that's right.'

'What time was this?'

'I don't know. Seven, maybe a bit later. I was late up because of last night. The cows were already at the bales waiting.'

'You are sure of this?'

'Of course.'

'What was he wearing?'

'Clothes. I dunno. Jeans. A jumper. I didn't pay attention.'

'Did anything about him strike you as unusual?'

'Like?'

'Was he distressed?'

'Not that I noticed. He was looking good I thought. The bruises are healing up fine.'

'What bruises?'

'He had a run-in with a steer about a week ago. His face is a bit messed up, but it's looking better.'

McMahon looks at the uniformed man and back at them.

'Thank you,' he says. 'That's all I need for now. Will you be at home later if I need to speak to you?'

'Certainly, Officer.'

They turn to go back to the van and she wonders if they'll let them get away. She holds Jim's hand. It's very cold.

Jim drives the Kombi up onto the grass and does a wide turn. When they are halfway up the hill she speaks.

'Well done.'

'Thanks. You didn't do so bad yourself.'

She is, she registers, in a kind of shock, shivering as if from cold. She wonders if she is about to be sick.

'I think, Jim, I am owed an explanation.'

Jim drives.

'I really think I am.'

'You are. I know you are, but you can't have it. Not from me. Please, if I could tell you I would. Don't ask, Jessica.'

'Before the week is out. Okay? And unless Kelvin is dead, which he doesn't seem to be, the stupid little fucker, stick to that story. We might have to find someone else who saw him too. I didn't like the way he spoke about Carl. I hope he's not involved in all this.'

thirty-six

He had not meant to sleep and he had slept too long and the waking was difficult. He ached from where he had fallen during that first terror-stricken flight. His face was scratched and sore and filthy, his clothes stiff with blood that was not his own, his head pounding from dehydration, every available uncovered piece of skin swollen from where the insects had been feeding. These things themselves would have been enough to spur him into movement but the sun, also, was well in the west, sending sloping shadows through the trees, and the prospect of another night, of even another hour of darkness, alone, in the forest, was more than he could bear. He had to go down, he had to have water. If the top of the mountain was supposed to grant some sense of power, he could not feel it.

He dropped off the side of the ridge, finding the beginnings of a gully and following its winding course until pools of water began to form beneath a tight-knit canopy. Even then he did not drink, holding off until he came to a place where at least there was the smallest flow. He laid on his belly then, suddenly quiet taking the liquid in small sips, staring at the magnified pebbles in the tiny pool, their many colours so perfectly matched. Afterwards he washed himself, rubbing the cool water around his neck and shoulders.

Once again he pulled out the compass and the map. The gully was running in completely the wrong direction. Since leaving the summit he had apparently been heading north. He did not want to risk coming back down on the same side he had come up. He climbed out eastwards onto another ridge, his footsteps on the dry bark drowning out all other sound. Every now and then he stopped to listen, unable to prevent himself from checking to see if he was being followed. He could still sense, or imagine he sensed, it did not matter which, the will of those who hunted, their malevolence.

After another hour he stumbled upon a granite shelf, bare of trees, the rock exfoliating in wide curving slabs, home to everlasting flowers and a single struggling blackberry with one half-ripe fruit. He stood for a moment, immensely grateful simply to be in the open. The sun's last rays still playing across distant hills. Far off there was recently cleared land, its bull-dozed winrows measuring out the contours. There was no such thing mentioned on the map, but then there wouldn't have been, it being too new, these would be places where they were going to plant pines, and if they were the same ones he'd seen between the Farm and Coalwater then he was indeed on Jessica's mountain and the creek in the valley below would be Gubra Creek. If he could make it there and follow it down-stream he would come, eventually, to the Farm. And if it wasn't the Farm, well, he'd come to something; there would be roads, people, shelter. He had need of food in a way he had never imagined. His body was shaking with the lack of it.

But the Farm was where he was going. He was running towards Jessica. He wondered if she would even speak to him. During this last day she had become in his mind a scold; it was her voice, like a mother, that catalogued his failures. What could he possibly say to her in reply? 'I'm sorry, Jess, but I thought the way you were going about this business with the forests was all fucked up. I didn't tell you, though, because I thought you wouldn't like it and might stop loving me. Besides, I thought I knew better, I thought I could go out there with a couple of guys and sort it all out with some sugar and diesel. But hold on there's more, because Carl got involved and he thought he could solve it with some nitroglycerine. But now he's dead and the cops are after me.' Despite any critique he gave to himself in her voice it was she he moved towards, desperately and with deep longing. She scared him, but not as much as the darkness and the forest, or the men who searched.

Perhaps she had been right about the summits of mountains after all, because down on the slopes, where he was, there were no longer any choices, there were just actions taken in response to other actions. He could see that, but also, from within his strange and heightened mood, he could see that it had always been like that. It probably was for everyone. Throughout his life he had thought he was making decisions, agonising over one thing or another, a girl, a job, this or that

319

town, but in fact he'd been impelled by unconscious forces whose roots were right here, in Eden and its surrounds. Forces so strong they'd even brought him back. The only way that he could ever see himself being free of their influence would be if he could do nothing at all for a time, if he could learn to say no to everything; if he could sit like a kind of petulant child and say no, I'm not going to do this, I'm not going to do that, I'm not going to run, or hide, I'm not going to pretend to be this or that person.

If a man could do that, sit in one place for long enough saying no then eventually, perhaps, everything around him would cease, all the threads of his life would wind down to zero. It might take years. Life would go on around him, oblivious, but in the end he might be able to look at it passing and see where it was that he fitted in. He could make a choice. For so long he had nurtured the illusion that he was separate *and* could choose. He had watched people trapped in their lives from the lofty perspective of his own, and all the time he was actually being turned by his own wheel, ground around and around like those blinkered oxen in India. Not only that but the people who were really in charge, it seemed, were utterly indifferent to him, had not even considered him as a person, just something in the way, to be used or discarded as was convenient. That he was important had been his own fantasy. It was, perhaps, an extension of the business about the mountain and the forest going on after he died, or no, not really, because the forest simply was, it simply existed in its own foresty way, unravelling its own foresty business. It was not consciously bending the world to its purpose. There was a difference.

Even as he thought these thoughts he ran, walked, hobbled. His legs did what they were supposed to do, but reluctantly, threatening to throw him off balance if he took his attention away for a second. His feet hurt. Only the creeping night pushed him on.

It was lighter when he reached the creek; outside of the forest cover it was not yet fully dark. He lay on the pale granite rocks with the clear water trickling over them, subsumed with a liquid delirium. This was Gubra Creek. Another kilometre down were some large flat rocks where a fire trail crossed. He had been there before, with Jessica.

He set off again, making what use he could of the extra light to rock-hop, oblivious of snakes, scaring the marsupials who'd come down for their evening drink. He was within an hour of her house. She would give him food and shelter, at least that, before she threw him out. He moved quickly, incautiously, only bringing himself up when he came to the fence, remembering he could not afford to be found.

He took the old fence trail uphill. By then it *was* dark, even darker amongst the trees, but his eyes had adjusted with the failing light and there was a small moon, five days old.

But the track was not a good idea; trees had grown up in the available space beside the wire and he had to push his way through them and the spiderwebs woven thickly between their branches, their threads sticking to his face and hands. He couldn't see and his movements made too much noise. With deep repugnance he turned off, entering once again the forest. But at least he was on the Farm; the trees he slipped through were tame, not the wild ones of the previous night.

On the top of the ridge he found the fire trail where it wound above the cleared valley on one side and Gubra Creek on the other. Below, next to the road, would be the main house; he could see the lights of someone's dwelling on the opposite hill. The trail dropped steeply down onto another shoulder and then another, then joined the road to Jessica's cabin.

Lights were glowing in the window.

thirty-seven

Suzy hears or smells him when he's still a hundred metres away. He left her there the afternoon before, when he was going to the main house to meet Carl and Andy. Only a little more than twenty-four hours has passed. She barks, her hackles raised, then runs along the road to meet him, tail wagging madly.

Jessica opens the door of the cabin.

'Is anyone there?' she says, standing in the light.

How much he wants her. He crouches, stroking Suzy, trying to calm her with his hands.

Jessica calls out, 'Suzy, Sooo-zie.'

The dog becomes more excited, yelping a couple of times but doesn't go back, waits for him, torn between the two people, coming in close, fascinated by his smell.

'Kelvin,' Jessica says. 'Is that you?'

He stands, 'Yes,' he says, and walks towards her.

'Come in then,' she says. 'Quickly, before anyone sees you.'

★ ★ ★

She knew he would come, and there he is, stepping out of the darkness. She wants to touch him, but recoils, confused, stepping aside to let him pass. She closes the door behind him. He stands for a moment by the bench looking at her, then simply collapses.

He's on the floor and she's squatting next to him. He's filthy in a way that is quite foreign to her, as if he has been in the woods for months, living with wild animals, his face scratched and torn, his clothes matted and dark. He opens his eyes.

'I'm sorry Jessica, I'm really sorry for not meeting you at the airport,' he says.

She has forgotten about that.

'I won't stay long. Can I have something to eat? I haven't eaten since yesterday, except for some nuts and raisins I got from Carl.'

He tries to push Suzy away but the dog won't leave him alone.

'Stop it Suze,' he says, but gently. 'Stop it now.'

'Where's Carl? What's Carl got to do with this?'

Kelvin is surprised. 'Carl's dead,' he says.

'No.'

'I thought they might have found him. I dragged him out into the creek so that they would.' His eyes shift away from hers. 'It was Andy who killed him, you know. He fell down a cliff but Andy –'

'No, you've got it wrong, Kelvin. Andy's dead, it's not Carl.'

'No, no it was Carl. This is his blood.' He holds up his arm for her to see but it could just as well be any part of him.

She has not, until then, realised the import of his filth.

'He talked to me and then he died. He died when I tried to move him, but it wasn't my fault, I don't think it was, not that bit anyway. He was already dead.'

His words have a curious effect. He's on the floor with Jessica crouched over him, the dog snuffling. He tells her this about Carl and she stands up and walks a few paces away. When she turns back she's crying. Just like that. He tells her Carl is dead and her face simply breaks up, her eyes go red and swell up and actual tears run down her cheeks. She's keeping her balance with one hand.

'I'm really sorry,' he says. 'I've really fucked up.'

Suzy will not be dissuaded. Suddenly Jessica understands what she's interested in.

'Out,' she says to the dog. 'Outside, now!' going over and holding the door, the dog slinking outside, tail between her legs, 'Disgusting animal.'

'She's all right,' Kelvin says. 'She's just a dog.'

'As for you,' Jessica says, turning her anger on him, 'as for you, you little shit.'

She looks at him through her tears, pathetic, filthy, and yet something else too.

'Take those clothes off. I'll run you a bath. Lucky for you I lit the stove. I'll get you something to eat, then you can explain yourself. It better be good, that's all I can say. It better be good.'

She has gone into the lean-to which serves as a bathroom, a place of pot plants and unguents. He can hear the water running into the bath. He is, he notes, lying on the floor.

He was beside Carl when he died. He had held him in his arms. He knows that it was probably the moving of his body which finally killed him. Even then he hadn't cried. There were no tears in him, only that awful distance.

She comes back and starts undressing him, pulling the shirt over his head. Her cheeks are still wet with tears and her nose is running. For some reason he doesn't mind that, for some reason this seems to be normal; proper, even. She stands and takes some tissues from the counter. He thinks she is going to wipe her eyes, blow her nose, but instead she comes to him. It's his eyes she wipes, not hers.

'Andy's dead?' he says.

'I don't know for sure,' she says. 'But there were some cops down at his place. Special Branch, I think. They were being very coy. The radio said there were two men dead, one seriously injured and one missing. I guess you're the one who's missing. They didn't say it was you but they asked for you. Jim told them he'd seen you this morning, that you drove my car to the dairy at seven.'

'Andy was a cop,' Kelvin says. 'He was working for Special Branch.'

She takes the clothes to the stove, empties the pockets and then burns them, everything she can find, every last stitch, everything that came out of them, the map, the string, what to do with the knife and compass? She leaves them on the bench.

She stands in the bathroom doorway.

'Are you an international terrorist?'

'Is this some kind of trick question?'

'They said it on the radio, that there was a terrorist involved who was wanted around the world. Is it you?'

He stares at his legs under the brown water.

'That would be Carl, I guess. It fits. He said he was going to tell me when this was over. He ran off a cliff, Jessica. I was following him. We were running through the trees in the dark and he kept going, straight out into the air. I grabbed a tree.'

He is in her bath, in the hot water and the scent and the safety of her house. Outside is the darkness. She has her hand on the doorjamb, her face flickering between emotions as if it is a physical register of internal thought. There has never been anything hidden about her. This red-haired, pale-skinned woman, perhaps even a little plain, but real, surrounded by her world.

He is taken, then, by such longing for her. Even from where he is, surrounded by all his failings, all his needs, he senses this feeling to be utterly genuine. Even though he is, at this moment, governed more surely by circumstance than at any

327

time in his life, he knows the feeling to be pure, unadulterated and true. If he could choose her, he would.

Carl is the terrorist? Carl is dead? Her Carl. Her Carl who wouldn't let her love him, who she had loved anyway, who had loved her but wouldn't tell her because of something in his past. It is so stupid, so vastly, enormously foolish that she can hardly stand and yet there, in front of her, naked in her bath, is Kelvin, delivered, as it were, out of the night.

Is his story equally stupid? Andy was a cop? They were setting a trap? Suddenly she doesn't care. His body is covered in bruises and scratches. His beautiful body. So large in her bath, the dark hair around his cock and balls. There are great rings under his eyes, his cheeks are drawn. Sleep will fix that. With a shave and clean hair he won't look too bad, there's only one nasty cut across the forehead. You could put that down to an accident, a run-in with barbed wire. He will pass muster in a high-necked shirt.

There is so much she doesn't know about the simplest things. When she first got to Sydney she thought she was hitting the big time, talking about the politics of the possible, but that had turned out to be so much bullshit. Macquarie Street was only about power. Issues were only issues in that they were stepping stones to making someone's career. For a moment she had been caught up in it, she had even thought she could cut it there.

Then she came back and Jim hadn't even asked her what

happened. Neither had Kelvin. And even though she wasn't exactly open to questions, she is so disappointed in that, as if what is happening here on this little bit of land is all that's important. Except that on some level it is. That's the paradox. These are the differences she has to try to marry. There has been another life going on without her, another life here she has failed to see. She raises her eyes to meet Kelvin's. She wants to hit him, she wants to hold him. Did she make a pact with God? She can't remember. Probably it's best to be on the safe side. She kneels beside the tub, takes the cloth in her hand and begins to wash his cheek.

acknowledgments

I have been blessed with a remarkable level of support in the writing of this novel. I am indebted to my editor Julia Stiles not only for the attention she gave to the manuscript, but also for her early belief in its potential. I am immensely grateful to the Queensland Premier's Department for granting me the 'Best Manuscript from an Emerging Queensland Author Award 2004'; would that all states granted writing the importance that Queensland does. I would like to thank David Woolston, motor-mechanic *extraordinaire*, for his advice regarding motors and their response to sugar in their fuel; Gary Crew, Ross Smith and John Purser for their early readings and comments. Lastly I am more than grateful to my wife, Chris Francis, for reading the manuscript in its numerous different versions. I am fortunate indeed to have someone who offers me such loving encouragement.